FACING THE TRUTH

Liam Ashford

Contents

1. Chapter 1 — 1
2. Chapter 2 — 9
3. Chapter 3 — 15
4. Chapter 4 — 25
5. Chapter 5 — 34
6. Chapter 6 — 41
7. Chapter 7 — 49
8. Chapter 8 — 57
9. Chapter 9 — 64
10. Chapter 10 — 71
11. Chapter 11 — 81
12. Chapter 12 — 91
13. Chapter 13 — 99
14. Chapter 14 — 106
15. Chapter 15 — 112
16. Chapter 16 — 122

17. Chapter 17 . . . 131

18. Chapter 18 . . . 142

19. Chapter 19 . . . 149

20. Chapter 20 . . . 159

21. Chapter 21 . . . 167

22. Chapter 22 . . . 175

23. Chapter 23 . . . 182

24. Chapter 24 . . . 191

25. Chapter 25 . . . 198

26. Chapter 26 . . . 206

27. Chapter 27 . . . 216

28. Chapter 28 . . . 223

29. Chapter 29 . . . 230

30. Epilogue . . . 239

CHapTer 1

Taylor

Thursday, January 31st, 2014

I cracked my knuckles and placed the pads of my fingers on the piano's silky surface, eager to make beautiful music with it.

My fingers danced over the keys, tapping each black and white slab in perfect rhythm, mimicking the tune written down on the sheet music in front of me. My fingers stretched apart as they moved from note to note, the sounds enveloping me like a snug blanket on a cold winter's day. The beautiful blend of the bass notes and the clicks of the treble notes sent chills down my spine. Right here, right now, there was nothing else in the world except me and this grand piano.

I wasn't practicing anything that Miss Lauriana had given me. On Thursdays she let me stay behind after school to practice my own music in her classroom.

Instinctively, my throat began to hum the notes of the lyrics I had written for the song I was playing. My performance had to be perfect - this was one of the songs I was going to play in the coming weeks in front of the entire school.

My fingers picked up in speed, tapping the keys as smoothly as I could muster. Since it was nearly four in the afternoon, nobody was at Vale high school except for the odd teacher that stayed behind for marking, or the occasional cleaner or two swapping the lining for the bins. Having memorised this part of the song by heart, I shut my eyes as I began to sing the chorus.

My fingers, and my voice, halted as a loud cough came from the doorway. Almost instantly, I knew it was Darko listening - he poked his head through the door, smiling as we made eye contact. He coughed again as he walked to me, his black sneakers squeaking against the tiles.

"Hey," he croaked before clearing his throat.

"Shouldn't you be in bed, or did your pneumonia heal already?" I teased. Darko wiped his nose with his jumper sleeve, chuckling to himself.

"It's just the flu. Jesus, man," he said before smirking, "I came because I wanted to hear you play. You know that your music makes me feel better."

His eyes darted to the black grand piano in front of me, then to my fingers. His green eyes flitted up to meet mine as he cleared his throat.

"Well? Show me those fingers doing their thing, Tay. The thing you were playing before sounded great, play that one."

My hands quivered over the instrument, its pearly white keys suddenly reflecting the harsh afternoon sunlight that shone through the tall arched windows behind me. My hands knew what to do - they've played the piano in dozens of theatres, stages, and plays before - yet they sat there limply on the keys. I adjusted my glasses and swallowed hard. The timing had to be right. I couldn't play this to him.

The song is about him.

"What I was playing is a... surprise for the performance," I said, gritting my teeth at my shallow lie. "I'll play some Beethoven, you love him."

He furrowed his brow before nodding in agreement. He slid his hand softly over the instrument, wiping the trace amount of dust from it, before grabbing one of the chairs that had been stacked by a cleaner. He sat next to the piano, facing me.

'God, he's so fucking cute.' I thought to myself.

It was hard being in love with your straight best friend; I just couldn't be completely honest with him.

I couldn't even remember when we started being friends. From what I had seen from the childhood photos my mum kept around the house, we did everything together when we were little. We ate together, we played hide-n-seek together, and we even bathed together.

During my first year of high school, something just changed. I realized that I looked at guys the same way I looked at girls. Soon, I couldn't stop thinking about Darko - something in me needed to know what he was doing, where he was and how he was constantly. I was head-over-heels for him, my best friend. Ordinary people don't fall for their best friend... right?

The problem? Darko was straight - I knew he was straight. The number of girls he had hooked up with and the number of girls that were always flirting with him... it was unsettling, not to mention heartbreaking.

I supposed I could at least tell him I'm bisexual. In an ideal world, your best friend would accept you no matter what; my world was different. Darko would never understand.

"Hey," Darko said before waving his palm near my face, "You okay? You zoned out there for a second."

I quickly whipped out of my thoughts and nodded. "Yeah, sorry, was just uh... trying to remember the piece."

It took every ounce of willpower to stop myself from reaching over, kissing him while tangling my fingers in his brunette hair.

My fingers began to regain their strength, and I started playing a slow version of Für Elise. Darko closed his eyes and swayed softly to the sounds the instrument produced, humming to the parts he recognised. His mouth curled into a warm smile, to which my heart responded by fluttering like a hovering hummingbird.

He kept his eyes closed after the song ended. I looked up at him, and he was smiling contently, eyes shut, like he was in a trance.

"I fucking love your piano skills," he muttered softly, opening his eyes after his statement, "you need to teach me sometime."

I chuckled. "Mate, this took me years to perfect. I can't just teach you how to play; it takes dedication and discipline."

Darko frowned before he looked at the instrument.

"Besides," I continued, "Don't you have motor races to worry about?"

Darko looked up, his eyes narrowing slightly. "I can ride my motorcycle whenever; it's not like it's taking up all of my time."

I rolled my eyes. "Fine. I'll teach you 'Für Elise' one day, all right?"

Darko's face lit up at the sound of my words. He nodded before a bright toothy smile appeared across his creamy cheeks. "I'll be the best pupil, my good sir."

I rolled my eyes before laughing. "Shut up, jackass."

That nickname is horrible. He's been calling me that since I got back from a performance in Sydney. He claims I'm too posh, that I was some noble sir with high status. My annoyance towards it seems to make Darko say it more.

I refocused on the piano, while Darko closed his eyes again. I began playing Beethoven's Moonlight Sonata, but a loud crash echoed from the classroom door, interrupting us. Craning my head around to see who made the noise, I realized it was Miss Lauriana, carrying a huge stack of orange papers that she was struggling to hold. Darko, who had opened his eyes and noticed Lauriana too, quickly shuffled to her and lifted the papers, causing her to sigh in relief.

"Stupid papers! I can't believe I walked into the door..." she mumbled to herself as she tucked a stray chocolate curl behind her ear. Darko placed the stack on her desk.

"Wait, Darko lifted that from me? I thought that was you, Taylor," She said before chuckling. "What are you doing here Darko? You haven't seen the insides of this room since you punched a hole through my drumset in year 8."

"Miss, I just came to hear Taylor. His music always makes me feel better when I'm sick."

Miss Lauriana instantly took three steps backward. "You're sick?"

Darko rubbed his nose. "Yeah?"

Miss Lauriana frowned. "Please stay away from me. I have younger kids to teach tomorrow; I'd probably quit if I have to deal with their usual behaviour while putting up with a cold."

Darko and I laughed as she checked her watch. "You boys should be getting home soon. It's past four thirty and it's beginning to get dark outside. Do you need a lift?" she said, gesturing towards the door.

"No thanks," we both said simultaneously.

"I have a car Miss," Darko stated. He turned to me. "Tay, you want a lift? The people on your bus are always up to something dodgy; I don't think it's safe."

The idea of being alone with just him, inside his car, talking about nonsense, made me smile like an idiot. He had taken me on car rides multiple times before, but the feeling never changes. There was something intimate about driving alone with him, I can't explain it.

I mean, it's intimate when I'm alone with anybody, but it's special when It's just me and him.

"Yeah, sure man. I'd love that." I said, smiling at him. He smiled back but quickly turned away. From the corner of my eye, I could see it - the faintest of colour change on Darko's cute face.

I turned to Miss Lauriana, who had just sat down at her desk. "Thanks for letting me stay behind after school, miss. See you tomorrow."

Miss Lauriana, who had just begun writing on the large stack of paper she had brought in, waved us a goodbye without breaking her concentration. "You're welcome here anytime. Close the door on your way out; I hate it when students leave it open."

"I think you just got a message," Darko said. Perplexed, I looked away from the window towards my phone in the central console, the screen alight with messages.

"Huh?"

"Your phone keeps vibrating, my good sir. Think someone's messaging you."

I glared at him. "I hate that nickname."

He nodded, a smug grin appearing on his face. "That's good to know, my good sir."

Groaning, I picked up my phone from the centre console and squinted through my glasses at the screen.

"Okay, three messages. They're all from Ana."

"What do they say?" he questioned.

"Three forty - Hey Tay, you still at Vale? Message me back ASAP. Three fifty-five - Taylor? Pick up your phone! It's an emergency! Ten-past four - For fuck's sake, you twit! CHECK. YOUR. DAMN. PHONE!"

Darko's eyebrows furrowed. "Is it something to do with your mum again?"

I shrugged at him as I dialed her number. I held the phone between us as she picked up.

"Hey, I'm on my way home right now. You're on speaker, Darko's in the car as well. What's wrong?' I asked.

Ana's voice was harsh. Her breath was rapid.

"Mum's collapsed on the couch and she's refusing to get up. She's conscious, but she's just ignoring me, staring at the roof, silently crying. She's been drinking a lot, Tay."

"Shit. Have you called an ambulance?" Darko suggested.

"I wanted to, but I don't think her Medicare card works any-more. Plus, I think the paramedics are getting sick of us. Just hurry home, I'm sure we can deal with this."

She hung up. I looked at Darko. He just shook his head, focusing on the road, speeding as much as he could.

The rest of the trip was silent, except for the rumbling noise of the asphalt road beneath us and Darko's random lung-hacking. When he pulled up to my house, he turned to me.

"Hey, I know this is an inappropriate time, but once your mum's feeling a bit better, you wanna stay over at mine?" Darko asked. I turned my head to face him, and he had that gorgeous smile on his face again.

God, that damn smile.

"Not inappropriate at all. I'd say yeah, but you might get me sick," I stated.

His face faltered a little at my comment, but like always, he had to say something to convince me.

"Well, my parents are out, and Stefan's at his friend's house. Please? I don't want to be alone while I'm like this."

I rolled my eyes. 'He's persistent,' I thought.

"Fine, fine, you ass. Come pick me up; I'll text you when it's over. I don't think you'd want me to catch a bus to your place that late at night." I said. He smiled.

I hopped out of the car and waved him goodbye as he reversed out of my driveway. He honked his car horn as he sped off.

Now, to deal with my mother.

CHAPTER 2

Taylor's pov

Thursday, January 31st, 2014

I shoved my house key deep into the front door's lock, fighting against the rust embedded within it, and turned it. Through the slab of oak-wood, I couldn't hear a thing.

Was mum feeling better, or did she pass out?

I twisted the doorknob and slowly opened the door.

"Ana?" I shouted, "I'm home!"

She poked her head out from the kitchen and whispered: "be quiet." She gestured for me to come to the kitchen.

"Sorry I was a little late," I whispered, "Darko dropped me off."

She was brewing some chamomile tea; mum's favourite. Ana had explained everything that had happened - mum came home, had a fit (she threw some plates; Ana had already cleaned them up), drank a bottle of whisky before blanking out on the couch. Ana had managed to get her to her room just before I came home, but Mum was still unstable.

"She said Dad's name before, Tay. She has been saying it too much; I don't think her pills are working anymore."

"Or maybe she's just not taking them," I stated, sighing. "I'll go check her out."

Ana handed me the warm cup of the tea as I slinked out of the kitchen. I made my way to mum's room quietly, being careful not to spill the warm beverage. I hovered over the door, leaning so my ear was just touching it, and there it was - the softest, most heartbreaking sobs were audible.

She misses dad so much; it's the most distressing thing to listen to.

"Mum... I'm here," I said as I softly pushed her bedroom door open, "are you okay?"

Mum slowly looked up at me from her bed, her eyes puffy from her tears and her face flushed. Her room was an absolute mess; there were pillows scattered everywhere, the blanket was twisted up, a glass had been knocked off of her bedside table, and there were many empty bottles of alcohol scattered at the base of her shelf, a buildup from the past few weeks. She began to sob harder as I approached her bed.

"Oh my God," she said suddenly, wiping a tear from her face. "M-Matthew, you're back! I - I... I thought you..."

Matthew? She... she just mistook me for my dad. Oh christ...

I felt my cheeks burn up as she clumsily stumbled towards me, wrapping me in a tight hug. My heart fluttered, but not in an affectionate way. I felt nauseous. I can't believe she just mistook me for him. Her soft sobbing sent ice shards through my chest.

Mum was stuttering all over her words, her palms were shaking as she began to speak, "You... you've come home. I-I've missed you. I love you so much-"

"Mum... it's not Dad. You're hugging me- Taylor."

I felt her arms falter as she looked up at me. Her eyes began to get watery again, and her smile faded into a sad frown.

About four months ago, dad and I were driving home from our routine Saturday morning fishing trip. We were meant to stay out for longer, but I was extra tired that morning because I had a performance the night before, so we cut the trip quite short. It was roughly 3am, so we were both exhausted. The next thing I knew, something had hit our car. The force... It's indescribable. I remember flailing half awake as our car tumbled and tossed and turned off the street into a thick tree. It was horrific.

According to the nurse that rescued me from the rubble, it was a truck that had hit us. It sped off on impact, completely ignoring us. A large glass shard from the windshield impaled Dad, and I managed to survive with just a broken arm, minor cuts, and bruises. I ended up needing stitching, and I never heard from that driver again. I barely even remember what the truck looked like.

We were all broken, mum especially.

"Oh... oh my God... I'm so sorry Taylor. I'm so sorry..."

"It's okay," I whispered, hesitantly.

It wasn't fine.

"Have you taken your pills today?"

She hung her head. After a minute of silence, she shook her head. "No. I haven't."

I sighed. "Mum... why not? You know they help you. We can't afford to go back to therapy."

She shook her head. I sighed again, wrapping her up in my arms. "Okay, from now on, every morning, I'm gonna watch you take those pills, and every day you don't, I'm taking away your credit card. I will not let you poison yourself with alcohol, okay? I love you... I don't want to lose you as well."

Mum began to cry again. I let her weep into my chest, my shirt becoming soaked with her tears. I started to cry as well; hearing mum like this, seeing mum like this, and have her bawl her eyes out on me... fuck, you'd be deranged if you didn't feel sad.

"Hey," I said after a couple of minutes, "Let's get your bed ready. Today has gone on for too long, and you need some rest. Drink some of the tea that Ana brewed."

She nodded softly, lifting herself from my (now soaked) torso. I gestured to the cup on her bedside table, and she immediately grabbed it, slowly drinking the warm liquid. After a few moments, she handed me the empty cup and looked me straight in the eyes.

"I love you, Taylor."

I wiped a tear away. "I love you too, mum. I'll put on some of my recordings, okay? I've got to head out. Get some rest."

I walked out and softly shut the door. Ana was waiting outside, her arms folded and her eyes puffy. I think she cried a little bit too; she must have heard what had happened.

"Is she going to be okay?" She questioned. I quickly nodded, and she sighed in relief. I handed her the cup, which made her smile weakly.

"I take it she liked my tea... huh. I always thought I brewed it wrong," she said, walking back to the kitchen.

"Are you okay with watching her? I told Darko that I'd sleep over at his place," I said, following her. Ana sighed.

"But you just hung out with him..."

I placed a hand on her shoulder. "I know, I know, but he has the flu-"

"But nothing! It's just the flu. He's 18; I'm sure he can take care of himself." Ana retorted.

"He can't. Before he dropped me off, he asked me to come over. He doesn't want to spend the night alone; his entire family is going to be out."

Ana hesitantly nodded as she placed the empty mug into the sink. Realising that she might make me stay home anyway, I spoke up.

"Besides, I need you here to keep an eye on mum. I've just calmed her down with some of the stuff I recorded for her. Can you be the best little sister? Please?"

Ana went to nod, but her stomach grumbled. She quickly grasped it and darted her eyes to the fridge. "Sorry, mum hadn't cooked anything yet, and I'm starving."

Ana stroked her chin, her eyes narrowing as she smirked. "How about this; you make me some food, and you can go."

"Sure," I said, smiling warmly, "I'll teach you how to make stir fry."

"Jeez Taylor, where did you learn how to make this? It's so good!" Ana managed to say through her mouthful of food. I chuckled.

"Food Science class. I highly recommend it." I said, making her snort. She checked her watch as I turned the TV on for her, putting some pre-recorded Futurama on.

"Tay, it's nearly 8," She said, "If you want to go see your boyfriend, you better go soon before he falls asleep."

I laughed at her joke, a mockery of how I was feeling inside. Darko's boyfriend.

"What makes him and me 'boyfriends'?" I questioned. Ana chuckled.

"Dude, I was joking. You do act a little gay around him though... is there something you're not telling me?" she said sarcastically. I laughed but was still preoccupied with what she first said.

Hehe. It was fun to say it in my head. 'Darko is my boyfriend.' Like that would ever happen.

"Anyway," I said, getting up from the couch, "I'll be at Darko's. Are you all good? Message me if you need anything."

Ana toothily smiled, a few bits of stir fry poking out from her maw, "I'll be okay. Besides, Futurama is on. I couldn't ask for anything more."

I waved and said bye to her as I walked to the front door, quickly shooting Darko a text. 'Hey bro, crisis averted. Pick me up soon?'

Darko replied almost immediately. 'Yeah, sure thing. See you soon, bro.'

I smiled at my phone as I waited on the porch. Darko never usually sends me hearts. It made me smile like an idiot while I waited for him.

A heart emoji's just a heart emoji, right? Like, they shouldn't mean anything? They're just groups of coloured pixels, they shouldn't mean anything serious...

'Should I send one back? Would it be too obvious that I like him? Do two guys even send heart emojis to each other!?' a voice echoed in my head. Impulsively, I sent him one.

He sent a smiley emoji back.

Surely that meant nothing.... right?

CHaPTer 3

D arko's pov

Thursday, January 31st, 2014

I'm in love with Taylor James Ferguson - but I can't be with him for so many reasons.

I've always loved that nerd, right from when we were toddlers. Although, back then it wasn't romantic love - not that at all. In retrospect, it was just 'platonic love' - we just played in the sand-pits together, and we cheated off of each other's homework, and we always picked each other during sports. We were tight.

Right when high school started, when everyone started to over-load in gross-teenage-pubescent hormones, was when I knew I really loved the idiot. I couldn't get him out of my brain - during class, I just couldn't stop thinking about him! His adorable smile, his cute black glasses that suited his face so well, not to mention his freaking amazing piano skills. Eventually, the only thing I could think about was him.

I can't be with him - which is slowly, internally, killing me.

He's never really talked about his sexuality, so I've never 100% confirmed it for myself if he was secretly into guys. I've always assumed he was straight, otherwise, he probably would have told me by now. Best friends should share all of their secrets... right?

I could never be with him anyway, on the off chance that he did like guys. My family would never approve of it. As they say, its 'a man and a woman must marry' or 'homosexuality is a sin, and gays must be cleansed.' They would never accept either of us or me in specific. They'd disown me if I ever came out to them. I'd be the family 'mistake.'

Not to mention, being in a relationship with him would ruin my reputation at school. I'm currently known as the 'popular-player-that-makes-girls-weak,' and if I were ever to date Taylor, all of that would get thrown off balance. I wouldn't be popular anymore, and I would probably confuse a lot of girls. Yeah, I hooked up with them and dated a few, but I did that to cover up my burning feelings for Taylor. I never dated any of them for too long, I just casually hooked up with them during parties, and if they got clingy, I just left them.

This boy is driving me nuts.

I can't risk telling him how I feel; there is just too much at stake. If he returns my feelings, my family will disown me. If they aren't returned, then I would not only embarrass myself, but my friendship with Tay would be completely broken, my social life would probably crumble, and my parents would eventually find out and disown me.

Either way, I lose. Either way, I get disowned.

It's midnight, and the house is silent. Taylor came over a while ago and slept a lot earlier than usual. He didn't tell me about the emergency that went down at his place. He was too quiet during dinner, and he barely spoke to me afterward. Well, he wasn't completely quiet - he responded when I talked to him - he just wasn't all... there.

He wasn't acting like his usual self. Something serious must have happened.

I'm sitting in the living room, absentmindedly scrolling through Netflix while devouring a block of hazelnut chocolate. I deserve to scoff down on this, being sick has drained me of my energy. I clicked "American Horror Story" and continued to nibble on my brown delicacy.

It has been a long day. I hate being sick. It sucks balls. Stupid Bella had to come to stupid school a few days ago and 'accidently' cough near me. I'm surprised she didn't give me Ebola or something.

God, that sounded so bitchy. You can't blame me though; if someone that was sick came to school and made no effort to keep their germs to themselves, you'd be a little pissed, to say the least.

On the bright side, being sick meant that my family had steered clear of me at home. Stefan avoided me like the plague, and mum and dad went out of their way to buy face masks. It's ridiculous; I have the Flu, not the damn Black Death!

I'm just glad that ever since I got sick, I didn't have to hear much of dad's preaching. Thank fuck for that.

You see, dad's the headmaster of this house. Whatever his opinions are, we're forced to follow them - it's how he managed to get all of us to believe in God and what not. I don't believe in God - I have nothing against Christian beliefs and I'm proud of who I am - but my brother, oh boy. He's like dad's prodigy. He's managed to make Stefan love God unconditionally, but he's also made him incredibly biased. He hates gays with a burning passion, just like my dad does. The worst part? He's openly hateful. They'll yell at any gay couple they see in public. They'll angrily rant about it to anyone that's willing to listen. They'll make sure everyone they talk to knows they dislike 'them fags.'

Don't I have the best family?

I switched the TV off and sluggishly chewed on a final chunk of the cocoa goodness before I got up and walked to the kitchen. I languidly swung the pantry door open, threw in my comfort food, and shut it.

That's when I felt a large, cold hand wrap itself over my stiff shoulder.

Instantly, my 'Fight or Flight' instincts kicked in; my brain decided to 'Flight' instead of 'Fight.' Because I was so drained and sick, I had little control over my arms and legs.

So, I ran into the pantry. Hard.

After I had recovered from the shock, I turned around to face my midnight assailant. Cautiously rubbing my probably-bruised skull, I squinted around in the darkness, groaning in pain.

Fucking hell, Taylor, you prick.

"Oh my God," Taylor said with the biggest grin on his face, "You should have seen your face! You ran straight into the pantry; I should have been filming that! Holy shit!"

Taylor was laughing his vocal chords off, clapping his hands like a drunken seal while squeezing his oceanic eyes so tightly they looked like they had just come into contact with a lemon. His laugh was like a siren; thank God nobody was home or he would have woken up the entire house.

I punched him in the arm and began to walk upstairs, back to my room.

"Well, it is fucking 12am, how do you think I'd react? I thought you were asleep! You could have called out my name instead of grabbing my shoulder! You could have been a robber or a rapist or God knows what else!"

Taylor ignored my comments and continued to snigger and laugh at me while I grumpily shuffled to my room. He followed en route behind me.

"Oh God, that's the greatest thing that's happened today!"

"Yeah, haha, so amusing, you asshole." I spat before shooting him a glare, to which he responded by laughing again. I rolled my eyes and climbed onto my bed.

"Anyway, speaking of your day today..." I said, quickly thinking of a subject apart from my very-manly-totally-dignified moment.

"Yeah?" Taylor said, wiping a tear from his eye. He was still grinning like an idiot, and I think I made him cry of laughter. He climbed onto his side of the bed and began to unfurl the sheets when I spoke. He doesn't like it when he sleeps separate from me, which is somewhat weird, but hey; don't question the miracle. I always end up waking up with him in my arms, and he never notices it.

"How was the emergency? What happened?" I asked.

Almost instantly, Taylor's smile faded into a frown. He faced me, and I saw his eyes begin to glaze, and his cheeks begin to flush like they always do when he's upset.

"You've been extra quiet since you got here. What happened? What's wrong?" I cocked my head to the side, like how a dog would when you ask it something, and furrowed my brows.

Taylor turned his head, glancing at me. He couldn't keep eye contact with me.

"Mum called me Matthew," Taylor croaked, his voice trailing off slightly as he faced his sheets again. "Matthew! My dad..."

Now it was my turn. My annoyed grimace turned into a slight frown, and I felt my cheeks warm up. Taylor looked up at me again, and we made the briefest of eye contact before his head fell, his gaze leading to his lap.

"Oh, Taylor..." I said. He looked up at me, his frown deepening.

"She was drunk again," he began, "This is the third time this week. I'm not sure how long Ana can keep putting up with it; it's only a matter of time before I find her locking herself in the bathroom again."

I placed my hand on Taylor's shoulder, which made him tense slightly. He relaxed when I began to speak.

"Taylor, I know losing your dad was hard on them. But you just need to know; they are trying to cope in a unique way. Your mum is drinking and Ana's depressed. You can't do anything except to help guide them."

Taylor looked away from me, his glazed eyes now becoming waterfalls. Teardrops began seeping out of his pastel blue eyes, and they dropped onto his cherry-red cheeks. As he turned back, I shot him a reassuring smile, but it seemed to make the tears fall faster. He hastily took off his glasses, throwing them onto his pillow, and began furiously wiping his face.

"I miss him so much," he said between sobs. "I miss him so fucking much."

I pulled him over and wrapped him in my arms. He sobbed quietly into my shirt, which soon became drenched in his tears. He inched closer and wrapped his arms around me, adjusting himself so he was crying into my shoulder instead of my chest. I leaned my head onto his shoulder as I rubbed his back while he continued to sob quietly.

"I promise Tay," I whispered into his ear after a few minutes passed. "Things will get better soon. I promise."

He unfurled himself and looked at me, a tiny tennis-ball sized gap forming between our faces. I stared deeply into his (now red) eyes as he searched my face. The way his eyes skimmed over my face, especially because he was so close, made my heart flutter.

It took every single ounce of self-control not just to lean forward and kiss him.

I couldn't kiss him, not now, not ever.

"You promise?" He said, his voice breaking the silence. I nodded, making him smile warmly.

He climbed off of me and wiped his eye with his hand. He picked up his glasses and sighed slowly.

"I'm sorry. I shouldn't have cried..." Taylor said, his voice trailing off as he continued to unfurl his sheets.

I furrowed my eyebrows. "Are you kidding? Don't be sorry about that; you know you can talk to me about these things."

Another adorable little smile washed over his lips. "Thank you."

I smiled back, and he seemed to do a double take. I mentally shrugged it off, and he climbed into the sheets. Why would he double take at it?

"You wanna do something? Today was stressful; it'd be fun to take your mind away from it for awhile." I suggested. Taylor raised an eyebrow.

"Like what?" he asked, puzzled. I shrugged.

I could say to him that I wanted to hug him so he was all fixed. I could say I wanted to kiss him until my lips were swollen, and I was out of breath. I could say to him so many things. But what did I come out with?

"I don't really know. You wanna watch something on Netflix?"

Taylor chuckled. "Sure thing. I cannot stand anything drama-packed right now though."

I laughed as I hoisted myself from my bed to the TV that was in my room. I switched it on, turned on my PS4, and clambered back onto the bed, controller in tow. We flickered through the films, but none interested us.

"Hey, what about this?" I suggested. Taylor lifted a brow.

"American Horror Story? It seems kinda gory."

"I was watching it before you made me shit my pants," I said, making both of us laugh. "It's quite interesting; It's got a lot of 'skin' though."

"Play it."

I lifted a brow, a smirk forming on my face. "Wow, that decision was made easily. I didn't even say what type of nakedness it was."

Taylor furrowed his brows as he turned to me. "What kind?"

"Just you wait and see," I said, wiggling my eyebrows at him. Taylor laughed, and I pressed play.

"Well, I don't know about you, but I am tired." He said, sleepily. It's 2am now, mum and dad got home a while ago, but they didn't come up to check on me. I heard their shuffling in the kitchen, then their talking as they went into their room for the night.

I had yawned before I said sleepily, "I'm not that tired. Besides, the fun bits haven't shown up yet!"

Taylor scoffed. "Fun bits? A set of twins got mauled, the couple found a leather suit in their new house, and their neighbor is a creepy fuck? How is that not the 'fun' bits-"

As if on cue, a man appeared on screen; he just got out of a shower, so he was steaming hot, wet, and distressed. The actor walked out of the bathroom, and the camera cut to an angle where his ass was visible.

Taylor stared at the screen for a moment, probably either taking in that he just saw a man's ass or deciding whether he'd keep watching. I wouldn't mind honestly, the guy did have a nice butt.

"Uh, ew. That was gross." He said flatly. "You hyped up the bareness so I could see a man's ass?"

"Well, you should have waited until I said what kind it was, dummy." I retorted. "Besides, to me, it looked like you were enjoying your view."

Taylor's nose curled up as my words left my mouth. His brows furrowed and he made a fake gagging noise. "Ew. Speak for yourself, jackass."

Yep. He's straight. Dammit.

I wiggled my eyebrows at him, causing him to scoff. "Whatever, my good sir."

Taylor turned to me, a strange look forming on his face. "Call me that again and I'll punch you."

I laughed, hard. "Ooooh, Mr Tough Guy now? Fine, I'll stop, since you've obviously so much bigger than me, and so muscly, and brawny, and intimidating-"

Taylor laughed. "Damn right I am."

I rolled my eyes. "Should we get some sleep though? It's nearly 3am... and we have school tomorrow. Well, technically today, but you get what I mean."

Taylor shrugged. "Meh. I don't feel like going to school tomorrow. Let's just watch the end of this episode..."

Taylor nestled himself comfortably onto his side of the bed. I smirked at him before my attention went to my phone, which was sitting on my bedside table. I picked it up and clicked the lockscreen on.

'Snapchat: From Nicole.'

"Who's that?" I heard Taylor say. I glanced at him, and his head was turned to face me, his eyes fixated on my screen. I shrugged. Why is she sending me stuff this early in the morning?

"Oh wait, I know who she is! She's that chick in our year that always gives you flirty looks in the hall!" Taylor said. I shrugged.

I unlocked my phone and opened Snapchat. Clicking the photo, I braced myself.

It was a very, very clearly defined pic of her with her enormous cleavage. The caption read "hey xx". The pic disappeared in an instant.

"Damn," I heard Taylor whisper, "Aren't you lucky?"

I smirked, before giggling lightly. "Yeah, definitely. She's so hot."

I felt something in me twinge when those words left my mouth. For god's sake, I hate being closeted. I would much rather see Taylor shirtless right now. I texted her 'hey x' before throwing my phone aside, watching the rest of American Horror Story with Taylor.

CHAPTER 4

D arko's pov

Friday, February 1st, 2014

God, I love Fridays.

The only significant part of today so far was waking up to Taylor's soft snoring on my shoulder with American Horror Story still looping on my TV. As much as I had wanted to stay in that little time bubble, to be with Taylor as he softly leaned his head on my shoulder as he peacefully slept, I knew I couldn't. We had school today.

The first few classes, as well as recess, were about as entertaining as reading the dictionary. Taylor and I were so tired from our TV-show marathon that we were barely awake until the end of the fourth period.

The lunch bell woke us both up, and thankfully, we were finally allowed to buy coffee. We bought three cups each, but it just wasn't enough. I'm never binge watching TV that late again.

We had just sat down with the rest of our group when we heard her voice. That whiney, dick-in-mouth-sounding voice.

"So, who wants to come to my paaaaartyyyy!?" An extremely irritating voice said as it approached us, the sound piercing my ear drums. I glanced away from my beloved coffee, and surely enough it was Lyra. She smiled at my group while tapping her fake pink fingernails onto our table, waiting for an answer. After about a minute of silence, Lyra scoffed in annoyance. She had rolled her eyes before she flipped her curly hair over her shoulder, wafting her cheap peach scented perfume all over the place.

Yeah, she does that. It's cringy.

Lyra Anderson looked and acted like the typical clichè high school bitch. She wore clothes too tight for her (although nobody seemed to mind) and she's mean to everyone. She tries to be nice to Taylor, Bella & I but.. she has her moments. She's dated nearly every guy on the school's rugby team and she's cheated on every single one of them. She has a boyfriend now, but who knows how long that'll last?

I talk a lot of shit about her, but she's actually one of my closest friends. I just... don't agree with a lot of her choices. Yeah.

Among the rest of the students, Lyra's known as the 'Party Queen' and, to some extent, she is one. Nearly every month, she's been hosting these grand parties that almost always end up on the news. Riots, underage drunken messes, fights, and drugs are a few issues off of the top of my head that end up being broadcast on TV's and radios and plastered all over social media. For some stupid reason though, her parties seem to get more popular by the month, and the one she's planning right now already has 200 people attending.

"So?" She asked in a hurried voice, "which one of you idiots wants to come?"

Our lunch bench was big. It was the typical 'popular' table, but to me, it wasn't just that. Owning a motorcycle and being a professional racer meant that girls were begging for my attention, not that I wanted any of it. The table, hence, usually had all of the racer kids and the cheerleader squad overloading its benches. It's just a huge coincidence that all of the popular kids sat at the same table. I ignore most of them anyway; they usually only gossip about some random horse-shit, Kylie Jenner or something else that's irrelevant.

I mainly just focus on Taylor and Bella; emphasis on Taylor.

I don't like Bella. She might be a good person to others, but to me, she isn't. I just don't like her at all.

She's only really here because Taylor is here; which fucking annoys me.

She randomly became friends with him in year 8, and now she's nearly always at his side. Sometimes, I wonder if they're secretly dating. They're always doing things together, she's always talking about him, and I'm pretty sure she doesn't like me, hence why she 'accidentally' gave me the flu. Ugh. Back the hell off.

"I'll go," Bella said, smiling at Lyra. Lyra's cake-face instantly lit up as she waddled over to Bella and wrapped her in a tight hug. I rolled my eyes.

"- but only if Taylor and Darko come too."

I exchanged a confused look with Taylor, and we looked at Bella with the same pained expression. Taylor hates parties - something about being in a room with dozens of strangers and loud music makes him feel anxious. He's okay when it's a small gathering, but he is not ready for one of Lyra's parties. Heeeellllllllll no.

Honestly, I'm okay with the party as long as there are hot guys, food, and sick music. Three of my favourite things. It's just weird that I'm one of her conditions to go.

"Yeah, I'll go," I said before clearing my throat, "but Taylor shouldn't go. Parties aren't his thing."

Taylor instantly shot me a reassuring smile. I think I just did him a massive favour.

"Yeah, what Darko said," Taylor quickly added, which made Bella frown.

"But Taaaaaay!" Bella said in a falsetto whine, before slapping him softly on the shoulder, "you promised me that you'd go to the next party Lyra hosted!"

Taylor confusingly lifted a brow at Bella. "I did?"

Bella scoffed and rolled her eyes. God, she can be so irritating sometimes! Can she keep her dirty paws away from him? When she's with Taylor, she always has her hand on his shoulder, or she's always leaning on him, or she's always whispering stuff to him which makes his cute mouth laugh or smile.

Yeah, I'm a jealous bitch. If I can't have Taylor, no-one can.

"If you don't come, I'll..." she trailed off, tapping her red nails on her white chin. She suddenly beamed and poked his chest with her pale finger. "I'll tell the world your secret!"

Taylor's face drained itself of colour as Bella's mouth widened in the largest grin I've ever seen on a human being before. What secret was she on about...?

"Don't you fucking dare," Taylor hissed coldly, which made Bella frown.

"Well then, go to the party!"

Lyra and I exchanged a knowing grin as we began chuckling to ourselves. Lyra and I both knew that Bella had Taylor under her finger. Whatever this "secret" was, Taylor was desperate to keep it hidden. If I didn't even know what it was, it must be big.

Wait, Bella knows something about him that I don't? Since when did Taylor trust Bella more than me?!

"Darko? Help me out here, buddy! Come on man!" He pleaded.

"Sorry, can't help," I said coldly. "Next time, don't share secrets with her."

Taylor, somewhat taken aback at my words, sighed deeply and glanced at Bella.

"Fine, I'll go, you manipulative ass." He said flatly.

Bella shot her arms up in triumph before shouting 'YES!'. She playfully smacked his arm again before giggling.

Lyra forced a laugh out of her thick lips. "So, you're all coming?"

Bella and I nodded, as did Taylor, albeit he did reluctantly. Lyra instantly beamed as she whipped out her phone and began typing furiously, probably writing our names down on her invitee's list.

"Sweet! See you all there!"

Lyra walked off, flicking a flirtatious wink at Taylor. Oh, honey... not you too.

Bella began talking to some random cheerleader that was sitting next to her, as well as that Nicole girl that sent me that photo of her last night. Taylor started munching on his lunch, and I stared off into space, engulfing my coffee and a giant chocolate-chip cookie. Nicole tried to get my attention but I pretended I was too lost in thought.

I can't believe Taylor's going to a party. A Lyra party. When I go to those, I get uncomfortably drunk. Now that he's going, he's going to need someone to look out for him. Usually, I'd assume Bella would be the one to look out for him, but she gets completely wasted at parties too. She drinks the night away and tries to hook up with as many guys as she can.

I don't particularly want to leave Bella and Taylor alone together anyway. You know since he trusts her more with this secret than he does with me.

I guess I have to stay sober to keep him safe... not that it's that much of a burden to me. Gives me more of an excuse to be with him, and to keep Bella away.

Snapping out of my thoughts, I only just noticed that Taylor had picked up his tray and sat next to me.

"Hey bro, sorry, they started talking about periods. It's not a good thing to listen to when you're eating red shit." He said, gesturing to his plate.

I glanced to his tray and then back to him. I let out a chuckle before lightly clapping his shoulder.

"Red shit? You shouldn't eat that stuff man. Sounds kinda filthy."

Taylor let out a snort as he glanced back over at Bella. Periods are nasty, and they shouldn't be disclosed in a cafeteria where people are eating. Every time I hear someone talk about them I just casually remind myself how blessed I am to be a male human being. It's good not to have blood seep out of your privates.

"So," he began as he threw a tomato-sauce-covered-chip into his mouth, "What is a party, my good extrovert? And how does one go about in a party, without wanting to throw themselves from a balcony?"

I had laughed before I munched on a tater tot. "I still can't believe that you agreed to go to it. Whatever that secret is, it must be important to you."

Taylor stopped eating and glanced at Bella, who was making dumb animal noises to the girl she was talking to. "I can't believe she's blackmailing me with that. She knows how bad it is."

I lifted a brow and stuffed another tater tot into my maw. "It must be bad, you haven't even told me about it, and I know EVERYTHING about you."

When Taylor gets nervous, his body does some weird shit. His hands quiver, he cannot make eye contact for the life of him, and he stumbles over his words a lot. Whatever this secret was, it was making him panic.

I threw another tater tot in my mouth as I side glanced him. "I doubt you'd tell me anyway; you obviously trust Bella more than me."

"I... I uh," he spluttered, seemingly lost for words. After a moment of his panicked mess of a sentence, he said evenly, "I'm sorry. If it makes you feel any better, it's got nothing to do with you. I.. promise. Yeah."

I rolled my eyes and smiled. "Whatever man. You're such a bad liar."

Well, obviously, the secret has something to do with me. Instantly my brain began to draw up false conclusions.

HA. What if the secret was that Taylor liked me? Or that he was gay?

That'd be funny. Too bad it's not going to happen. It's probably got something to do between them. Maybe they finally 'tied the knot'. Ugh.

Ignoring my statement, he began filling himself with the last of his food. I picked up my last tater tot and leant closer to him; eyebrow furrowed, lips pouting.

"Can't you just tell me, dude? You literally cried on me last night, I thought we were past having no secrets between us," I said, gritting my teeth at my words. 'No secrets.'

Taylor began to protest when the siren rang. The cafeteria erupted into a panic, the various students hurriedly eating the last of their lunch as they scurried to class.

"Gotta go, bye!" Taylor said quickly before grabbing his bag as fast as he could. He slipped and faded into the ocean of teenagers almost instantly, earning him a frown from me.

He might have gotten a free ticket out of that, but I am going to know his secret, one way or another.

Taylor's pov

Holy shit. Bella is now dead to me. Dead. Deader than my great grandpa. Completely dead.

How dare she use my secret to blackmail me? She KNOWS I hate parties so much. She knows how nervous I get. Why the fuck does she want to drag me into that horrid mess that is Lyra's parties? WHY?

I ran from Darko the moment I could. Apart from him knowing I have a secret now, he's also pissed at me because I didn't tell him what it was. YAY. I could probably throw Bella onto an electric fence right now.

I can't fucking tell him that I'm in love with him! Now he's suspicious, and it's all Bella's fault. ARGH! You think you could trust someone...

I angrily walked to Biology when I felt a hand on my shoulder. Seeing the red nail-polish, I instantly recognised that it was Bella.

Greeeaaatttt.

"Dude, thanks for waiting for me. Real sweet of you." Bella spat sarcastically. I shrugged her hand off and continued walking.

She bolted in front of me and folded her arms.

"Taylor, what's wrong? If this is about the period talk, then I'm sorry-"

"No, you ass, while I am annoyed that you talked about that stuff, I'm more concerned about how you forced me into saying yes to Lyra and making Darko suspicious. Like, I mean seriously?" I threw my arms in the air and groaned. "Why?!"

Bella smiled sweetly before placing a hand on my shoulder. I leant away slightly from her, confusion spreading across my face as she opened her mouth.

"Oh my god dude, hear me out." She began. I hesitantly nodded as she half smiled.

"Okay, using your secret against you was a terrible thing to do, and I'm sorry. But, I did all of this for you. Why did you think I asked Lyra if I could get you AND Darko to come? I'm trying to get you two to go to the party, man. Together? Do you see where I'm going with this?"

I furrowed my brows in confusion, which made Bella rock her head back and groan dramatically. Her orangey-red hair tumbled behind her back as she did so.

"I'm trying to set you two up, you door-knob. You know? After a few drinks, Darko probably wouldn't be able to tell you from a guy or a girl. This party could be your big moment, dude!"

I widened my eyes at the imagination of Darko and me getting naughty at Lyra's party, but I then narrowed it and directed my gaze at Bella.

"I'm still annoyed! Now he know's something's up! Way to keep my secret under the radar, jackass!" I shouted to her, earning a few looks from passerby's. She glared, but then turned away. She began walking to class when she began to speak again.

"Like I said, I'm sorry. If you want to hear the plan, I'll tell you all about it in Biology. You just have to trust me."

Rolling my eyes and mentally preparing myself for whatever plan Bella was conjuring, I trudged my feet towards class.

CHAPTER 5

T aylor's pov

Friday, February 1st, 2014

"So, what do you think of the plan?" Bella whispered to me as she flicked through her biology notes, snorting and giggling when she came across the "human reproduction" section. I shrugged in response. In all honesty, I didn't hear a single word Bella had said to me. Whoops.

I was too busy ogling Darko from across the room, admiring from afar the cute little things he does when he thinks nobody's watching him study. He sat there, absentmindedly nibbling on the tip of his pen as he read and took down notes from his laptop, occasionally asking Lyra for help. The little smiles he would do once he figured out an answer, or the tiny giggles he spoke when Lyra told him one of her party tales drove me freaking wild.

I'm surprised Darko & Lyra hadn't hooked up yet, but I'm euphoric that he doesn't see her in that way. They got close during one of her earlier parties when he was a drunken mess one night, and she helped keep him safe & away from the other cheerleaders. Ever since then, people have been shipping them together. "Darko & Lyra, the match made in Heaven!" I hear his teammates say teasingly to him on occasions. Bleh. I don't think Darko even knows what shipping means.

Lyra is my friend. Darko is my secret crush. I can't do anything about my burning jealousy without exposing myself - so I'm sitting here, mentally weeping because of them behind my thick black-rimmed glasses.

Bella, realizing I was ignoring her, followed my gaze and figured out who I was focusing more on. She saw the pain in my eyes when she saw them laugh about something.

"You're jealous, aren't you?" she whispered as she joined me in my stare. I nodded, and she rolled her eyes.

"Jealousy is a bitch to deal with; I've learned my way of dealing with it, you've just gotta find your own way without outing yourself."

Bella's jealous over something? Jealous of what?

"Anyway," Bella began, snapping me out of my gaze, "You want a recap of the plan?"

I shrugged. "Fine, but be quiet, or you'll trigger Mr. Fisher."

Bella had snorted before she leaned in close. "Okay, so, Lyra's party is when shit's gonna go DOWN. My plan, put short, is just to get drunk. You need to get at least tipsy; otherwise, my plan isn't going to work - it's foolproof. Once you're drunk, and he's sufficiently drunk," she nodded her head towards Darko, "I'll work my magic."

I raised an eyebrow. "That's the thing, Bella. How can I know this will work? He's straighter than a flagpole, and both of us getting tipsy ain't gonna change that? Not to mention I hate the idea of getting drunk? Did you forget I have an alcoholic mother?"

She pulled off another eye roll. This time, it was accompanied by a groan.

"I know you're gonna be uncomfortable about this plan, with your mummy issues and your skepticism," she said in an annoyed tone, "but I know what I need to do to make him reveal his 'undying gay romantic feelings for you' if they even exist. You've just got to trust me."

I sighed. Bella has been there for me almost as often as Darko has been. During my first year of high school, my lunch money was always snatched from me from this group of bullies. Darko didn't know about it, and I didn't want to tell him because he'd probably get beaten to a pulp. They did it every day for four months straight. The only reason it stopped?

Bella came along.

During my victim phase, Bella was dating one of my tormentors. She saw what they were doing, promptly dumped the douche, and blackmailed the entire group. She's been my 'protector' of sorts since then since she's always able to find dirt on people and use it against them.

I have no choice. I trust Bella wholeheartedly - whatever she was planning I just had to trust her. She knows what's best for me.

"I trust you," I said to Bella, which made her face light up, "Just don't do anything dumb, okay? I don't want this to blow up in the future."

Bella smirked, "Now, any other problems that are going to worry you?"

I placed my hand on my chin and stroked it, "How will I know if I'm drunk? Like, I've never been drunk before. This is all new territory for me."

Bella smirked, "you'll know when you're drunk, trust me, and if you can't handle being drunk I'll make sure Lyra lets Darko know, okay?"

I smiled. The idea of getting drunk and allowing Darko to help me when my head is stuffed up is making me excited about the party. Don't get me wrong, drinking is bad and I shouldn't be doing it, but it's just for one night. It's necessary for Bella's plan. I have to step out of my comfort zone.

Bella smiled toothily before thundering "Now, nerd, get back to work before Fisher dissects you!"

I had grimaced before I shook my head. "Ew. You and Darko seem to have a habit of giving me weird nicknames. Nerd? You know I'm not that smart..."

Bella shrugged. "You wear nerdy glasses - therefore your nickname is 'nerd.' It's just the natural order of things," she said before sighing, "anyway, I gotta finish this chapter before Mr. Fish-head throws me over a cliff."

Uhm, rude? My glasses aren't nerdy. They're fashionable. Learn the difference, Bella.

I turned my focus away from Bella and directed my attention back to the most beautiful thing in the room, but I felt my stomach drop when I looked.

Unusually, he was staring straight back at me, his eyes flickering back between Bella and I. Normally, I'd flinch back and pretend I wasn't looking at him, but something was off. His cheeks were slightly pink, and he had this pissed off face expression. Furrowed brows, upturned mouth, murder in his eyes. He has never gone that shade of red before...

Oh no.

He couldn't have heard the plan. The people behind us couldn't even hear us speaking, so there's no way that Darko could have heard it. Something else was riling him up, something about Bella and me talking.

Was he... jealous?

Realizing I was looking at him, he quickly darted his gaze back to his laptop. His face grew even pinker as he pretended like I just hadn't caught him staring. He quickly looked up and nonchalantly covered his face with his hand as he noticed I was still staring. He attempted to talk to Lyra, but she had her headphones in her ears, and she was furiously typing away on her iPhone.

Was he... embarrassed? Why would he be embarrassed if I caught him staring?

Darko's pov

Oh fuck. Taylor just caught me staring at him.

All of Biology I've been making goo-goo eyes at him while he's been talking to Bella. I have no idea what on earth they've been whispering about, but it's pissing me off. Taylor is mine. MINE. Bella can fuck off. Stop talking to MY man.

And, how dare she call him a stupid nickname? I'm the only one that gives them to Taylor. Can she not? Find your own quirk, you blonde git. Stop stealing my stuff.

Taylor just had to be the observant person he is, and he had to look up to see what I was up to, just at the moment I was starting to become enveloped in my burning jealousy.

Why didn't I flinch back when he locked eyes with mine? Why did I do the dumbest thing and attempt to hide my face after I got caught the second time? Ugh, Darko, why do you do this to yourself?

"Wow, you look like shit," Lyra said, unplugging her headphones, "Oh wait, that's just how you usually look. My bad."

I smirked. "Well, at least I look better than you and your twelve different faces of makeup combined."

Lyra scoffed before facing me, a pretentious grin forming on her face as she flicked her hair. "Don't play the insult game with me,

Sports boy. At least, not to the person hosting the next big party. One click of a finger and you're uninvited."

I sighed. "Fine, I'm sorry. I'm just a little tense, that's all."

Lyra sighed too. "Yeah, whatever. I'm sorry too I guess, my boyfriend won't fucking text me back, and it's putting me on edge too. Like, he was just online a minute ago, and he hasn't responded to my text that I sent thirty seconds ago. Do I mean nothing to him?"

Containing my laughter, I looked away from Lyra and refocused on my laptop. While Lyra and I are friends, she can be one of the most annoying people on this earth, and not to mention clingy. Typically, I would have hooked up with her by now, for the sake of keeping my identity a secret, but it would backfire horribly. She'd become clingy, she probably wouldn't stop messaging me, and she'd play those mind games girls play where they're pissed off and you have to Rubix-cube yourself into figuring out why they're angry. She's that kind of girl. No wonder her boyfriend is ignoring her.

I am not gonna tangle myself into the web of Lyra Anderson. So, instead of being her boyfriend or her worst enemy, I took the friendly approach and now people won't stop 'shipping' us together, whatever the hell that means. Maybe Taylor knows what it means; note to self, ask Taylor later on.

I looked up from my laptop and glanced at Taylor again. He was giggling at something with Bella again, rocking his head back. Why does he have to be so cute for? Stupid Taylor being so damn adorable, messing up my concentration. Why was his smile so eye catching? Why was his laugh like music to my ears?

Biology sucks. Taylor sucks. I wish I were straight so I could get over my feelings. Nothing hurts more than falling for someone who would never want to be with you.

Not to mention, that stupid secret has been eating me out since lunch.

"Hey Darkie," Lyra said, snapping me out of my over-thinking thoughts, "don't forget to ask your parents that you're going, okay? I don't need another angry mum complaining about their son at my doorstep a day after the party."

I side-glanced her and laughed. "Okay, first of all, it's Darko. Darkie sounds awful on soo many levels," I said, which made her giggle. "And secondly, yeah sure. I'll let you know tomorrow."

"Sweet. Make sure to tell Tay-Bæ to RSVP too."

Tay-bæ? Oh god, that's so cringy. Taylor would probably fling himself off of a cliff if someone called him that to his face. Lyra gives out the worst names, and that's coming from me; the king of bad nicknames.

"Yeah, sure, I'll let him know."

CHAPTER 6

T aylor's pov

Saturday, February 2nd, 2014

Saturdays are my favourite days of the week. Zero chores, zero responsibilities, zero obligations and all the time in the world (well, technically, 24 hours only, but still). All I did today was play piano in my room, writing new songs and rehearsing old ones.

This particular Saturday though, I had one chore. One thing nagging me at the back of my head that I needed to fix.

I needed Ana's advice about the party.

It was late, about eight at night. Ana had come into my room a while ago, enjoying some brother-sister bonding time. She was painting her nails while I continued to play on my piano.

"Hey... Ana?" I said nervously, tapping the tips of my fingers softly on my piano keys, "can I ask you something?"

Ana, who was sitting on my bed in my room, lifted a brow. She placed her black nail-polish brush back into its bottle before she began fanning her hands. "Uh... sure? What's up, Tay?"

I had tapped a few piano keys before I uttered, "Let's say some-one was blackmailing you, and to keep your dirt hidden, you're forced to do something you're uncomfortable with. What would you do?"

Honestly, I don't trust what Bella was planning. What she told me yesterday in bio was too vague; she was purposefully keeping me in the dark. I'm sure Bella's trying to get Darko and me together, but her method's dodgy... It's my first party, and she's already trying to make me drink! There are already enough dangerous things to worry about at a party, yet she's trying to throw me in the deep end. I just.. my gut is telling me that something's not right. What if something goes wrong?

Ana softly chuckled before saying, "I'd do the thing that the person's forcing me to do, but I'd make sure first that it won't make me feel like shit. What is this person blackmailing you with, bro?"

"The blackmail has to do with... school. Nothing too big," I said, gritting my teeth at my lie, "and the uncomfortable thing is a party. I've been 'invited.'" I said, using my fingers as quotation marks.

Ana began blowing her nails softly before she snorted. "You? At a party? Don't make me laugh, Tay; if you went to a party, you'd probably explode from your nerves. You weren't built to be overly social."

I shook my head before grinning. "Yeah, you're right about that. But, I have to go to it. I have no choice."

Ana looked at me, a half-smile appearing on her pearly face, "So, regardless if you go or not, something's gonna happen?"

I nodded. Ana chuckled, before refocusing on her nails. "Nice one, bro. Way to get yourself into that kind of situation."

I rolled my eyes. "Well, I have until next Friday to make a decision. That's a week from now until the party - AKA my next nervous breakdown."

Ana sighed. "Does that mean I have to babysit mum again?"

"Hey, I'm only one call away. Besides, if I'm not responding and something drastic does happen, you know you can call Darko's family. Or, you know, an ambulance." I said.

We both sighed. Friday is going to be a busy night for both of us.

"What are you even going to do at a party? You've never been to one!" Ana stated as she started applying another coat of the matte black paint onto her thumb. I sighed.

Honestly, I have no idea what to do. What do people do during parties? Are they like the parties in high school movies where everybody gets drunk, everyone dances like an idiot and everyone gets laid? Because if they're like that, then I don't care if Bella exposes me. Parties like that are definitely not my thing.

Well, it is Lyra's party. It's going to be wild, no matter what. Great. Hopefully, it gets shut down early, so I don't have to worry about it too much.

"I have no idea," I began, which made Ana snort, "do you have any pointers? You've been to more parties than I ever have been."

Ana looked at me, a mischievous smile growing on her face. "I do have some pointers, but are you willing to get out of your comfort zone?"

I hesitantly nodded. Ana had laughed before she refocused on her nails.

"Well, first thing's first, you have to get at least tipsy. It makes everything seem way more fun than it actually is, and it helps with your confidence, which I'm sure you'd need," Ana said, as she continued to paint.

"Funny, Bella told me to get tipsy too. I guess it's something that needs to happen. It's just a little daunting, is all," I groaned, dragging my hands down my face lazily in annoyance. "Wait, you've drunk alcohol before?"

Ana glanced towards me, her brows furrowed. "Of course I have, but it was only once or twice, and I always made sure one of my girlfriends was looking out for me."

I nodded. At least Ana is responsible for her drinking habits, unlike someone else in this household.

"Also," Ana added, "I don't trust that Bella girl. I have a feeling she's hiding something from you." she said evenly.

I raised an eyebrow. "Like what?" I questioned. "She wouldn't be the type of person to hide something from me."

Ana shrugged, "I don't know. Just, something's off about her. Keep an eye on her, okay?"

I had sighed before I nodded. "Fine."

We sat in a comfortable silence after that. Ana finished her hands, and she moved on to her toe-nails, making sure not to get any on my pristine white sheets. I refocused on my piano and began practising an Adele song.

After I had finished the song, Ana asked, "So, I'm taking it that Darko's going?"

I nodded. Ana noticed it and reciprocated with a smile. "If you get extra nervous, just stick with him. He has been to plenty of parties; he would know how everything works. And plus, I'm sure he'll be more than willing to keep you safe."

I glanced away from Ana and smiled at those last few words she said. 'More than willing to keep me safe'. That's one of the best things about Darko - regardless of how he's feeling or what else is happening around him, I'm always his top priority. He's always really protective of me, and he's always making sure I don't hurt myself.

This would be so cliché if he were gay and in love with me. Oh, but a man can dream...

Oh, wait, shit. I just realised; If Darko's going to be at a party, that means he's going to try and hook up with someone. UGH. Great. Now I have to suffer through jealousy while being drunk. YAY. Maybe I'll get so drunk to the point where he has no choice but to make sure I don't die during the night. Then he'll be forced to stay with me, preventing him from finding some dodgy girl to stick his-

"Oh, by the way, " Ana said, interrupting my train of thought. "Sorry if I act a little loopy from now on, mum took me to a doctor the other day. He prescribed me some anti-depressants."

A huge grin spread across my face as I turned around. To my surprise, she was already behind me, and I wrapped her in a warm hug. "I'm proud of you Ana. Thanks for taking my advice."

Unlike our mum, Ana knew she had a problem and was willing to get help. I caught her a few weeks back, sitting on the bathroom floor crying her eyes out, her black mascara dripping down her cheeks. She showed me her scars and told me there and then that she had depression. I made it my duty to make sure she got the help she had needed before it got any worse; before I lose another family member.

"Anyway, " Ana said, releasing me from her hug, "I'll leave you to practise your performance songs. I gotta make an 'urgent' call with Kaitlyn. You need anything?"

I shook my head before smiling. "Nah, but thanks. Have fun with your bestie." She left the room, softly shutting the door behind her. I heard her shuffle towards mum's room, their mumbling voices piercing through the drywall, then to her room, closing her door behind her.

I put my sheet music into my folder and climbed into bed, pulling out my phone and connecting it to my speaker. It was nearly eleven, but nobody cared if I played my music, as long it wasn't too loud. I pressed the shuffle button and lied back, staring at the tiny cracks and paint smudges on my old roof. My tall paper lamp that was next to my bed glowed a beautiful quinacridone gold, which dimly illuminated my room, calming my senses. Once the speaker recognised the song that came through, it began echoing the relaxing melody within my four walls.

Smooth jazz. Yes.

I closed my eyes, and the first thing that popped into my head was Darko. The way he looked during lunch. The cute giggles he let escape him during Biology. The way he daydreamed after Lyra left our table. Everything about him made me smile like an absolute idiot.

Oh, the things I would give if he were here with me right now, whispering sweet nothings into my ear, while exploring me with his hands. The things I would give for him to be fucking gay. AGH!

Personality aside, Darko was quite the looker too. A jawline that could smite trees, emerald eyes that grass would be envious of, and a nearly perfectly toned body that every unfit guy dreams of. His smirk alone could make anybody drool.

I remember once; I was half asleep in his bed as he had burst into his room with only a towel around his waist, dripping wet. He was furiously rubbing his head, and his eyes were bloodshot. He had told me that his bathroom's shower head had burst from the wall mid shower, launching directly into his skull. While I was helping him fix it, half awake, shirtless and groggy, he got up to get a wrench from the garage, and his towel fell off, exposing... everything. Oh boy. He was so big.

I threw a hand in my pants.

"I can't believe I'm going to a party," I said aloud, dragging my free hand down my face. 'A party'. I already felt nauseous. What if something happens at the party? What if I don't fit in with the other party-goers? What if I embarrass myself in front of Lyra, Bella and especially Darko?

Feeling the stirring, I sighed in relief. Thanks to my thoughts about the party, there also was an unsettling amount of anxiety. I never thought it was possible to be horny and anxious...

I turned over, took my hand out, grabbed my glasses and turned off my lamp, placing the spectacles on my bedside table. Switching the song to something more melodic, I turned the volume down, so it was just barely audible. The soft, quiet sound of rushing water filled the dark space in my room, calming me down slightly. Soft shades of the moon's light peeped through my thin white curtains.

I closed my eyes. Visions of Darko materialised in my mind then faded; then a party scene popped its way into my head then back out, then... my dad appeared. Standing tall, wearing his classic red flannel and jeans, and his famous toothy smile.

What would dad do if he was here with me? Would he encourage me to go to this party? Would he even consider letting me go out?

He so would.

Dad was a firm believer in the "try everything once" motto, and he would most definitely want me to go. I can see the scene now - I'd go up to him and ask reluctantly, he'd laugh and pat me on the back before saying, "son, just fucking go. Live your teenage life! Enjoy every single aspect of it; don't make mistakes like me."

God, I miss him so much.

Dad faded away in my mind, and visions of Darko without a towel came back. My hand travelled down back to my groin as I felt it. Jesus. I wish it was his hand that was down there.

Suddenly, my phone started to buzz uncontrollably, startling me.

"Oh for fuck's sake," I said, getting my hand out. I lifted myself up and grabbed my phone, squinting at the blinding light of my lock-screen. It was Darko; he was calling me.

I picked it up, a sly smirk forming on my lips. "Hey, I was just thinking about you -"

"Taylor, I was just robbed."

CHapTer 7

D arko's pov

Saturday, February 2nd, 2014

I needed to tell him. I didn't care about what others had thought anymore.

Weighing out the pros and the cons, it suddenly dawned on me; I would rather hope and pray that Taylor felt the same way than live a depressing life that my parents and other people control. If he didn't return my feelings, I'd at least have that weight off of my shoulders.

I was going to tell Taylor about my feelings on his birthday, which was the week after Lyra's party, then come out to my parents. I wasn't going to say it to his face, oh jeez, definitely not to his face, but in a card. His birthday card. How poetic, eh?

Fate had other plans.

I had the gift, and I had the card; it had been prepared and ready to go. I even hid it in my car, so my family wouldn't find it. It was a small porcelain piano figurine with a slip of paper dotted with musical notes, and a 'Happy Birthday!' card with my feelings written in it.

Now it's gone. I hate this fucking neighbourhood.

"Robbed? What, how and when?!" Taylor said his voice prickling with concern through my phone's speaker. I had sighed as I ran my fingers through my hair. My hand clutched the phone firmly as I began to explain what had happened.

"I was taking out the trash from my room when I saw a figure lurking near my car. They were clutching a large box in one arm, and when they saw me, they pulled out a knife. A fucking knife! They... they threatened to stab if I tried to come near them. I couldn't recognise the voice, but it was feminine," I uttered through my panicked breaths. Taylor let out a gasp when I said the assailant whipped out a knife.

"Could you see what they looked like?" Taylor questioned.

I shrugged, then when I realised he couldn't see me, I answered, "no. Whoever they were thought this through; they were dressed head to toe in black. The thief was quite tiny, though."

"What did they steal?" He asked, hurriedly. I sighed, glancing towards my car from my front porch.

"My entire glovebox. Your birthday present was in there. Whoever it was got away."

There was silence on the other end of the phone. After a tense few seconds, Taylor asked, "you bought me something?"

Psh, yeah, and it's gone as well as my confession of love. Fuck my life.

"I'm sorry dude. Stupid robbers are so fucking inconsiderate. Like, is it even possible to steal an entire glovebox?" I spat rhetorically.

Taylor had snorted before saying, "Dude, forget about my present. The most important thing is if you're okay right now! If a robber waved a knife at me, I would have shat my pants!"

I let out a short giggle before I looked at my car again, the sight of the cracked passenger seat's window making me frown.

"You're right. I'm fine now that I called you," I began, "speaking of which, I'm sorry that I called you so late. I thought I'd let you know about it, bro."

"It's okay. I'm just glad you're safe," Taylor said.

My mouth curved into a warm smile at the sound of his words. I could call him at 4am for no reason, and he wouldn't be mad at all. Such a sweetheart.

I just hope I can get the piano figurine again; the shop was nearly out of stock.

"Well," he said, "I'm gonna head back off to bed. Lemme know if anything else happens. Night Darko."

I smirked. "Sure thing. Goodnight, my good sir."

Hearing a loud groan, I quickly hung up the phone before he could protest. Mum poked her head out of the front door, a cup of tea in her wrinkly hands.

"Hey," she greeted, "I've just gotten off the phone from the police. They're going to look further into it, but they say that they can't do much right now. I'm sorry Darko; if you need cash to replace your glovebox-"

"Oh no, Ma, it's okay." I said, interrupting her, "I have the money, it's just the contents of it were hard to replace. It's okay."

Mum crept out of the doorway and wrapped me in a tight hug, her tea miraculously not spilling in the process. "I love you; you know that right? I'm sorry that this happened to you, dear. You were so brave."

I smiled, before saying I loved her too. She released me from her grip, a weak smile forming on her lips as she wrapped her beige cardigan tighter around her tiny body.

"After this tea, I'm gonna head back to bed. If you're gonna stay up, please get a coat or something," she said, her eyes darting to my torso, "it's way too cold to be wearing only a singlet."

I smiled at my mum, who had sipped more of her black tea. A strong gust of crispy night air swept past us, making both of us shiver. I turned to her.

"I'm surprised Stefan and Dad slept through that," I said suddenly, "Thank you for coming outside."

She half smiled at my words as I looked back at my car. After a few moments, I turned to her, gave her a quick peck on the cheek and announced that I was going to bed. I need to sleep this off.

Maybe this was the universe's way of telling me that I shouldn't tell Taylor or my parents. Maybe I was just being too selfish and just wanted what was best for me, instead of what was best for everyone. UGH.

Maybe it's best if I just didn't say anything to anyone. I need to re-think this all.

Sunday, February 3rd, 2014

I fluttered my eyelids open, then immediately snapped them shut while I covered my face with my hand. Out of all of the annoying places the sun decided to peek through my curtain, it decided to shine directly in my eyes. Thanks, sun, you prick.

I sat up on my bed, groaning as I stretched. I went to check my clock when I heard unfamiliar voices coming from the downstairs kitchen. Quickly pulling on some shorts over my boxers and slipping on a shirt, I snuck out of my room, sitting on the staircase. I began to eavesdrop.

"Like I said, I'm sorry, but there's nothing else we can do," a police officer said to my parents, his deep voice invading the living room. Stefan was in the kitchen eating a toasted sandwich while the officer talked to my parents.

"Surely you can dust for fingerprints or something!" Mum said, turning to dad. The officer frowned as he let out a sigh.

"For the third time ma'am, we did already! The culprit must have been smart and wore gloves; there was no trace of any fingerprints anywhere. Apart from the wrench and the wire cutters we found, there was nothing else peculiar about this."

Dad groaned, and mum sighed. Out of options, they had no choice but to dismiss the officer, of which swiftly left the house. I crept down from the staircase, pretending not to have heard that exchange. A wrench and wire cutters? Did the robber plan this robbery?

I guess that figurine and my card are lost forever.

Stefan looked up at me from his phone. "Mornin'. I'm sorry about your car; I heard what had happened."

I casually said 'yeah, thanks' as I peeked into the fridge, grabbing the carton of OJ and pouring a glass. I sat next to him as mum and dad entered the kitchen.

"I'm sorry son," dad said, "for now, keep your car here. I'll see to a replacement of your window. For now, use your motorcycle."

I stuck my thumb up as I took a huge gulp of orange juice. Dad left the room and parked himself in front of the TV, his legs lifting up as the chair reclined. Mum groaned as she opened the fridge.

"Do you want some toast like your brother or something else?"

I looked at her, setting the orange juice down onto the coaster on the marble island in the kitchen.

"I'm not that hungry, but thanks. I'll just have some juice."

She nodded. "Don't forget, it's Sunday. We're gonna go to church after this, so get ready. We're leaving in twenty minutes." She said as she left the room, leaving Stefan and me alone. He munched on his peanut-butter-and-jam toastie while he scrolled through his phone.

"You're oddly calm about this. If someone robbed my car, I would be so pissed off about it. To you, it's just like... a mild inconvenience." Stefan uttered. I shrugged.

"There was nothing great in the glovebox anyway. Besides, I have cash. I'll replace it later." I said. Apart from the present, nothing else was in there except for a few elastic bands and paper scraps. It really was just a mild inconvenience. I had the money, and I had a second means of transport anyway; my motorbike. It just means that I'll need to leave my car at the repair shop for a day or so.

There was a comfortable silence after that. We both just sat there, Stefan reading something on his phone while he ate as I sipped my drink. If Stefan knew about the card, I wouldn't doubt he'd tell dad the first opportunity he got. I came to a conclusion last night that I'll come out to Taylor first, then my family last... once I get the present again.

"Are you going to Lyra's party next weekend?" He said suddenly, looking up at me. I nodded, which made him smirk. I furrowed my brows.

"Please tell me you're not going too," I said, groaning when he hummed in response. Why did he have to go? You think he'd get enough entertainment from when he backstabbed me and got me into heaps of trouble with dad after one of Lyra's previous wild parties.

I was at one of her parties, and I didn't know that Stefan was invited too. Before the party though, I had a fight with Taylor. I had hurt him; before you ask, no, not physically (I would never intentionally hurt him that way) but... emotionally. Saying that 'I said some crappy stuff' would be the understatement of the century - I'm not sure what point I was trying to make, but I began bringing up his dad in my angered state. He ended up crying and saying that I was just like his mum.

Anyway, at the party, I couldn't stop thinking about the fight, replaying all of the things that were said and the things I didn't say. Thanks to the 'wise' words of Lyra, I downed half a carton of beer and ate two pot-brownies, thinking that it was the best decision at the time.

It wasn't for obvious reasons.

On the bright side, the drinking did help make me stop thinking about the fight. On the downside, the drinks-and-drugs combo turned me into an embarrassment. I vomited at least twice, I was a drunken swaying mess, and I was very flirtatious to guys (people shrugged off my advances because I was drunk and high, thank God.)

That was when Stefan saw me; A dazed, drunken dumbass lying half-conscious on Lyra's front lawn, covered in vomit. Not my proudest moment. I think dad's still pissed off at me for that, even though it happened months ago.

"I won't snitch on you again," He said, a small smirk appearing on his lips, "If you try and help to get me in with Lyra."

I furrowed my brows, nearly choking on my juice. "What? You want to get in with her?"

Stefan glared at me. Sensing he'd probably hit me, I added, "I... didn't realise she was your type." I'm surprised that he'd be interested in her. Eh, to each his own I guess.

He snorted. "Yeah, Lyra's cute. Besides, I'm way better for her than the douche she's currently seeing. I mean, look at him!"

He showed me his phone, and to my surprise, he was on Lyra's Facebook profile. Her profile pic was her with a creepy looking guy named Steven; his eyes were bugging out, he had a raccoon-coloured Mohawk, and he had an unsettling, toothy smile. I frowned at the photo, which made Stefan laugh.

"Fine, fine, he's gross," I said, making him giggle louder. "I wonder what she sees in him."

Stefan grunted before rolling his eyes. "He's filthy rich, that's why."

"He's still disgusting," I said, "no money in the world can fix that."

"No shit bro. I, on the other hand, however, am a sexy beast, that even the likes of Lyra will have a hard time resisting."

I slid my finger around the rim of my cup. "Well, being physically attractive won't be a problem, Lyra would date anything with a pulse and a dick," I said, making him snort. "While I would say that her being in a relationship is a problem, I don't think that they're actually connecting."

Stefan lifted a brow. "What do you mean?"

I smiled, thinking back to biology yesterday. "They're dysfunctional, and Lyra has crazy expectations of him. If anything, I can see her dumping him at the party, grabbing as much attention as she can. You'd have to swoop in then."

"Sweeeeeeet," Stefan said, finishing the last of his breakfast. "I guess I won't snitch on you then. Again, I mean."

"I'm still salty about that by the way," I said, making him roll my eyes.

"Well then, next time don't drink and get high under age, you idiot. I'm just being a good big bro. Don't act sinfully."

With that statement, Stefan left the kitchen. I had drunk the last of my drink before I went back to my room, to get ready for church.

CHaPTer 8

Darko's pov

Thursday, February 7th, 2014

"ARGH! I HATE THIS PIANO!"

I shouted in frustration as I threw my arms up in the air. I slammed my head down onto Miss Lauriana's piano keys, a terrible clash of notes erupting from the instrument as my head crushed them. Taylor patted my back as I pseudo-wept.

"Like I said, learning things on the piano takes practice. You'll get the hang of it eventually." Taylor said soothingly, rubbing my back. I craned my head, my eyes meeting Taylor's as my ear rested on the keys. I had groaned before he let out a soft chuckle.

It's been four days since Sunday; four days since my glovebox was thieved. While I had managed to replace my glovebox, the porcelain figurine was one of a kind - the store had closed down. Apparently, I had been their sole customer for the entire month. There was no chance I, nor anybody else, could ever buy something from there again.

Why does the universe hate me? All I want to do is make Taylor happy on his birthday. Can't something go right at least once?

Come on Darko, I thought to myself; you didn't give up motor-cycle riding today to disappoint Taylor. You can do this!

"I guess so," I said weakly, lifting my head up slightly, "I just... I wish I could make Fur Elise sound as amazing as you can."

A smile appeared on his face, making him turn to face the in-strument. He cleared his throat as he adjusted his glasses. "You're such a suck-up."

"Pshh. If I were, I'd be spit-shining your shoes."

He had grimaced before snorting. "Now that would be gross. Anyway," he said as he placed his hands on the keys, gesturing me to join in too, "ready? I'll play the intro again; then you copy me."

I quickly nodded. Taylor began playing the first few notes of the song, making sure it was slow enough for me to remember the sequence. Once he was done, he turned to me, gesturing to the ebony keys. I finally managed to copy his fingerwork correctly, making a smile appear on both of our faces.

"Yes!" Taylor said cheerfully, "keep playing that part over and over until you can do it without thinking about it."

I nodded, smiling, and kept replaying the notes as I did before. I shut my eyes, letting my mind wander as the notes flitted into my ears. This week had been incredibly busy for everyone. Lyra's been busy preparing for her party, Taylor's been prepping for his performances at school, and Bella's... well, Bella hasn't been at the school for a few days. Quite weird.

Meh. I'm not complaining. Her being 'off the grid' gives me more one-on-one time with Taylor. My favourite time.

"Uh, Darko? You're playing the wrong notes..." Taylor said, snapping me out of my thoughts.

I glanced down, and I was playing everything one note lower down than I should have. I swore profusely, throwing my head back as I did. "I'll never learn this. I have stupid fingers."

Taylor chuckled. "Don't beat yourself up. Nobody gets it the first time. Believe it or not, I was once terrible at the piano."

I snorted. "Yeah I know, but that was in like grade two. Everybody is bad at an instrument when they're seven - you've always been talented!"

An enormous grin formed on his lips before he shrugged. "Like I said, you're such a suck-up, Darko."

I rolled my eyes as I refocused on the keys in front of me. Taylor focused on the instrument too, but he didn't play anything - he just sat there, staring.

I had lifted a brow before asking tentatively, "hey, you all good?"

Taylor remained unresponsive. He was literally fine three seconds ago, why's he suddenly acting up? Am I sucking up to him too much?

"Earth to Taylor?"

Taylor, seemingly to have snapped out of a trance, faced me, blinking his eyes rapidly for a few moments. Stifling back a laugh at his strangeness, I grinned, making him lift a brow this time.

"What's wrong?" he said. I let out a chuckled before I pointed at his face.

"You tell me, bro."

Taylor narrowed his eyes, perplexed. After a few tense moments, his face washed over with realisation. "OH! I was just thinking about the party tomorrow. Sorry about that."

I smiled, but then let it fade when Taylor turned away, touching the piano keys, his hand quivering slightly. He let out a soft, sharp breath of air as if he'd been holding on to it too long. I cocked an eyebrow up.

"Are you nervous?" I asked. He nodded.

"Tay... parties are nothing to be worried about," I said sombrely, making him glance back toward me. "If you're this nervous about it.. then just skip it."

Taylor groaned. "You know I can't do that."

I groaned before saying flatly. "Right, the secret. The one you still refuse to tell me."

I wish I knew this stupid secret. My curiosity has been eating away at me for a week now. It's like owning a diary and only writing down 'oh, the weather was good today'; it's bloody pointless. Taylor never keeps things from me; the longest thing he'd kept hidden from me was his Christmas present, but even then he told me about it. UGH.

"I-its... complicated. I only told Bella because she's the only one that can help with it. You will know, eventually man. I just have to work it all out first."

I huffed before sinking my head onto the keys again, letting the horrible wave of notes stream past my eardrums.

"Fine."

Silence filled the room after the screech of the piano left. Taylor sighed before placing his hands back on the piano, facing me.

"I'm sorry, alright? Anyway, this isn't about me today, forget my nerves, the party, everything. My mission is to teach you this song; I did promise last week, after all."

I snorted before focusing on the piano. "Fine. I just can't get my damn fingers to go in the right spots."

Taylor sat there, bringing his fingers up to his chin, slightly narrowing his eyes.

"Maybe we should use stickers? I remember you used to use them," I suggested. He waved at me dismissively, before his eyes widened. He turned to me, a soft grin spreading his lips.

"I have an idea. Trust me."

Suddenly, Taylor stood up and stood behind me. He leant forward, his head directly next to mine, and his arms snaked around, his hands resting on top of mine. His soft fingers curled over my now shaking fingers. His silky palms send electric bolts through my arms to my chest.

"We can't use stickers, Miss Lauriana would kill me," he said, his voice so tender on my ears, "this method is better. Stick out your pointer finger."

Feeling his warm breath on my neck made my heart race in my chest. He's literally on top of me. His stubble on his cheek was bristling with mine. His soft hands guided my hands, my pointer finger tapping the piano seamlessly as he moved from note to note. This is freaking intimate. Oh my god.

Ah shit. Of course, I felt a stirring in my groin. Thanks, dick, for being subtle. If Taylor takes one glance down, I'd probably cry of embarrassment.

I was too lost in my thoughts to realise that I was playing the beginning part correctly. Taylor's hands synchronised so well with mine that he just continued the rest of the song. His hands gripped around my two index fingers, playing the possible notes with such grace and fluidity. His proximity, his warmth, his touch... Jesus. There was nowhere else I'd want to be right now.

As 'my' fingers danced around on the keys, playing the final notes, we both just sat there for a minute, letting the mood envelop us. He rested his chin on my shoulder before whispering, "Well, you certainly don't have stupid fingers now."

I chuckled, before saying "Well, they would be stupid without yours. Thanks, mate."

Much to my dislike, he lifted himself from me and sat back down next to me. That was freaking intense. My heart is about to explode; my head is spinning, my hands are shaking. He looked at me, and for a moment there, I could see the faintest glint in his eyes.

I can't stand this anymore. Gay, straight, bi, whatever the hell he might be, this situation is just too surreal. Maybe he is gay, or maybe I'm over-thinking this entire thing.

I'm going to kiss this boy, right here, right now. This emerald eyed, nerdy pianist. My best friend.

I leant forward, lips ready, eyes shut, heart racing...

...just as Miss Lauriana walked in, distracting Taylor's attention. He turned to face the door just as I got too close.

He looked at me, a perplexed expression spreading on his pearly face. "Uh? You good there bro?"

I regained my posture, my face heating up, probably showing a very bright pink. "Yeah, just uh... a little dizzy all of a sudden. Sorry for nearly falling on you."

He smirked. "You better be, Darko."

He got up and walked over to Miss Lauriana. I placed my elbows on the keys, resting my head on the balls of my palm. Why did I just do that? WHY? Good God, I feel like shit. I nearly kissed my best friend - my straight best friend!

I got up and walked to the door. Taylor, clearly confused, shouted, "Darko! Where are you going?"

My mind blanked. I quickly thought back to the party, how Lyra asked me the other day to help pick her an outfit. That'll do for an excuse.

"L-Lyra uh," I said, stammering, "she just texted me. S-she uh, wants me to help her pick out a dress. She's having trouble finding one. Yeah. Trouble."

Taylor lifted a brow, looking at the piano, then back to me. "Are you sure? We still have time to learn another song if you want-"

"Nope! Sorry! Maybe next Thursday. Bye!" I said quickly, rushing out of the room.

I can't be near him right now, as much as my heart wanted me to stay there. His warm, his touch, his talent; it's dangerous - Miss Lauriana coming in just as she did must have been a sign or some sort of warning.

Maybe I should just stay away for a while.

Chapter 9

T aylor's pov

Friday, February 8th, 2014

It's now Friday.

Friday - the glorious day most students looked forward to - the day that marks the temporary end of their academic prison sentence. Weaving myself through the throng of teachers and students that littered the front of Vale's campus, I reached the school bus where Ana was waiting for me.

Everyone's mind was set on one particular thing this particular Friday. My mind, Darko's mind, everyone's mind - It had been 'the talk' of the week, the thing everyone was anticipating.

It was the dreaded day of Lyra Anderson's party, and I'm absolutely shitting my pants.

'For god's sake, Taylor, breathe,' I thought to myself when Ana smiled at me. Darko told me to keep repeating this to myself, which was sweet of him, but it's just not working.

Ana and I squeezed into the bus, which was packed to the sides like a can of oversized tuna. The party was the only audible subject. The girls were freaking out over what clothes they'll wear and what makeup they'll be showcasing, while the guys were betting on who would get laid the most and who would get wasted first.

Me? I wasn't thinking about any of this. Yesterday, after Darko left suddenly, all I could think about was Bella's vague plan - how she was going to 'make' Darko like me. She's been MIA for days now; no school, no texts, absolutely nothing. She still hadn't fully explained the plan yet, which is making me anxious as all hell.

What the hell was she doing?!

When Ana and I got home, I ran to my room and locked the door behind me. A few moments later, Ana knocked tentatively on my door. She asked, "the hell? What's wrong dude," a few times before she left - probably leaving to get ready for Lyra's event.

Mum was going to go see her therapist for most of the night, so Ana was able to come. Thank goodness she is - if anything bad happens I can go straight to her.

I sat there on my bed, nervously tapping away at the sheets, checking my phone every few moments. I kept my eyes locked onto my digital clock, watching the seconds tick by, hoping that by some chance time will freeze so I don't have to go to this godforsaken party. The quick flashes of the colon separating the hours and minutes seemed to torture me - every single flash indicating a second had passed, which means a second closer to the party.

Rumours about the party spread around the school like wild-fire. Apparently, Lyra was going all out - she apparently hired a stripper, bought a shit tonne of booze, and I think she talked to a drug dealer because there were rumours of weed and ecstasy being 'provided' at the party.

There's too much illegal stuff happening there. If my dad left me anything, it was my morals.

Oh God, I can see it now; everyone's going to be drunk and drugged out of their minds, going skits, dancing like idiots while they make out with anybody that is willing.

Note to self; never tell Bella anything ever again.

I should have never told her how I felt about Darko. If I never told her, then I never would have been blackmailed last week, and I would never have locked myself in my room, acting like a pissbaby because I'm a nervous wreck. If I had just kept my mouth shut, then I wouldn't have gotten myself into this mess. Now I have to go and get tipsy because otherwise, Bella is going to ruin me.

TAYLOR, WHY DO YOU DO THIS TO YOURSELF?!

A soft knock reverberated on my thin bedroom door, snapping me out of my thoughts. Nearly shiting my pants at the sudden sound, I called out.

"What do you want Ana?!" I yelled. After a tense moment, a voice began to speak.

"Actually... it's Darko. I came after Ana called. Can I come in?"

Did Ana call him? Ugh, WHY?

I groaned. Of course, she called Darko. Of course, Darko had to come in at this exact point in time to check up on me, to see how much of a nervous wreck I am, as if he is going to miraculously fix how I feel. Soon, we're going to drive to the party as if nothing had happened.

This is so cliché. At this point, the only person that was going to make me go is Bella, and she's off the grid right now, thank God.

"Yeah, sure, whatever, Just let me unlock it," I said, my voice breaking a little. I slowly got up out of my bed, unlocking the door. Darko looked daggers at me.

"Please don't tell me you're still nervous from yesterday," Darko asked. I shrugged.

"Why are you freaking out over this? I've said to you too many times just to breathe." Darko said, leaning on my door frame, an angry look on his face forming.

"That just doesn't work for me! I'm socially awkward; you know that!" I said, accidentally raising my voice. Darko's eyes widened.

"I'm sorry," I said, slumping slightly, "Just go. The only reason I'm going to this stupid thing anyway is because of Bella; since she's been MIA for the past few days, I'm gonna take advantage of it."

"I just wish you could come. I kinda hoped you weren't ditching the party - "

"Uhm, excuse me, Taylor? You're not ditching the party, are you? You remember what we talked about in AP Biology?" a feminine voice pierced through the house, cutting him off mid-sentence.

Oh shit.

Darko and I both looked out from my bedroom, and we both saw Bella hovering in the doorway, glowering. Ana had just opened it for her.

"Oh thank god! You're finally out of your room," Ana said, "I knew calling your best friends would coax you out."

"Yeah, thanks, Ana. Appreciate it." I said flatly. Ana had rolled her eyes before she trudged off to her room, leaving us three alone.

"Bella, where the hell have you been the past few days!? I've sent you dozens of messages, and you've missed out on too much schoolwork! Why do you pick your phone up to my sister, but not me?" I yelled. Bella shrugged non-chalantly.

"My old phone broke, and mum wanted me to take a few days off of school. I was gonna call you anyway, but since your sister already was, I didn't bother to."

"So much has happend!" I began, before gesturing to Darko, "Darko got robbed, he learned how to play Fur Elise-"

"Wait, what?" Bella asked, before looking at Darko, "you were robbed?"

Darko nodded, "yeah. Had Taylor's birthday present in there. We still don't know who it was."

Bella nodded thoughtfully, before saying evenly, "I hope you find out who it was."

There was an uncomfortable silence. I put my hands in my pocket while Darko whipped out his phone. Bella was eyeing my clothes carefully, before looking at me condescendingly. "You're going to the party in that?"

Well, I was contemplating about faking my death a few moments ago so I didn't have to go, so...

I looked at my clothes and glanced back at her, not knowing what to say. She had huffed before she walked out of the doorway, into my bedroom. Darko followed her. I groaned and rolled my eyes as I followed them.

Of course, she came. Now that she's here, I can't just ditch the party in front of her; Darko's here. If I were to ditch it right now, she would tell him my secret straight away. Fuck my life.

"Hey, why don't you wear this?" I heard Darko say.

I turned around, and Darko lifted up a white shirt with a wolf pattern on its torso. He held it up, inspecting it before he scrunched it into a ball and threw it at me. Bella fished out a pair of black jeans that was in my closet and tossed them to me.

"Pair those up with your red Converse, and you'll look good!" Bella chirped. I glanced down at the clothes I was given, before rolling my eyes.

"I don't know guys...that look is for people that look cute without trying."

"You always look cute!" Darko and Bella said simultaneously. I cocked an eyebrow at Darko, who was looking daggers at Bella, who was looking at me, smirking.

"Uh, that's flattering and all, but-"

"Just put on the damn clothes, you big baby," Bella spat. She turned on her heel and walked to the door, before glancing to her side.

"Uh, Darko? Let's give Taylor some privacy," she said, before looking at me, "Unless you want to see Taylor undress."

Darko turned around, staring slack-jawed at Bella, while I mouthed 'fuck you' to her. She chuckled before walking out the door, Darko following her.

If I could scream, I would be. I DON'T WANNA GO. I. DO. NOT. WANT. TO. GO.

I nervously adjusted my glasses as I slipped on the clothes that they had picked out for me. I opened the door and gestured to myself, earning a smile from both Darko and Bella.

"Damn, you look good," Darko said. Bella, out of sight from Darko, wiggled her eyebrows at me.

"Heh, thanks, Darko," I said, earning a soft smile from him.

Bella's nose turned upward. She had narrowed her eyes before they focused on me. "Taylor, when was the last time you show-ered?"

My eyes widened at her words, and I felt my cheeks burn up. Quickly ducking back into my room, I fetched a towel and shoved past the two, making my way to the bathroom.

"I'll shower now," I said quickly as I walked. I made eye contact with Bella as I reached the door.

"We're gonna go and get ready," Darko said, smiling, "We'll be back in an hour or so to pick you and Ana up. See you then, man."

I nodded before slipping into the bathroom, locking it behind me. I hastily turned on the shower before sliding down the door, quickly taking off my clothes, still fuming that I managed to get myself in an inescapable situation.

CHAPTER 10

D arko's pov

Evening. Friday, February 8th, 2014

"WHAT DID YOU SAY?!" Lyra exclaimed, shouting over the music which was blaring on enormous speakers. She cupped her hands behind her ears, absentmindedly bobbing her tiny body to the booming music as she talked to me. I sighed.

Bella, Taylor and I had gotten to the party a few hours ago - somehow between then and now, I ended up separated from them. I went to look for them, but Lyra intercepted and dragged me onto the dance floor instead, where a swarm of tipsy teenagers were dancing. Strobe lights obscured my vision while the heavy trap music deafened me. Several sticky elbows kept bumping into me as the beat quickened. It didn't help that I was already buzzed.

"I SAID, HAVE YOU SEEN TAYLOR AND BELLA?" I yelled. Lyra, finally understanding what I had said, shook her head. She pointed to the living room, where the other jocks and cheerleaders were congregating.

"TRY ASKING THE JOCKS! THEY HAVE EYES AND EARS EVERYWHERE!" Lyra shouted, smiling.

"ALL RIGHT, THANKS! GREAT PARTY BY THE WAY!" I responded. Lyra shouted 'THANKS!' before turning around to grind on another partygoer.

If there's one thing Lyra can do, it's dance like a stripper. It's like she was born to do it.

I shoved my way through the crowd, being careful to not get the sticky sweat from others on me. The combination of a crowded dance floor and very humid weather meant for a horrifically steamy, sweaty atmosphere. No wonder the jocks were inside - they'd be roasting under their varsity jackets.

I wiggled through the glass door that lead inside Lyra's house and was immediately greeted by the football team. Two of them, Michael and David, were chatting while taking long sips from their beers. Another one, Owen, was on his phone, and another two, Trent and Duncan, were smoking. I cautiously approached them.

I swear these guys haven't got a brain in their heads. Take Michael and David for example; they are as dumb as a box of rocks, not to mention they are incredibly irritating. For example, David breathes really, really loudly and Michael is the most conceited person I know. They're insane.

All right, breathing too loud might not sound that bad, but trust me. He sounds like a broken bagpipe sometimes. It gets unbearable.

Owen is a puzzle wrapped in an enigma. Nobody knows who he really is; apart from his name, all people know is that he's constantly on his phone, calling or texting somebody. I've heard rumours that he's a spy.

Trent, Duncan and I have a history together. We've gotten into fights, mostly because Trent's an insensitive idiot, and Duncan blindly follows him. Trent is a known homophobe in the school; he's always making remarks about gay guys being the scum and filth of the Earth. Needless to say, his bigotry has earned him a few punches to the face. He doesn't like me and I really don't like him.

Duncan has a criminal record; he's been known to set things on fire, beat people to a pulp, and be proficient with a switchblade. It's unclear how Duncan even made the school's football team - people say he threatened to stab the coach or burn his house down.

"Guys," I said flatly. Michael, Trent, Duncan and David all turned to me. Owen glanced up at me, but I didn't hold his attention for long.

"What do you want, faggot protector?" Trent spat, smirking. He roughly ruffled my hair before he nudged Duncan on the arm, bursting out into a fit of laughter. David and Michael looked at each other, perplexed.

"Huh? I thought his name was Darko," Michael said, scratching his head. Duncan and Trent laughed even harder as David rolled his eyes.

"They're just making fun of him again, you retard," David said, wheezing. Trent had wiped a tear from his face while Duncan continued to howl. Michael gasped in realisation while David nodded in approval.

Good God, I don't have time for this. I should totally punch Trent in the face.

"Oh my fucking god you knobs, it wasn't that funny. Calm down." Owen said suddenly, earning a glare from Duncan and Trent. He cocked an eyebrow before glancing back at his phone.

Owen is my favourite person right now. I couldn't have said it any better myself.

"Have any of you seen Bella and Taylor?" I asked, barely containing my laughter. Duncan and Trent tore their eyes away from

Owen, before setting them on me. Duncan nudged Trent this time, a creepy smirk washing over his lips.

"Ooh, yeah, I've seen Bella. Seen that fat ass of her's jiggling as she walked around with that nerd."

Trent sniggered. "Bella's so fiiiiine, dude. Imagine her as a lesbian - that would be so frickin' hot!"

Ugh, typical horny straight teenagers.

Yeah. Trent has no problem with lesbians but has a vendetta against gay guys. If he knew that I'm gay, he'd probably have a stroke. He acts all macho but he really is terrified of gay guys. Like, scared of them.

"You're both useless, as per usual," I said dismissively. I turned towards Michael and David, who had randomly started playing thumb wrestle. "Have you two seen them?"

David let out a long breath of air before saying, "I haven't seen them, sorry."

I gritted my teeth. "Michael? What about you?"

Michael furrowed his brows, concentrating. "Wait, yeah, I have seen them! They went and got a drink before heading off into one of Lyra's rooms. I definitely think that they're gonna do something nauuugghhttaaaaayyyyyy!" Michael said, wiggling his eyebrows at David. David started laughing, and Trent looked on in disgust.

"Guys, that's so gay. Don't do that again. Fuck."

I should punch the shit out of him. If Taylor weren't missing right now, I would have.

I yelled thanks to Michael before leaving the living room.

I've been looking in each of Lyra's bedrooms for about ten minutes now, and I still haven't found either of them. Why does she have so many bloody rooms? Which one are they in!?

I stood in Lyra's hallway, slumping against her peach coloured wall. I whipped out my phone and checked my messages; neither of them has replied to my texts. I sent, like, fifteen of them. He's never one to not reply to me, and Bella knew that I was meant to help take care of him, so why hasn't she texted me back either?

What if Bella was purposefully ignoring me so she could have Taylor all to herself?

That bitch. She's probably making out with him somewhere. Disgusting.

I forced myself up and I walked out of her hallway into Lyra's kitchen. Grabbing and downing a few more beer cups to calm myself, I spotted Stefan standing in a corner, swishing his cup absentmindedly as he stared out into the backyard, his eyes focusing on the makeshift dance floor. I walked up to him.

"Hey bud," I said, making him look up, "I'm gonna assume you haven't talked to Lyra yet?"

Stefan shook his head. "Nah, she's too busy dancing. I don't think she'd want to talk to me anyway; I've seen her talk to like, four different guys tonight. What chance would I even have?"

I furrowed my brows, exhaling softly. "Dude, go find her. Don't be ridiculous; knowing her state of mind right now, she wouldn't turn down a conversation."

Stefan shrugged. "I don't know man..."

I grabbed his shoulders and looked him in the eyes. "Big bro, take advice from me. Take a chance, and go talk to her. Besides, I made a promise to help you get in with her anyway. Don't make me waste my precious time."

He nodded. I clapped his shoulder and looked out into the dance floor with him.

"Oh, by the way," I asked, turning to Stefan, "you haven't seen Taylor or Bella at all by any chance?"

Stefan shook his head. "Nah, sorry man. I've been too preoccupied with Lyra all night."

I smiled. "Don't worry about it."

Stefan smiled at me before narrowing his eyes slightly. "Have you been drinking?"

I shrugged. "Yeah. I don't feel drunk yet though, but I've had quite a few."

Stefan rolled his eyes. "Lemme guess, you're planning on getting really drunk, aren't you?"

I nodded. Stefan let out a short sigh, before saying. "Text me when you wanna leave. I'll drop you off at home."

I smiled. That's actually the nicest thing Stefan's ever done.

"Thanks, bro."

We stood in a brief silence. As much as I'd like to talk to Stefan, I still needed to find Taylor and Bella.

"I'll catch up with you later, all right?" I said. He nodded before returning back to his cup.

I stepped away from Stefan and walked back out into the back yard, the dance floor seeming more swamped than it was before. I eventually spotted Lyra again, who was still dancing. She noticed me looking at her and immediately beelined through the crowd towards me. She wrapped me in a tight hug when she got to me, squeezing the air from my lungs.

"I haven't seen you in forever!" Lyra said, laughing. I furrowed my brows, confused, as I pried her arms from me. I glanced down at my shirt, and a portion of her makeup had smudged onto it.

Horray.

She's acting awfully nice; she hasn't insulted me once or called me anything terrible yet.

"Uh, you saw me like an hour ago? We were dancing together?" I said, perplexed.

Lyra's eyes widened in realisation as she let out a prolonged chuckle. "Oh my god, you're so right Darkie."

Ah, there we go. There's the terrible nickname.

Gritting my teeth at the horrid nickname, I looked back to where Stefan was, who was still sadly swishing his drink. He quickly shot up and started making himself look presentable when he noticed I was talking to Lyra.

"Lyra," I said, making her look up at me, "You know that guy over there?"

Lyra followed to where I was pointing and noticed Stefan. "Oh, that cute guy? What about him?"

"Well, his name's Stefan and I'm sure he's feeling a bit lonely. You mind cheering him up?"

Lyra smiled immediately before nodding. "Uhm, you never need to ask me twice to talk to a cute guy! This is so gonna piss Steven off!"

She quickly wiped her face and straightened out her shirt. She flicked her curly highlighted hair behind her shoulders before looking at me, her chocolate eyes expectant. Some strange brown substance lined the corners of her mouth. A few beads of sweat, either forming due to the humidity of the room or her dance moves, tricked down her forehead.

"How do I look?"

I smirked. "You look sweaty."

Lyra narrowed her eyes.

"Uh, I mean, you look sexy! Except, you have sweat on your forehead and some brown stuff at the corner of your mouth; you better wipe that off."

Lyra quickly wiped away at her forehead and lips, before smiling. I only just noticed it, but her eyes had a slight crimson colour to them. Her pupils had dilated.

"Oh yeah, I forgot to tell you! Someone brought over cupcakes and brownies, and they're making everyone really happy! In fact, I saw Taylor grab one of them!"

Shit. Taylor must have eaten weed brownies. Knowing him, he probably thought they were just ordinary brownies. Now he's lost and high as fuck.

Wait.

LYRA HAS SEEN TAYLOR! YES!

"Wait, you've seen Taylor? Where did he go?!" I asked Lyra, her words hitting me like bricks. She giggled before she pointed towards an obscure bedroom, one that I hadn't checked.

"He went in that room, like, ten minutes ago. Bella went in afterwards too, but she was acting really weird. She like, checked like a billion times before she went into the room and she put a 'do-not-disturb' sign on the door. Like, we're at a party, who's gonna bother reading that?" She said. She turned away from me and began walking to Stefan. I shouted 'thanks', earning a dismissive wave from her as she approached Stefan. His face lit up when she reached him.

Stefan now owes me a favour, and now he can't snitch on me.

I turned around and briskly walked back to the bedrooms - specifically the one Lyra pointed out.

I leant on the door, my ear pressed to the thin slab. Apart from the generic trap music that the DJ was playing, I couldn't hear a thing. I fully expected to hear moaning or to hear the bed rocking, or some kind of gross thing that Bella would be doing to him. The subject of torture - to hear your crush having sex with one of the people you despise the most.

Instead, all I heard was silence. They must have gone to a different room.

I sill wonder what Bella was referring to when we were at Taylor's house earlier. 'Do you remember what we talked about in Biology?' For all I know, they could be referring to how they were gonna lose it to each other. You know? Lose their virginity. They're so obviously together, judging by the amount they of time they spend together, and all the secrets they keep from me. Taylor probably doesn't even need me here at this party, since he's got his girlfriend to do all of the protecting.

God, I'm so salty. They're probably, like, talking to each other. As friends. Nothing more. Probably.

I got off of the door and slumped down, resting my back on it. The 'DO-NOT-DISTURB' sign was still hanging loosely on the doorknob by a lacey, red ribbon. The font was cringy and the parchment was covered in tacky kisses and hearts.

"Disgusting," I muttered under my breath.

I clutched my head. The alcohol was finally starting to set in; my body felt so warm and cozy, and the music began to sound amazing. My vision blurred slightly as I looked around in the hallway around me. The music started to fade as my eyes went in and out of focus. I took a deep breath, letting the air of the party circle my lungs for a few moments. My angry thoughts faded away to the back of my head.

Suddenly, soft shouting erupted from behind the door, snapping me back to reality. It was Taylor's voice. I stumbled up and hovered my ear on the door again, listening. The thoughts shot back to the front of my mind.

There was silence again.

What if Taylor was in trouble? What if Bella was doing something horrible to him? Taylor was probably high and most likely drunk, so Bella could literally do anything she pleased and Taylor wouldn't remember a thing the next day.

That's it, I'm barging in. If another couple is in there, this is gonna be so awkward.

I grabbed the doorknob and thrust the door open.

The lights were off.

"Taylor?" I asked, clumsily feeling the wall for a light switch. After a tense moment, I found a switch and flicked it.

I froze. Every single muscle in my body seized up at the sight of them. I felt like throwing up.

Bella was on top of Taylor. The air was sticky and warm, the stench of lust almost grabbable. Bella shrieked, while Taylor's cheeks burned a very bright crimson red. His face was painted with her lipstick, and her hands were in places they shouldn't have been.

"Fuck. Fuck! D-Darko, I... I can explain!"

Chapter 11

A few hours beforehand

Taylor's pov

Evening. Friday, February 8th, 2014

Sweat beads trickled down my forehead as my eyes darted around Lyra's backyard. It's been exactly one hour, ten minutes and thirty-seven seconds since Bella, Darko and I got here; One hour of my life I'm never getting back ever again.

I leant on a thick pole in the back of Lyra's garden. The strobe lights flashed brightly in my eyes, the music was tasteless, and there were so many people I didn't know. An overpowering scent of sweat, alcohol and vomit permeated the air, making my nose curl. From where I'm standing, I can see only a handful of familiar faces; Darko was getting a few drinks with Bella, and Lyra was greeting her guests. I drummed my fingers on my thigh as I nervously waited for my friends to return.

"Hey," Bella said, two cups in her hands, "I got us some beer."

I reluctantly took the cup from her, before peeking over her shoulder. I narrowed my eyes as I scanned the backyard.

"Where's Darko?" I asked. Bella glanced behind herself before shrugging.

"Well, he was behind me," she said casually, "Maybe he went off to dance. I don't know."

I had nodded before I scanned the dance floor. Darko's face was swallowed by the enormous group of unfamiliars swaying and bobbing to the repetitive beat the DJ was blaring. He's disappeared, without a single trace.

"Well? Are you going to drink?" Bella asked, gesturing to my cup, snapping me out of my musings. I glanced at it.

I really shouldn't be drinking this, but everything in the universe was telling me that I should. Lyra told me to, Bella told me to; heck, even Ana told me to. All I could see when I glanced down at the cup was my mother's face. That exact face she made when she thought I was Dad.

"I... I don't know..." I said, trailing off. Bella frowned slightly, before downing her drink.

"Don't forget about the plan, Tay," Bella said. I looked up at her.

"Speaking of," I said, narrowing my eyes slightly, "can you finally tell me every single detail of the plan?"

"I will," Bella began, "if you just drink the damn beer."

I sighed, before looking at the cup again.

I don't want to stoop to my mother's level, but I want to know Bella's plan.

'It's just one drink,' I kept reassuring myself, 'It's just one drink. You will be all right.'

I lifted the cup to my lips and chugged. The icy liquid burned against my throat, making my face twist with disgust. It was as bitter as the sun is bright. Why do people enjoy this?

"Yuck," I managed to say, hastily wiping my lips. Bella chuckled. I was about to dry-heave, but she placed her hand on my shoulder.

"See? That wasn't so bad. Good boy." She said almost patronisingly. I grimaced at her, the aftertaste of the beer stinging my tongue.

"So? The plan?"

Bella chuckled. "The plan was to see whether Darko would get jealous over you, and what better way to do that by hooking up with someone?"

I narrowed my eyebrows, barely able to contain my disgust. "Hooking up with someone? First, you make me drink; now you want me to fuck someone? Are you out of your mind!?"

Bella rolled her eyes before sighing. "Let me finish, Taylor."

I huffed before folding my arms over my chest, my ears waiting for Bella. "Fine. Continue."

"Finally. Okay, so, the reason why I need you to drink is so you can get rid of that self-loathing, negative mindset that you seem to have right now. You being drunk not only would make you more comfortable, but it's also gonna make you more confident. I could find you a girl or a guy that would, at most, want to kiss you, and with you being drunk you wouldn't hesitate. I'd make sure that Darko can see it; if he sees it and reacts, then you know where he stands. Got it?"

I narrowed my eyes. "Aren't you going to get drunk too? How would you be able to make sure this plan of yours works?"

Bella scoffed. "Who said I was getting drunk? I had one beer, Taylor, not an entire keg. I'm staying mostly sober for you tonight."

I pondered it. "What if we can't find a guy or a girl that's willing?"

Bella smirked. "I have a failsafe. Don't worry."

I narrowed my eyes again. Failsafe?

"You're definitely bisexual, right?" Bella questioned. I hastily stepped closer to her, putting a finger to my lips.

"Yeah...? You mind not saying that any louder mate?"

"So, you like boys and girls, right?" Bella repeated, completely ignoring my request. I sighed.

"I like Darko, but yes, I find both boys and girls attractive. Why?"

Bella had creased her eyebrows before nodding. "Don't worry."

Silence spread between us. The music was there, sure, and the chatter of the other crowds filled the space between us, but Bella and I didn't say a word. The awkwardness was palpable.

Why the weird question? I had told Bella about my sexuality last week; why the sudden need for confirmation? Did she want me to be comfortable with her plan, or did it have to do with the failsafe she had?

Growing uncomfortable with the silence between us, I cleared my throat. "All right," I said, "let's go do this."

Bella had smiled, before walking off to get another two cups of beers. When she returned, she gestured towards my phone.

"By the way," Bella said, "I'm gonna need that."

I stared at her, perplexed. "Uh, why?"

"Just trust me," Bella said, her voice slightly slurred.

"Okay..." I said tentatively. She gave me the two cups as I handed her my phone.

"Drink up," She said, slipping it into her bag, "you'll feel better soon."

I forced myself to drink four beers. My head is beginning to spin, but hey, Bella was right; the party is becoming more enjoyable now. The music sounded like bliss, and everybody seemed more attractive than usual. I've had two girls chat me up, but Bella ushered them away before I could fill them in on the plan.

Bella and I went inside. She dragged me along to a table where a few unfamiliars were playing beer pong, which made us both laugh. The guys were way too buzzed to throw straight, so they were missing the cups horrifically, but they still thought they won.

The dudes cheered when the ball rolled off the table, gulping the cups' insides as the game ended.

"What just happened?" I asked Bella, who was smiling at the mess in front of us.

"To be honest, who knows. They're having fun, so it doesn't matter."

The boys finished their game and stumbled back outside. Bella nudged my arm playfully.

"Hey, you want to go dancing? I'm sure we can find someone there." She asked. I sheepishly smiled.

"I can't dance..."

Bella's eyes beamed up, and she grabbed my hand, dragging me to the dance floor outside. "Oh my god, I've got to teach you!"

I rolled my eyes but went along with Bella. There was no way I was getting out of dancing, so I might as well try it. Bella was right; this alcohol does make you more confident.

Bella dragged me onto a tiny spot on the dance floor, slowly bobbing to the beat. She gestured to me, before moving my shoulders. I chuckled bashfully, standing in front of her like a vegetable.

"Come on!" Bella said, "Start dancing!"

I snorted but complied anyway. I began bobbing my knees like how Bella was, making her stop to laugh at me.

"Oh my gosh Tay, you dance like my dad."

I smirked before dabbing. "Your dad must be an excellent dancer, then."

Bella and I laughed, but I froze when I looked past her shoulder. About ten people away, I could just barely make out his face.

Lyra was dancing with Darko. That in itself isn't a bad thing, but what she was doing made my chest splinter into pieces.

She was slut-dropping, twerking, and grinding. On him.

And he looked like he was enjoying it.

Bella noticed that I wasn't having fun anymore. Her eyes had followed my gaze before they returned to me. She stepped closer to me, her body only centimetres from mine, and placed a soft hand on my shoulder.

"Tay?" She said tenderly. I snapped out of my dystopian reverie and focused on her.

I don't know what it was, either my jealousy of Lyra or the alcohol melting my brain, but Bella strangely looked beautiful. Her blonde hair turned into a myriad of colours thanks to the DJ's strobe lights. Her skin radiated a soothing kind of warmth. Her eyes twinkled with worry. Her lips danced with enticing crimson lipstick.

"They're just dancing. Ignore them." Bella said. I shook my head, before taking a few steps back. I took a deep breath in, wiping off a few beads of sweat that had formed on my brow.

"It's too loud out here," I said, looking at the backyard door, "Can we go inside?"

"Taylor? Taylor!"

Bella and I had gone inside when a familiar scent enveloped me. I walked around, Bella struggling to keep up with me, as I weaved myself through the crowd. I stopped when I reached the kitchen, a big smile forming on my lips.

"Ooh, brownies!" I said, nearly squealing. I darted to where the tray of the brown delicacies was, before picking up two. Bella slapped them out of my hand before I could inhale them.

"Tay! Don't eat those!"

I stared at her, dumbfounded. My eyebrows creased as I glanced at my hands, which were coated in brownie remains.

"What..? Why the fuck not?!"

Bella gestured around her to the other partygoers in the room. "Do you know what's in these?"

I lifted a brow. "Chocolate, eggs, butter, flour-"

"No! Weed!"

She nodded towards a guy who was giggling to himself in a corner, his lips completely coated in brownie crumbs. I ran my fingers through my hair before sighing sharply.

"First the drinks, then the dancing, now the brownies. Why can't anything go right tonight?!"

I groaned dramatically.

"You want to take a breather?"

I nodded furiously. Bella grabbed my hand and dragged me out of the kitchen.

"Come with me."

I collapsed onto the bed that was in the room that Bella took me to. On the way, I drank another beer, bringing my total to seven, I think. I was buzzed, my gut was stupidly warm, and I was disorientated. Everything seemed fuzzy, even with my glasses on.

I really need to pee.

"There," Bella said, closing the door, "I put a sign on the door. Hopefully, nobody comes in."

Unable to form a cohesive sentence, I grunted loudly in response. Bella trudged to the bed before sinking into it.

"I'm sorry I couldn't get the plan to work," Bella said, her voice laced with genuine remorse. I turned my head to face her.

I'm not too sure what it was, but it happened again; Bella randomly seemed attractive. I'm still unclear whether it was the alcohol affecting my vision, but, she was suddenly gorgeous. The soft orange lighting of the bedside lamp amplified her facial features. A strange urge in me felt the need to touch her face.

"It's fine," I said, smiling weakly. "It's a shame though; now I'm drunk for no reason."

Bella laughed, her smile making my heart skip for a second. Why the hell am I suddenly attracted to her?

"Taylor, I need to tell you something."

I quizzically lifted a brow. "What's up?"

Bella looked out into the room, solemnly. She let out a short sigh before glancing back at me, lifting a stray lock of blond hair away from her face. "I saw something bad on the dancefloor."

"Bad..?"

"Yeah, bad," Bella restated, "It involved Darko."

My heart began to race. "What happened? Is he okay!?"

Bella sighed again. "Yeah... he's more than okay."

I let out a sigh of relief. "What's wrong then?"

She frowned slightly. "He and Lyra were getting a bit too... friendly. I saw them hugging and talking, before pointing to the rooms. I don't know what they're up to, but..."

I blinked rapidly, my breath speeding up. "What are you suggesting?"

Bella held her breath. "He's definitely straight, Taylor. He hasn't sent you a single message the entire night, and he's way more interested in Lyra. I'm sorry."

I felt my cheeks burn up. "No! This - this can't be happening..." I yelled. Bella wrapped me in a hug as I let a single tear fall down my cheek.

"I'm sorry Taylor..."

She released me from her hug, and for the first time, we stared deeply into each other's eyes. I was so angry at Darko, and myself, for letting my feelings trick me into a false sense of hope.

Darko is straight; I have to face facts. I can't keep clinging on to the hope of him falling for me. This plan was a mistake, and going to this party was a mistake.

"Bella, I - "

Bella leant forward and kissed me. Her lips burned against mine, her lipstick smearing on me. She twisted her fingers in my hair, deepening the kiss. My eyes widened, but they slowly faltered. She placed her hand on my crotch, making a moan escape my lips.

I couldn't tell whether she was pitying me, or whether she was genuinely kissing me. I could care less; my head was spinning, my heart was sore. Any distraction was welcome to me right now.

She lifted herself from me, slightly out of breath.

"I... I probably shouldn't have done that..." Bella said. I was lost for words. Her eyes flickered from mine to my lips.

The door suddenly crashed open. Bella shrieked at the sharp sound while I faced the door, but what I saw made my heart stop.

Darko shouted my name before seeing Bella and me on the bed. His eyes widened, his breath quickened. A sweat bead ran down the side of his cheek.

He could see Bella's lipstick smeared on my lips. He could see her hand on my crotch. His eyes glazed over before tears began to fall. Bella retracted her arm.

"F-fuck! Darko.. I- I can explain!" I managed to splutter out though my drunkness. He slowly shook his head before backing out of the room, slamming it shut. The sound sent shockwaves throughout my entire body.

"I-I should go after him!" I muttered to Bella.

"Stay. Nothing you can say right now would change anything." Bella said evenly. She went to touch my hair, but I flinched away. I clutched my head.

"Like you said," I said, "If I kissed a girl, and he saw and reacted in any way, then I would have an answer. I have my answer."

"But you're drunk! You're not even going to remember any of this tomorrow, so why bother?"

I thrust my arm out of her grip. Stumbling towards the door, I glanced back at her, my eyes stinging with regret.

"Because he needs me."

CHAPTER 12

Taylor's pov

Evening. Friday, February 8th, 2014

Have you ever done something you regretted so much, it physically hurt you inside?

That's exactly how I felt when Bella's lips touched mine. As soon as those crimson pillows left me, I knew that that was something I shouldn't have ever done. I love Darko, and although I'm unsure as to how he feels, I should have never thought about another person in that way.

It broke me when Darko walked in. When he ran out, slamming the door into its frame, it felt like a dozen swords nosedived into my chest. Something shattered in me.

I regret ever going with Bella.

Darko feels something for me, I just know it. He wouldn't have run out like that if he didn't. He reacted like how a wife would if she walked in on her man with another woman. He was hurt that I was with Bella. If he didn't feel anything, he would have just said sorry and shut the door, and probably waited outside so he could tease me after.

He feels something. It's the only logical explanation.

Resisting Bella's protest, I ran out of the room, slamming the door behind me. My breath quickened as I looked around frantically for Darko. I needed to find him and explain everything to him. My shoes slammed hard into Lyra's tiles as I searched the house - every step I took, I felt a little more sober. I ran to the backyard, but Darko was gone.

I should have pulled back when Bella kissed me. I should have shoved her away and ran out of that room. I should have never gone to this party in the first place.

I should have been kissing Darko instead.

I stopped searching and slowly slid down a wall. I ran my fingers through my hair, catching my breath.

Where would he be?

"Darko!" I shouted as I burst through Lyra's front door. I leant over her porch fence, squinting out into her yard. A few people lingered around the place, but none of them was him.

"Damnit. Where are you?" I asked myself. I clutched the porch and took in a few breaths.

That's when I felt my stomach flip. I hunched over Lyra's porch fence and vomited. The disgusting liquid tore at my throat, the bitterness burning my tongue.

I'm never drinking alcohol again.

Wiping away at my lips, I turned around. Trent and his group were walking out of Lyra's house when they spotted me. Trent screamed "YUCK" before making a gagging noise. He sauntered up to me.

"Well, look who it is; the little piano freak has shown up. Should we steal his lunch money, like old times?" Trent said, turning to face his group when he said that last sentence. Duncan sniggered while Michael and David distractedly squinted around the yard.

Their eyes were red. Owen just shrugged while tapping away at his phone.

I felt my hands begin to shake again. Yeah, these were the guys that bullied me, and Trent was Bella's ex.

"H-have any of you guys seen Darko?" I asked hesitantly, gritting my teeth at his statements. Trent just smirked before looking at Duncan.

"That's funny," Trent stated before asking, "Darko asked us a similar thing about an hour ago. Where were you and Bella?"

Duncan sniggered before nudging Trent's shoulder, "The better question is, what were they doing? Look at his lips man; they're smeared with her red lipstick."

Eyes widening, I impulsively wiped at them with the back of my hand. The stain just smeared even more. Trent and Duncan both laughed at the sight of me. Great.

"I didn't know you had it in you to kiss my ex," Trent said, "and, judging from your up-chuck just then, you're drunk too. Gunning after Bella and drinking irresponsibly; I guess you really are as pathetic as you look right now."

Duncan whistled low as he nodded behind me, "Speaking of which, here she comes."

Oh no. No, no, no. Not her again. These pricks and Bella surrounding me? I might as well crawl into a ball and die.

I began to walk in the opposite direction, but Trent grabbed my arm.

"Why don't you stay and hear what she has to say, Joker?" He said menacingly. A fear suddenly setting in, I stopped and turned to face Bella.

"Taylor." I heard her say. I stared at her, wriggling my arm out of Trent's grip.

"What do you want?"

Bella shoved her fingers into her bag, before producing my phone. "I figured you'd want this back."

Crap, I forgot about that.

I snatched my phone out of her hand, swivelling around, desperate to leave. I can't stand to see her face right now; I just feel so angry.

"Where are you going?" She said. I ignored her, trying to shove past Trent. If she says one more thing to me, I'm going to go off at her.

"Tay? Don't ignore me!" She shouted coldly. That's it. I don't care if Trent's going to punch me in the face; Bella needs to shut the fuck up.

"Don't ignore you?" I said mockingly, swivelling around to face her, "you fucking manipulated me just so you can get in my pants, and now Darko's god-knows-where! You ruined tonight for me!" I blurted out. Randoms around me turned to face me, most of their faces a strange mix of amusement and confusion. Trent, Duncan, David and Michael stood there, unsure of what to do. Even Owen looked up at me from his phone. Bella stared at me, her face hard as stone.

"Tonight was meant to be a good night! We danced, we had fun," she said, her voice solemn. "Whatever. You don't care about me. You won't even remember any of this tomorrow when your hangover sets in."

She turned to walk away. Just before she was out of earshot, she turned around.

"Everything I did was for us." She shouted. She flipped her hair as she walked out of my sight.

If she isn't the definition of over-dramatic or extra, then I don't know what is. It was definitely the alcohol that made her seem better than what she actually is.

She stormed back into the house, her heels fading into the background music. The randoms outside with me went inside, as well as Trent's group. Trent glanced back at me before he walked through the doorframe, his face telling me he was still shocked. He scoffed before going back in.

I collapsed onto Lyra's porch couch and turned on my phone. Unsurprisingly, I didn't get a single message or call from Darko. In fact, my entire chat with him has disappeared. All of my messages had been cleared.

Real subtle Bella. Real subtle.

I called him. The ringing seemed to go on for forever.

He didn't pick up.

'Hey, it's Darko,' His voicemail said, 'well, you probably knew that already since you called me, haha. Anyway, send me a voice-mail, and I'll get back to you when I can!'

God, he sounds happy. I cleared my throat.

"Darko," I said, trying my hardest not to start crying. "please call me, or at least text me where you are. The night has turned to absolute shit. I don't know, I... I just need to explain everything to you. Please, I'm so sorry you had to see that. I regret kissing her."

I let my head fall into my hands. There was nobody outside; either the crisp air was far too cold for the likes of Lyra's guests, or I made things incredibly awkward after yelling at Bella.

Why did Bella deceive me? Why did she keep me away from Darko, when the entire point of me going to this god-forsaken party was to get in with him?

Did she... like me?

A woman plopped herself suddenly next to me, rudely snapping me out of my musings. I was about to go off at her, thinking it was Bella, but when I looked up, my jaw snapped shut. It was Ana, and she was watching me, her eyes soft. She placed a hand on my shoulder.

"I told you that Bella was nothing but trouble."

I scoffed before facing away from her. She sighed, before folding her arms.

"Are you alright? I heard what had happened. I brought you some water." she said, her voice relaxing and quiet on my ears. I let out a long sigh before she passed the drink to me. I let the icy liquid slither down my throat, feeling it soothe my raging stomach.

"I feel like shit, to be completely honest, but thank you."

Ana smirked slightly. "Yeah, that makes two of us. You're welcome."

I furrowed my brows. "You too?"

Ana shrugged, before leaning her head on my shoulder. "I've been to better parties. Besides, it seems this party upset too many people. Bella's just started crying, you're obviously drunk and confused, Darko was just driven home by his brother, and Lyra's beyond hungover already. It isn't a real party to me if the randoms are the only ones enjoying it."

I nodded. So that's where Darko went. Why won't he answer his damn phone?

We sat out there for a few minutes, enjoying the silence of the night. Ana's hair tumbled down my shirt, her blonde locks unrelenting as the wind swept them up into my face.

"What should I do?" I asked Ana. She sat up, before turning to me.

"Well, one thing is that you shouldn't go back inside the party. I'm pretty sure you and Bella killed the mood."

"Oh. Whoops." I said sincerely. Ana giggled before lightly slapping my arm.

"The party was shit anyway," Ana said, "I texted you, but you never picked up your phone."

I sighed. "Yeah, you can blame Bella for that too. I was stupid enough to give her my phone, thinking she had some greater plans for it. It turns out, she had her own agenda and didn't want others getting in the way."

Ana half smiled. "Anyway, back to your question. I don't know how to answer this, to be completely honest. Maybe we should just go home and sleep it off. Hopefully, Darko just gets over walking in on you kissing his mortal enemy."

I lifted a brow. "Mortal enemy? What makes you say that?"

"Lyra and I are closer than you think. She always bitches to me about how pissed off he gets when he sees you and Bella together."

I frowned slightly. I didn't know Darko hated Bella that much.

Why does he dislike her? She's done nothing to him directly. Its all been about toying with me.

I let out a short sigh before I felt a question tugging at the tip of my tongue. "Hey Ana, can I ask you something?"

Ana sat up, facing her whole body towards me. She nodded. "Sure, what is it?"

"Have you ever thought that maybe," I began, unsure how to say this casually, "Darko could be a little... gay?"

Ana lifted a brow, before breaking out into laughter. "Oh, that was good Tay."

I narrowed my eyes. Ana stopped laughing. "Oh, you were serious. Sorry."

Ana sighed. "Tay, I wouldn't know. From the years and years I've known him, he hasn't ever shown any interest to dudes. He might be closeted, but it just wouldn't make any sense if he were. He's been with too many girls to know if he swung the other way."

I nodded, before looking off into Lyra's front yard. Ana lifted a brow, before asking, "why do you ask?"

Oh. Not because I'm so confused as to whether Darko feels the same. Maybe I'm overanalyzing, but I can't help but entertain the idea that he's secretly gay. It just answers so many questions.

"Uh, no reason." I manage to say. Ana sighed.

"Okay."

I half smiled. Thank goodness she doesn't want to dig.

Ana stood up. "I'm gonna go say bye to my friends, and then I'm gonna call an uber. Wait for me here, okay?"

She smiled, before disappearing back into the house. I whipped out my phone. Still no message back from Darko. I called him again, but there was no answer.

'Just give him space,' a voice said in my head. 'the more you message him, the more he's going to stay away.'

I couldn't do anything but hope that he was okay.

CHAPTER 13

D arko's pov

Midnight. Friday, February 8th, 2014

That's what their secret must have been.

I fucking KNEW they were interested in each other. I fucking knew it. No wonder they wouldn't stop giggling in biology. It was all just a complicated plan so they can hook up!

I ran out of the bedroom, my tears hot as they fell on my reddening face. I ran to where I last saw Stefan, not caring about the people I've shoved past or the strange looks I was getting. After a few minutes of searching, I found him talking to Lyra in a quiet corner.

"Stefan, we need to go, now," I said, not caring whether either of them saw my tears. Stefan did a double take at me, wiped my cheeks and asked what was wrong. I ignored his questions and grabbed his wrist, yanking him away from Lyra. He hastily waved goodbye as I dragged him out of the house.

"Where is your car?" I cried out. He pointed to a few houses away from Lyra's house before tossing me the keys.

"Go unlock it. I need to go say goodbye to Lyra first."

I nodded. Snatching the keys out of the air, I rushed to his car. I crashed into the passenger seat, leaning forward to shove the key in the ignition.

I sat there, wiping away the stray tears that Stefan missed. After a few moments, Stefan reappeared and sat in the driver's seat, seemingly at a loss for words.

"You mind telling me what happened?" He finally said. I shook my head

"Just drive."

"No," he said, turning the car off. "Tell me what's wrong! You can't just yank me out of a conversation with a girl I'm interested in and not tell me why!"

"Stefan," I said, my voice crackling, "please, just trust me."

He leaned back in his chair, running his fingers through his chocolate hair. "I'll drive, but you need to tell me what happened when we get home, okay?"

I shook my head. "I can't do that."

"Why can't you tell me?!"

"BECAUSE I DON'T WANT YOU TO HATE ME!"

He sat there, slack-jawed. "Darko, you are my little brother. I can never hate you."

I can't tell him. He's too homophobic. I'm so worried that if I say something now, he would throw me out of the car and drive home to tell dad everything.

"Just trust me. Please, just drive. I'll tell you when I want to."

Stefan sighed, defeated. "Fine."

Thank god he's given up. Thank God.

Stefan pulled away from the kerb and began driving. He flicked on the radio, a strange mellow melody filling the air in the car. He hummed along while I leaned my head on the car door, facing out the window. After a few traffic lights, he spoke.

"Would you like to hear a distraction? Something to keep you entertained for a few minutes?"

I turned to face him. "Like what?"

"My love life with Lyra, which you might have ruined, by the way."

I shrugged. "Whatever, sure."

Stefan smirked. "She was really beautiful, man. Looks aside, she is one of the sweetest, happiest girls I've met in a long time."

'Yeah, probably because she was drunk and high,' I thought to myself.

"Wait till she's sober before you make that judgement," I said, making him frown.

"Mate, let me be happy."

I snorted. "Fine."

"Anyway, yeah, she was so cute and adorable. When she walked up to me, she made a remark about how similar my name was to her ex's - Steven. After I had complimented her outfit, she told me that I was already doing better than him. She said I was better than her ex!"

"Ooh wow," I said, flatly. Stefan smiled, unaware of my sarcasm.

"Oh my god, that reminds me," He said, cruising down an empty street. "While I was talking to Lyra, this really feminine guy walked past me and gave Lyra a hug. He was really fucking gross, man! He had makeup on, bright pink hair, and had painted nails."

He shook his head. "Fuckin' fags."

I sat there, frozen.

"Stop the car."

Stefan lifted a troubled brow. "What's wrong?"

"Stop the fucking car."

"Okay okay, jeez," He said. He veered the car next to the curb. "Done. What's wrong now?"

"I feel sick. I'll walk the rest of the way home."

"Mate, it's five minutes away, just let me drive you." He said. I ignored his protests and unbuckled my seat-belt.

"I need air. I'll see you at home."

I got out of the car and slammed the door. I could hear his muffled protests, but I kept walking.

One more gay remark from him and I would have punched him right in the nose.

I knew I was lost, but I didn't care.

I aimlessly wandered the streets, using the streetlights as checkpoints for my feet. I put my entire focus into moving one foot in front of the other; it helped block out Bella and Taylor. I crossed a ditch, some dilapidated buildings and a broken fence until I stumbled upon it.

An abandoned playground. Oddly, it seemed familiar.

The place was in ruins; the swings and slide were rusted and broken, weeds protruded from hundreds of cracks in the concrete surrounding the playground, and the sandpit had dense shrubs growing in it. It looked like it came straight out of a horror movie.

I walked up to the slide and touched it when I heard a child laugh. It was a boy, but it was faint.

"The hell?" I said, squinting around the playground in near darkness. By this time, my eyes had adjusted to the moonlight, but it was still quite hard to see.

I whipped out my phone - twenty percent battery left. Great. The flashlight is going to kill the battery. I put it back in, deciding to conserve it for when I want to go home.

I walked over to the swing and sat on the large seat when I heard the laughter again; it was two little boys' voices. Ignoring the instruction I just gave myself, I whipped out my phone and turned on the flashlight. I scanned the playground, but there was nobody there. The only sounds I could make out was the wind blowing through the trees adjacent to the park, and the cars driving and beeping on a nearby road.

"I must have drunk too much at Lyra's," I said to myself. I put the phone away, but as I did, the swing chain snapped, and I found myself spiralling onto the ground. Somehow, I scraped my knee.

"Ow! For fucks sake," I said, clutching my leg. I got up and turned on my flashlight. I spotted a worn down park bench and hobbled to it.

It creaked when I sat on it. I wiped away at my knee with a stray tissue I had in my pocket when I heard the giggling again. This time, it was right next to me, on the bench.

I flinched, punching the air next to me while scrambling to get away. I scraped my elbows, back and ass on the splintery wood as I punched the backing of the bench.

Nobody was there.

"What the fuck," I said, clutching my fist. I flicked on the flashlight and looked where the giggling was, and my heart dropped.

I squinted at the bench, and faintly written on it was 'Taylor and Darko, Best Friends Forever!'

That's when it hit me; I knew this playground. I swung my flashlight around, and after a few moments of searching, I found a nearby sign. It was broken, and vines had encircled it, but the painted letters were still readable.

'Joelle Park.'

This place was where Taylor and I first became friends.

I looked at the slide again. A vision of toddler me and toddler Taylor formed; we were sliding down the slide together, giggling like we didn't have a care in the world.

I faced the swings, and another vision popped up; toddler Taylor and I were swinging high on the swings, our combined weight making the frame creak and tilt.

Freaking out, I faced the bench again. Sitting on the bench was a sad toddler version of me with a scraped knee. Taylor was embracing me tightly as I wept into his shirt. Nostalgia filled every part of my body.

Suddenly, everything faded away. I couldn't see the visions anymore; it was just an abandoned playground again. I slumped on the bench and touched the carving.

That's when it all started hitting me.

When I touched it, Bella crept into my mind, and she wouldn't go away. All I could see was her and Taylor kissing. The scene at Lyra's replayed over and over again in my mind. Tears welled as I clutched my head, tangling my fingers deep into my hair.

"FUCK YOU!" I shouted. "FUCK YOU, BELLA!"

I lied on the bench, sobbing. Hot, painful tears burned my flushed cheeks as they fell from my eyes. The bench under my head became wet with tears.

'Taylor is straight, Darko,' a voice similar to Bella's said in my head, 'And there's nothing you can do about it. He's mine.'

The voice was right. Taylor is straight. Being in love with him has done way more harm than good. I'm just hurting everyone with this.

I'm too selfish.

I felt a hand on my shoulder. Quickly snapping myself out of my crying, I scrambled away, nearly falling off the bench. The hand gripped my shirt, yanking me up.

"Careful," it said, "You'll hurt yourself, baby bro. Well, judging by your knee, you already have."

I squinted, but the tears made it impossible to see in the darkness. "Stefan? H-how did you know I was here?"

I heard him snort. "I followed you, made sure you didn't see me. I'm worried about you, man."

He leapt over the bench and sat next to me, grabbing and pulling me into a rough hug. I sobbed into his jacket while he patted my back.

"I'm here man," he said softly, "I'm here. Come on, let's go home."

He helped me up, and we walked to the car. As I got into the front seat, my phone began ringing. I looked at it, and it was Taylor.

"Are you going to answer that?" He asked, turning the car on. I shook my head.

"No."

I let it ring, but he left a voice mail.

"Should I get out of the car?" Stefan said. I nodded, and Stefan got out. At least he's respecting my privacy now.

I played the voicemail. Fuck, Taylor sounded shaken.

"Darko, please call me, or at least text me where you are. The night has turned to absolute shit. I don't know, I... I just need to explain everything to you. Please, I'm so sorry you had to see that. I-"

My phone died before he could continue. I shook my head before throwing my phone. Stupid fucking battery.

Stefan noticed me throw it. He poked his head inside. "Can I come in?"

I nodded. Stefan climbed in and buckled his seat-belt.

"Let's go home."

CHAPTER 14

Taylor's pov

Saturday, February 9th, 2014

"Taylor, wake up, or I'm going to throw your breakfast away!" I heard Ana shout from the kitchen. I groaned loudly.

My eyes fluttered open. Clutching my throbbing head, I rose from my bed slowly, rubbing my temple with my palm in a vain attempt to ease the pain. My mouth was as dry as stale bread.

"I'm coming! Gimme a sec!"

I stumbled out of bed, shuffling towards the kitchen like a zombie. I rubbed my eyes as I walked in, the harsh white morning light reflecting from our white furniture. Slipping on my glasses, I noticed that Ana had cooked a delicious looking breakfast - perfectly scrambled eggs, crispy bacon, golden toast and a huge cup of hot chocolate. There were two plates, one for her and one for me. She was sitting down, a chunk of bacon in her mouth.

I know Ana. She always does something unusual or extraordinary when she either wants something from me, wants to know something or to coax me into doing something for her. Her cooking me food is considered unusual - I'm the one that makes her breakfast, always.

She pointed to the empty seat with her fork. "Come on, sit!"

"Wait," I said, squinting through my glasses, "Let me go brush my teeth and freshen up first."

She let out a sigh. "Fine! Just hurry, I kinda need to talk to you about something."

There we go. I knew Ana didn't make this for the sake of it.

I quickly walked to the bathroom, brushed my teeth, washed my face, and slipped on some new clothes. I walked back to the table. Ana was texting on her phone.

I sat down and began scoffing down the eggs. "That class I told you to go to is really starting to pay off," I stated. Ana chuckled.

"I glad you like my cooking," she said, gratefully. I smiled.

"So, what did you want to talk about?" I asked her. She lifted a brow.

"Isn't it obvious? The party, stupid!"

She drummed her fingers nervously on the table. That's weird. Of all things, Ana isn't a nervous person.

"I uh," she began, "have some questions I need answers to."

"Ask away," I said. I was in the middle of biting my toast when I realised what kinds of questions she meant.

Good god, I am not ready to tell her.

"Why did you think Darko might have run away?" She asked calmly. I shrugged.

"I don't know why, Ana," I said. "Maybe he just didn't know what to do and panicked. I know I would have if the situation was flipped."

"Why did you want to talk to him so badly about it after he ran away?" She asked, her tone becoming less and less calm. "I'm just confused as to why it's such a big fuss - don't guys usually cheer their friends when they get in with girls?"

I shrugged again. "I don't know. Darko looked hurt, I could see it. Just felt like I should clarify what happened."

"Interesting," She said, picking up her fork again. Absentmindedly poking the last of her eggs, she looked up at me, her face serious.

"Why'd you ask me if Darko was gay?" She finally said.

I shrugged for the third time. "I don't know. Maybe Darko is, it's the only real explanation to me as to why he ran away after seeing me with Bella, but as you said, he can't be. You know him too well."

She nodded, putting more eggs in her mouth. After swallowing, she stated, "sometimes, you never know a person completely, even if you're living with them."

Fuck, she's talking about me. She's been doing too much digging. She must know something!

After a few long seconds, she put down the fork and looked up at me, her face almost pale.

"Taylor, do you like girls?"

I lifted a brow. "Yeah? I'm not gay, Ana." I said. It's half the truth. I'm bi, so technically what I just said was the truth. Hopefully, that's enough for her.

I told one person, and that's already backfired on me. I don't want Ana to backfire on me; she's one of the only things that make me happy in this world.

We sat there in silence for an uncomfortable amount of time. Ana finished her plate and brought it to the sink. I was too busy thinking about last night to eat properly, so I was still chugging on, eating my breakfast as fast as a snail would.

She washed her dish. When she was done, she stopped and gripped the bench hard. Her knuckles turned white. She hung her head low, before speaking to me.

"I've been thinking a lot about last night, and there are still too many unanswered questions," She states, her head barely moving. After a second, she lifted it, her eyes looking directly at mine.

"I'm not going to beat around the bush, Tay."

She let go of the bench and sighed.

"Taylor, are you bisexual?"

I sat there, my mouth completely lost for words. Although I couldn't see it directly, I knew my hands were gripping my fork so hard that the knuckles were on the verge of bursting. I stood up, my nerves seizing control over my legs. I need to get out of here.

"I uh, I gotta go," I said, making way for the door. I stopped in my tracks when Ana began to speak. Her voice was choked up.

"I didn't think much of it, Taylor. I just thought of it as a joke because I always saw how close you were to Darko. Even at the party, your focus was on him. I just assumed you had best friend beef."

She looked at me again, running her hands through her blonde locks. "Do you remember anything that happened when we got home?"

I shook my head; my jaw was still wide open at that my sister guessed my sexuality. Every part of me wanted to leap through this door frame and forget that she ever asked me, but I knew that it was finally time. I turned to face her.

"What happened?"

She smiled weakly, walking over to me. She grabbed my hand and brought me back to the table before opening her mouth to speak...

Ana's pov

"Muuuuuuuuuuum! We're home from the party!" I exclaimed, dragging Taylor in by the wrist. He was able to walk, but he kept accidentally falling asleep while standing. Poor big bro. The uber ride seemed to make him really tired.

Mum walked out of the living room and wrapped us in a hug. "How was the party, dears?"

I smiled sheepishly, nodding my head to Taylor. "Rough night. He needs to sleep."

Mum chuckled. "Go put him to bed. You can come and join me watching tv after if you'd like?"

I shook my head. "Sorry, I'd love to, but I'm too tired. Maybe tomorrow we can binge watch something, okay?"

I gave her a quick peck on the cheek before dragging a very drowsy Taylor to his bed, wrapping him tightly in the sheets. I took off his glasses and swept the stray hairs hanging over his face that was hanging over his eyes.

"Goodnight, Tay," I said, quickly trying to leave the room. I flicked the lights off, but when I got to the door, Taylor said something that made me stop dead in my tracks.

"I love you too Darko... I should have kissed you instead."

"... You thought I was Darko, Tay. I didn't know what to think of it, but now I do."

She grabbed my hands again, her grip tender. "Taylor, are you Bi?"

My eyes began to glaze over. Hot tears had pooled in my eye sockets before they began cascading down my reddening cheeks. I have to tell her now, whether my mind knew that I shouldn't or not.

"Yes Ana, I am. Please," I said, my words shaky, "please don't hate me. I didn't want you to find out like this-"

Ana wrapped her arms around me, her hug fierce. I wept into her shoulder, my tears soaking her shirt. I felt an enormous weight leave me, my breath stabilising with every sob. I can't believe I just admitted that to her. I'm finally out to my sister. I'M FINALLY OUT TO HER!

"I will never hate my big bro. Dad would be so proud of you for being so brave - I know I am."

She released me, squaring my shoulders with her hands. She looked me straight in the eye.

"I love you, Taylor, don't you dare forget that. Your sexuality is never going to change my sisterly love for you."

I smiled. "Thank you, Ana, for being so accepting. I honestly thought you were going to be so angry about it."

Ana furrowed her brows. "Uhm, no? Do you know what this means? WE CAN TALK ABOUT BOYS TOGETHER!"

We laughed, the tension in the room vanishing almost completely. She smiled, lifting herself up and collecting my empty dish to wash.

She reached the counter before stopping. She looked at me, her eyebrows creased, then suddenly, her eyes beamed.

"Wait," she said, her lips widening into a smile, "oh my god, it makes total sense now."

I lifted a brow. "What do you mean? Huh?"

She squealed, nearly waking mum up. "It answers everything! You must have a big as hell crush on Darko then!

CHAPTER 15

D arko's pov

Sunday, February 10th, 2014

"Mate, stop daydreaming and focus!"

I snapped out of my musings, prying my eyes away from the red dirt beneath me and faced my biker friend, Connor. His bushy brows were furrowed, and his calloused hand was stretched out towards the track.

"We're about to race," he said, his thick Australian accent reverberating in my ears. "You ain't getting out of this one that easily. Don't forget about the bet ya made last week."

"Bet? What bet?" I asked, confused. He groaned, before shaking his head. I have no idea what is happening right now, I've been too focused on Taylor and Bella to remember or think about anything else.

"You're seriously so forgetful mate," he said, "I wonder about you sometimes. You should be more like the other guys, they remember everything, like elephants-"

"Can you just tell me what I fucking forgot?" I said, snapping at him. He looked at me, his face a mix of confusion and shock.

"Jeez mate," Connor said, exasperated. "Who shat in your corn-flakes?"

Connor tends to make up phrases as he pleases, and usually, none of them make any sense; but, he's used this one before. I think it translates to 'Who pissed you off?' I don't even know. Connor is as good with phrases as I am good with nicknames.

"Bella did," I muttered to myself, out of Connor's earshot. It has been a few days since the party, and I haven't been able to shake off what happened. I guess I hoped my Sunday racing would help me forget, but it doesn't appear to be working.

I shrugged, realising he was still waiting for an answer. He sighed, before rubbing his bald head with his palm.

"Ya made a bet after the fit ya had las' week about coming second in a race, mate. The bet was, and I quote from you, 'the best idea in the world'," Connor said, using his fingers as quotation marks. "If ya place first, ya get to pick one of the other racers and they have to do whatever ya want," He said, gesturing to my other friends on the track.

"And, if ya didn't place first, whoever did gets to make you do anything they want."

"This sounds stupid," I said, sneering at the group already gathered at the race track. Half of them were either bike junkies or newbies. I groaned.

"Hey, you made it up, not me. You said something about it being 'revolutionary', whatever that means. I'm just reminding you. You know what happens here if bets aren't followed through," he said, nodding his head to the area's entrance. "You aren't allowed to come back."

I shrugged. I wasn't in the right headspace to race, but a bet is a bet. I just have to win, so none of these guys gets to use me for the rest of the day.

Maybe this race was good for me. Maybe, this race will help me forget about Bella and Taylor. Gunning and focusing on winning might just be the cure for my fixed mindset.

"Sure," I said, making Connor smile, "Let's go."

I wheeled my motorcycle to the edge of the makeshift starting line (It was a checkered fabric tied loosely to the base of two posts on either side of the dirt track), put on my carbon black helmet, and slipped my fingers into my leather gloves. To my left, three brutes that I hadn't seen before gruffed at the track ahead. Their bulky builds squished their bikes beneath them - they won't be a problem for me to pass, especially on the track's turns.

I looked to my right, and it was just Connor there. He was a good racer, but he's too small and old to turn corners properly. Adjacent to him, there was enough space for another rider or two to enter, but nobody did. A few newbie racers gathered on the side of the banks, as well as a few girls, to watch.

Looking at the racers, as well as the fans on the sidelines, has blocked off all of my negative thoughts from the party. All I care about right now is winning this race and having as much fun as I can while trying to do so. Racing is my cure.

I looked to Stefan, the temporary referee, who shot me a warm smile. Stefan usually doesn't come with me to the races, but our usual referee broke his leg. Usually, Stefan would just laugh if I told him before, but he's been acting really supportive ever since I broke down on Friday night. He said he was more than willing to help referee - either it was he wanted to see me race or he wanted to make some quick cash. I'm hoping it was more for the former rather than the latter.

He never acts like this in regards to me. It's really refreshing; I like it. He's been getting really involved in stuff I like as of recent.

He's even pretending to be a real sports presenter - it's both equally sweet and entertaining.

"Aaaaall right, ladies and gents," Stefan shouted in a presenter-esque voice, "Today, we witness my little bro verse these three burly buds and his old friend, Connor. If Darko wins, he gains a slave for a day, but if any of the other contenders win, Darko becomes a slave. This track is triangle shaped, and there will only be one lap. I repeat, ONE."

I glanced over to the brutes again, who were all smirking at me. I narrowed my eyes before flicking a brow at them.

"See you at the end of the race," I shouted. The brutes laughed. Their fate is sealed - underestimation of my talents is what gives me an edge.

"Now racers," Stefan said as a woman clutching two flags strutted to the centre of the starting line, "Get ready!"

I flicked up the kickstand with my ankle and pulled the clutch lever with my fingers.

"Get set!"

I pressed the shifter down to first gear. I let the motorbike roll forward.

"Go-"

"WAIT!"

Stefan stopped himself. The woman on the runway lowered her flags, and all of the racers, myself included, turned around.

A guy zoomed in on his bike, weaving his way around the stray people wandering the place, before stopping perfectly at the starting line. He wore a helmet with a flame pattern painted on it - I couldn't make out his face at all.

He lifted the tinted glass on his helmet, just so only his mouth was visible. "Sorry! I want to join!" He shouted. Stefan shrugged.

"Sure."

Stefan restarted his count down. "Aaalll right! Get ready every-one!"

Everyone revved their engine, but I was too focused on the stranger. There was something familiar about him, but I couldn't pinpoint what it was.

"Get set!"

The other motorbikes sounded like they were about to explode. The stranger gripped his cycle's handlebars confidently, looking directly at me. He shot me a quick wave before focusing on the track ahead.

"GO!"

Oh shit.

The other racers sped off in front of me, leaving a huge dust cloud in their wake. I quickly released my clutch and let the motorbike roll forward, before hurriedly twisting the thrust on my handlebar. My bike took off like lightning, catching up to the three brutes with ease. They all let out a frustrated yell when I passed them, waving to them as obnoxiously as I could.

That's what they get for underestimating me.

I faced forward, the brutes now far behind me. I banked the first turn with ease, zooming forward like a hungry cheetah chasing its prey. Two more turns to go.

Soon enough, I caught up to Connor. He noticed me and sped up, but when we got to the second turn, he hesitated, giving me just enough room to slip by him. He shook his head, flicking his middle finger up at me as I passed him. I laughed to myself - at least he can take being beaten better than the three-muscly-mus-keteers I passed effortlessly beforehand.

Now, that just leaves one turn, one dash to the finish line, and one more person to overtake.

Ahead of me rode Mr Mysterious. His fit frame hugged his motorbike, his gaze fixated on the track ahead of him. I caught up with him, my bike parallel to his. He turned his head slightly in my direction.

"Hey!" I shouted, before opening my helmet's glass cover. "Nice helmet, I think I'll call you hotman."

He shook his head, but amidst the racing, I could hear his laughter. "Whatever Darko. See you at the finish line!"

He suddenly raced ahead, countersteering perfectly against the final bank on the track. I smirked. Finally, some fun competition. I didn't even care as to how he knew my name - adrenaline was overpowering my critical thinking.

I cleared the final corner and twisted the thrust on my bike hard. Soon enough, I caught up with him again. He noticed me catch up and sped faster. I did too. We both kept going a foot further than the other as the finishing line drew nearer and nearer. Stefan's excited figure became more visible the closer we got.

"Aaaaaand, the winner is..." I could hear Stefan shout on his megaphone. The finish line inched closer and closer before I realised it was underneath me. The small crowds on the edges erupted into a cheer, but as I turned around, I realised they weren't cheering for me.

"The new kid won!" Stefan announced.

I stopped my bike, awe and shock washing over me as I turned around, seeing the crowd praise Mr Anonymous. I rode my bike back to the track, watching as Connor and the three brutes pass the line. I parked my bike near Stefan's car. Another race started, leaving just me and Hotman watching on the sidelines.

"So, I believe you're my slave?" Hotman said, slipping off and stuffing his gloves in his pocket before facing me. He was still wearing that flaming helmet.

"I believe you're right. Good job on winning, Hotman. It's not every day a newbie beats me."

"That's such a bad nickname," he said, his voice muffled under the helmet. "And, I'm not a newbie. I've been racing for ages, just not at this particular track."

I lifted a brow. "Who are you, anyway? Unless you want me to refer to you as Hotman for the rest of the day, I suggest you take off your helmet."

He chuckled. "Sure. Just brace yourself."

He unsheathed his helmet. His short brown hair twisted tightly on his head, sweat beads trickling down from the heat. His hazel eyes twinkled as they met mine. His smirk flashed his perfectly white teeth.

I didn't expect this at all.

"Owen? Since when do you ride?!"

He smirked before shrugging. "I've been riding for years. Just goes to show how much people know about me..."

I smiled, realising that this is one of the first proper conversations I've had with him. "I'm surprised you aren't texting. You're always on that phone of yours."

Another smirk from him. "All for good reason."

He turned back to the track. His bushy brown eyebrows furrowed when the three burly bikers zoomed past us, stopping at the finishing line. "Those three are douchebags. They tried to make me crash during the race - I was legit terrified. They got out a crowbar and tried to swing it at my front tire."

I craned my head toward him, my eyebrows twisted with concern. "Dude, you know that's illegal, right? You can go get them fined or even suspended from The Tracks!"

Owen shrugged. "Meh. Something tells me that if I said anything, I would really regret it."

He nodded towards the starting line, and they were all there, resting on their bikes. One was cracking their knuckles and neck bones, the other was hollering like a pig at the flagwoman, and the last was flicking a switchblade between his fingers with perfect precision. Owen laughed when he saw my fear-stricken face.

"Yeah, I'm pretty sure you'd end up with a fucked up face if you said anything bad about them," I said, my mouth still slightly agape. Owen laughed.

"Who was that other guy that raced?" he asked. "You seemed familiar with him."

"He's an old friend of mine," I said, smiling at the pun I just made. "Emphasis on the old."

His lips smirked. "He seems like a cool dude."

"Damn right I am, kiddo!"

We turned around, and Connor was sauntering up to us, his helmet under his arm. He flashes a toothy smile at me, before clapping Owen on the shoulder.

"Good job out there on the race track, kid. You're pretty good, Darko might have finally met his rival."

Owen smiled sheepishly, rubbing his fingers through his hair. "It was great fun. It was good to meet you."

Connor smiled at Owen, before regarding me. He faced me, his face solemn. "Sorry about those three idiots that joined the race, Darko. Thank goodness your friend won, otherwise, you'd have to deal with their shit instead."

Connor shook Owen's hand. "Don't forget the prize of that bet."

He walked off, leaving us in comfortable silence. Well, it was comfortable, until Stefan began shouting my name from the Referee stand. I groaned.

"Hey, I've got to go, Owen," I said, smiling at him. "It was good racing you. Just know next time, I'll be the one in first place next time we race."

Owen rolled his eyes before smirking. "Whatever man. Don't forget, you still owe me that favour."

"Whatever, Hotman. I'll see you next time?" I said, smirking over my shoulder as I walked away from him. I could see him cringe at the nickname, but a smile forced its way through his thin lips.

"Sure man, next time. See you around."

"Stefan? What did you need me for?"

I wandered to where Stefan was calling me from. He grunted while waving his free arm up, showing me he acknowledged my presence. He was counting the money he got from refereeing. "Dude, look at this moola! I should referee more often; I could afford Lyra flowers and chocolate at this rate!"

Well, I guess he cared more about the money than seeing me, it seems.

He held up a thick stack of $5 notes. I rolled my eyes. He's so infatuated with her; ever since the party, they've been talking non-stop online. The only reason I know they've been talking is because Stefan keeps giving me minute-by-minute updates. Apparently, they have more in common than I had originally anticipated, right down from their favourite foods to which movie they last watched while making out with someone. I have never cringed more in my period of life - but on the bright side, at least Stefan is happy.

"Is that why you dragged me here? I was making a new friend. I'm sure your bragging could have waited."

Stefan shrugged, his eyes never leaving his hands as he was counting the money. "No, I called you here for two things. One - praise. I don't think I've ever seen a motorbike race before, but you made it seem enjoyable. Kinda upset that you didn't win, but meh!"

I smiled. So he didn't care only about money. That's a relief.

"And two?" I asked. Stefan smiled sheepishly.

"The other reason I called you here is that you know Lyra way better than me and I want to buy her something special with this money."

He looked up at me, his face contorting to mimic a puppy dog's gaze. "Can you please help me get Lyra something special?"

I rolled my eyes. "You're such a sap."

Stefan's eyes pleaded. After all the stuff Stefan's done for me - watch over me while I sobbed in the playground, support my racing, ask constantly if I was okay - how could I say no?

"Sure, let's go now," I said. Stefan nearly squealed.

"YES!"

We walked out of the building. Stefan walked me to his car. He helped me push my bike into the trunk of his Ute, strapping my baby in with as many harnesses as I could find. I threw myself in the front seat, Stefan joining me on the driver's seat.

Stefan was telling me all of these ideas about what present he was thinking to get Lyra, but I wasn't paying any attention in the slightest. I was busy staring out the window, looking out for Owen. I found him, and he produced an adorable toothy smile for me before throwing his helmet back on. He stuck his thumb up before racing those three biker men again, Owen leading ahead of the racing pack.

A slight flicker appeared in my chest. For a second, I completely forgot about Taylor.

CHAPTER 16

Taylor's pov

Monday, February 11th, 2014

The school bus screeched to a halt in front of Vale High School, making Ana and I jostle violently in our seats. It was a stormy day - dark, foreboding cumulonimbus clouds filled the sky, blocking whatever sunlight they could snatch from the waning sun. As we and the other students spilled out of the withered bus, rain started to spray from the sky, pelting everybody. Ana and I rushed to a shaded spot near the front of the school, smoothing out our uniform and wiping off any droplets of water that clung to us.

"Yuck," Ana said, rubbing a few drops from her skirt, "what a horrible way to start my big bro's eighteenth birthday."

Yeah... I'm now officially eighteen. I've been too caught up in my own drama even to remember my own birthday. If it weren't for Ana parading into my room at one past twelve this morning, exclaiming how old I was now, I probably wouldn't have remembered at all.

"I like the rain," I said, wiping my glasses free from the droplets. "Just, not when I'm caught in it."

Ana smiled, but then frowned when she noticed how glum I looked. "Taylor, what's wrong?"

I snorted. "Oh, nothing, apart from this birthday being the first birthday without dad being here with us."

Ana froze for a few moments before extending her hand out, tentatively touching my shoulder. Her fingers made my muscles relax - I hadn't realised that I was so tense after blurting that out - before she sighed sharply.

"He's still here with us, Tay," She said, a half-frown forming on her lips. "This is going to sound cliche as hell, but, he will always be here with us. Don't let the memory of him ruin your day."

I wanted to scream at her. I wanted to shout from the rooftops that I didn't want to celebrate my birthday because all I could think about was the tradition dad used to do with me. We'd eat a huge dinner and play some upbeat songs on the piano before dad and I drove out to the beach where he'd give me life-changing advice. Every year, he's told me something worthwhile and meaningful, and it's been my guiding light.

That light is gone, and I am lost in the darkness. Maybe that's why I forgot my birthday today; my subconscious didn't want another reminder of dad.

"Taylor?" Ana said, her voice laced with concern, "What are you thinking about?"

I shook my head. "It's nothing, don't worry about me."

Ana frowned, retracting her arm from my shoulder. She straightened her posture, fixed her outfit for the last time, before resting her eyes on me.

"I know you may be in a dark place today, Taylor, but trust me - after school, I'm going to make sure you have the best birthday ever. Please, just trust me."

I looked at Ana, her eyes full of hope. I can't let her down.

"I can't wait," I said, forcing a smile on my lips. Ana's face lit up, a huge grin that exposed her teeth formed.

"Yay! I'll see you when you get home. Don't forget; I get home early because of my therapy, so everything will be ready when school ends. Don't be late or I will kick your ass!"

She smiled before walking off, joining her group of friends. She waved bye to me as she walked off, the clicking of her shoes fading to the point where the sound matched the rain drops falling onto the concrete floor below me. I turned and walked into the school, my smile fading into a melancholy line as I walked to Form room.

I pulled out my phone and checked out my timetable. Monday is my least favourite day for many reasons, but this particular Monday is far worse than all my previous ones. I haven't spoken to Darko or Bella since the party; the only one out of my friend group that has messaged me was Lyra, and it was for Math help.

My social life isn't the best right now, and it's my fault.

The form teacher wished me a happy birthday - not out of kindness, but because he had a calendar on his desk with everyone's birthdays marked down. He gave me a short smile before resuming back to his laptop.

I glanced around the room. Amongst all of the acquaintances that littered the area, I couldn't find Darko or Bella anywhere. Not that I minded - the less I see them today, the less I have to worry about being in an awkward situation with either of them.

Today is going to be lonely; I can just feel it.

The bell rang, and I scooted out of my seat, leaving the room to walk to Biology. The period went by very slowly - I was alone for the entire lesson, not to mention that we were doing some revision of cell respiration. I put in my headphones and blasted music until the next bell sounded.

Woodwork. My second favourite class.

Apart from playing my piano, Woodwork was the one other place I could let out my creativity. I've finished several projects - a fish carving, a piano keychain, and a plaque - and I was working on my final project - a scale model of an orchestra.

I dug my knife into the wood, prying off splintery chunks. This class was the perfect place to release anger - I had so much pent up from Lyra's party, it felt good to let it all out here.

'Stupid Bella,' I muttered, digging the knife hard into the side of the wood. 'Stupid Darko, stupid dad, stupid everyone-'

The knife slipped and dug deep into the palm of my hand.

Screaming, I dropped the knife, clutching my wrist. Blood spluttered from the centre of my hand, dribbling onto my work bench. The blade tore muscles in the heart of my hand. I winced, whimpering at the pain.

"Ah fuck! Sir - I've cut myself!" I shouted, flagging my teacher's attention with my free hand. He ran over, med-kit in tow, before cringing at the sight of my palm.

"Oh my gosh Taylor," he said, rummaging through the first aid box, "How did you do this?!"

"Knife slipped," I said, wincing when he applied antiseptic to my cut. Fighting back the urge to scream, I gritted my teeth as he wrapped my hand in gauze.

"Stop carving," he said, taking the knife away from me, "You can work on another project - you can start this one again when your hand heals."

"Oh shit, what happened to your hand Tay-Tay?!"

It was recess. I was trying to eat a cookie when Lyra sat with me, her face ashen as her eyes saw the blood-stained-gauze on my palm. I winced when she touched it.

"Hey! Don't touch - that hurts like hell!" I said, quickly retracting my arm. Lyra held a hand to her mouth, shocked that I'm injured.

"I cut myself accidentally while doing woodwork. My birthday just keeps getting worse and worse by the hour," I said, bringing my cut hand to my chest. Lyra frowned.

"That sucks, Tay. Happy birthday by the way - even though it doesn't seem very happy right now. I got you a gift, but I left it at home. Soz."

I smiled. At least Lyra was here at school to remember my birthday, and that she remembered to get me a gift. A tiny part of me knew that she hadn't gotten me anything and that she was covering up her slackness, but I didn't care. Objects aren't that important to me.

"How was your party?" I said, resuming half of my attention to the food in front of me. Lyra smiled.

"It was going great, until... you know. You, Bella & Darko had that beef. On the bright side though, I did find a cute guy!"

My eyebrows furrowed. "Wait, I thought you were dating Steven?"

Lyra laughed, hard. "He's old news, Tay. I have a new, better version of Steven."

Lyra looked past me, grinning. "And here he comes now!"

I turned around, and my jaw nearly dislocated from the shock. It was Stefan - he was sauntering up to my table with a huge bouquet of orange hibiscuses and red roses. Lyra squealed when Stefan reached my table, plucking the bouquet from Stefan's arms.

Since when were these two a thing?

"Oh my fucking God Stefan!" Lyra said, smelling the flowers delicately, "how did you know these were my favourites?"

Stefan smiled sheepishly, running his fingers through his hair. "I have my sources. I promised you I'd get you flowers."

I'm surprised Stefan didn't wince when Lyra used The Lord's name in vain.

Stefan turned to me, his lips forming a half smile. "Happy birthday dude."

I smiled before saying 'thanks' to him. He nodded.

"Where's Darko? He hasn't been in classes; is he sick at home or something?" I asked. Stefan lifted a brow.

"No? He's been here all morning, man."

Stefan scanned the cafeteria before pointing to a corner. "There he is."

I stood up and my jaw dropped again.

Why on Earth is he hanging out with Owen? What the hell is happening?

They were sitting along together, hunched in a corner, smiling and talking to each other. Darko was laughing his face off while Owen had appeared to be reciting a story to him. I groaned, before sinking down into my chair, cupping my face in my hands.

Does Darko even remember that it's my birthday today? Why the fuck did he ditch form and biology? Was he spending the entire morning with Owen? They don't even talk, nor are they even friends!

I felt my stomach tie itself into knots deep in my chest. Did my kiss with Bella affect my friendship with Darko that much?

I shook my head. 'No Taylor, it didn't. You're just overthinking again; you need to stop,' a voice in my head said, snapping me back to reality. Darko isn't ditching me. Darko is allowed to have other friends. I need to breathe.

Maybe I'll ask him why he's talking to Owen. It's odd enough to see Owen without a phone in his hand - it's even weirder seeing my best friend talk to him out of the blue.

The siren rang, sending the cafeteria into a frenzy. Stefan walked off with Lyra, leaving me alone on the table. I don't want to go to English. It's so boring.

English went by too quickly.

Usually, I fall asleep in English. I'd be listening to my teacher doing her job, but there was something weird about her voice that made me completely drowsy. In under five minutes, I'd be out cold, eyes shut, head slammed on the desk.

Today was different.

Either it was the subconscious melancholy I felt about my birthday keeping me awake, or the sharp, burning pain in my hand that kept me conscious. Regardless, I didn't sleep and learned for once in that class.

Physics came around, and I was so ready for it. The teacher has arranged us in groups of two - horrible seating plans might I add - but it wasn't a problem for Darko & I. We would sit together, fuck around, forget that we were in a learning environment and be total idiots.

This was the perfect opportunity to ask him why he's been with Owen. Hopefully, he doesn't ditch me for Owen again.

I had sat down in my chair and waited. After a few minutes, Darko didn't show up. The teacher started doing the roll rcall. He went down the list, stopping at Darko's name.

"Darko Ulyanov?" he shouts. There was a stony silence in the air as my physics teacher waited for a response. After a few moments, he let out a sigh before resuming the list.

"Wait!" A familiar voice said, "I'm -we're - here!"

Darko bursted into the room, out of breath, with an equally exhausted Owen behind him. The teacher nods, before resuming back to the roll call. I sat there, waiting for Darko to branch away from Owen, but he never does. He walked and sat with Owen.

My bag was still on my table. I shoved it off, my bag crashing onto the floor with a loud thump. The teacher, as well as Darko and Owen, looked up at me.

I furrowed my brows before pointing to Darko's chair. Looking directly at Darko, I mouthed, 'what the fuck?' before shaking my head.

He whispered something to Owen, something I couldn't make out, before he got up and walked to my desk. He kneeled down by my side so our teacher didn't notice him out of his seat. He began to whisper.

"What's wrong?"

My face scrunched in anger. "What's wrong? Why the hell have you been avoiding me all day to be with him!?"

I pointed my hand at Owen, who was staring at us, an eyebrow raised. Darko looked back to him, then to me.

"What? I haven't been avoiding you all day?" he said. I scoffed.

"Yeah, you're right. Not all day, all of the fucking weekend too. What, did my kiss with Bella offend you that much?" I spat loudly, getting the teacher's attention. The other class members were oohing and egging us on to fight.

"Boys, that's enough-"

I flipped the bird at the teacher. He stared at me, his eyes filled with disbelief. A student gasped.

"That's it; you're getting a detention!"

He sat back into his desk as he filled out a detention slip. Darko just stared at me, not knowing what to say. I narrowed my eyes at him, shaking my head.

"I'm sorry about Friday, Darko, but you can't just ditch me. Do you even know what day it is today?"

Darko's eyebrows furrowed. He shook his head.

"What day is it?" He said, slight annoyance in his throat. I stared at him for a few uncomfortable moments. He shook his head.

He doesn't care at all. All of his attention has been on Owen, that he's forgotten. I felt my gut wrench, like Darko had reached in and was yanking my insides. I could feel sharp pains stab at my heart and pressure push down on my shoulders. My eyes stung with angry tears.

"I can't believe this," I said, stifling back a laugh, "My best friend forgot about my birthday."

I picked up my bag and rushed to the teacher's desk, hastily snatching the detention slip out of his wrinkly fingers before bursting out of the room. I could hear outburst erupt from my class, but I didn't care. It faded the further I got from the class, and soon enough, all I could hear was the relaxing raindrops strike the roof of the cafeteria.

I fucking hate myself for kissing Bella now, more than I did on the night.

I hate my birthday.

CHAPTER 17

Taylor's pov

Monday, February 11th, 2014

"I can't believe this," I said, stifling back a laugh, "My best friend forgot about my birthday."

I picked up my bag and rushed to the teacher's desk, hastily snatching the detention slip out of his wrinkly fingers before bursting out of the room. I could hear anarchy descend from my class, but I didn't care. Their loud talking faded the further I got from the class, and soon enough, all I could hear was the relaxing raindrops that struck the roof of the cafeteria.

I fucking hate myself for kissing Bella now, more than I did on the night. I hate my birthday so fucking much!

I crashed onto my cafeteria table and unfurled the crinkled detention slip my physics teacher wrote for me. This is the first detention slip I've gotten in years.

Why the hell did I stick my finger up at the teacher? I wasn't angry at him - I was angry at Darko for forgetting about me, and Owen for stealing my best friend.

I sat there, glowering. I wanted to tear the green parchment up and ditch it in the bin. I scanned the writing. Apart from him spelling my name wrong, a particular section caught my eye. I felt my stomach lurch. The big, black, bold letters made me run my fingers through my hair.

'AFTERSCHOOL DETENTION; CLEANING DUTIES FOR AN HOUR AND A HALF.'

Ana is going to kill me! It takes an hour to get home from the school bus - I'm going to be so late for her birthday plan...

'Maybe if I run back to physics now and beg for forgiveness, I will be okay!' I thought to myself. Picking up my school bag and my detention slip, I ran to the cafeteria door.

As soon as I reached it, however, the siren rang. The thunder of student's feet sounded as they all approached the cafeteria. Accepting my fate, I trudged back to my table, slamming my head onto its metal surface.

'Could this day get any worse?' I thought to myself. I felt like crying.

"Hey... Taylor? Jesus, what did you do to your hand?" A familiar blonde's voice asked. Yeah. My day just officially got worse.

I lifted my head up. It was Bella.

"Are you okay?" She asked, seemingly genuine. Not bothering to speak with her, I rolled my eyes, picked up my bag and began to leave, gritting my teeth when my cut grazed my bag's strap.

"Hey- WAIT!" she shouted, making me freeze in my tracks. I side-glanced her.

"What do you want?" I grumbled.

"Please," she said, looking down at where I was sitting before, "Sit back down. I want to apologise for the other night."

'This should be funny,' I thought. I shook my head, my lips forming a sardonic smile. Snorting, I strode back to the table, slamming my bag onto it, and stared at her, my eyes waiting. She cleared her throat. What could she possibly say or do that would fix everything?

"Taylor," she said, unable to keep eye contact with me, "I'm... I'm sorry for how I behaved at Lyra's party. I shouldn't have kissed you, or got you drunk, or embarrassed you in front of Trent. I know how much you hate drinking because of your mum, and I know how much you hate Trent. I shouldn't have put you in those situations. I'm an idiot, manipulative, stupid, and I shouldn't have treated you like that. You're my best and only true friend. I'm... I'm so sorry."

She made eye contact with me. Her face was flushed, her cheeks red, her lips quivering slightly as she breathed. She was extremely nervous - nervous about what, though?

"And, I, uh," she said, moving a stray lock of blonde hair away from her face, "I know this won't make up for much, but I got you a birthday present."

She fished through her schoolbag before she produced a small, ribbon-wrapped box and an envelope with a wax seal.

"Happy birthday, Taylor."

She smiled, her eyes flickering between the gifts and me. I sat there, slightly bewildered. The one person that I thought was going to make my day go from bad to worse has actually done the opposite. Something is telling me that Bella's words were genuine.

I untied the box and lifted the lid. My eyes widened as the gift gleamed under the silk that cushioned the gift.

There was a little, beautiful, porcelain piano statue. I picked it up, my eyes eagerly inspecting it.

The fluorescent lighting in the cafeteria radiated off of the gift's shiny surface. Its keys were carved with perfect detail - it looked like it could be a real piano. It had intricate vine carvings on the back of it, as well as on the bottom. The base of it also had two letters and a short phrase engraved on it.

'D.U. May you cherish this.' this must be from the creator of the gift.

"Bella..." I said, a small smile creeping up on my lips, "This... this gift is beautiful. Thank you."

A grin spread across her rosy lips.

"Before you open the card," She said, her eyes looking at the red wax seal, "I didn't want to make your birthday about me, but, I wrote some personal feelings in that card. I know you have no right to return my feelings, but..."

She half smiled.

"I hope you do."

As I opened the card, Bella calmly packed up her bag and walked off. My confusion wore away as I read the letter, covered with intricate cursive writing. Parts of the letter were smudged away, almost entire paragraphs.

Weird.

"Dear Mr birthday boy,

I'm not going to bore you with the gritty, cheesy nonsense that I've blessed you with every year prior to this one. Actually, this card has a much deeper meaning to it. By the time you'd have received this letter, I'd have walked away or you're opening it at home.

I... I've been meaning to tell you something important.

It's been eating away at me for a long time now. I... I have no other way of saying it without beating around the bush. Brace yourself, you're probably never going to expect what I'm going to say next.

Taylor... I love you.

I know, we're best friends, we should tell each other everything, blah blah blah - I didn't feel comfortable sharing this with you, mainly because I never knew how you'd react to it. I should have come clean about who I was and about who I am. I figured you'd hate me, or you'd just stop talking to me, or something like that. I just needed to tell you, my feelings were beginning to get in the way of my academic life, as well as my social life.

God, I feel like such a coward for telling you through a letter. Hopefully, after I have given this to you, you'll still talk to me.

Love, your best friend, Bella."

I squinted, hard, at the end of the letter. Something was odd about Bella's name - around it was blurrings of other letters. I could barely make out the letters behind her name. I could only make out that there was a K there.

Did Bella forget how to write her name?

I shook my head and smiled, folding the letter back into its envelope before admiring the porcelain present. Maybe all of my priorities have been wrong. Maybe, I've been pining over the wrong person. Sure, I won't forgive Bella immediately, but she's giving me a good reason to try. Hearing the bell ring, I packed up my stuff and walked to Music class, a spring in my step and a warmth in my chest.

"Playing the piano with just one hand, Taylor? That's unconventional if you ask me," said Miss Lauriana as she walked past me. I showed her my injury, making her gasp.

"Yeah, I'd play with both, but I don't think you'd want to clean up blood from the keys." We shared a short laugh.

"How's your birthday going?" She asked, sitting down next to me. I sighed, rolling my shoulders back.

"It's been... different. Aside from all of the drama, it's just going to get harder after this class ends. I really don't want to go home.

Mum's going to be going through her usual antics, Ana's going to be disappointed in me because I'm gonna be late, and Dad..." I said, stopping at my last word. Miss Lauriana placed her hand on my shoulder, her smile sympathetic.

"Say no more," she said. "I get it. Why is Ana going to be disappointed in you?"

I sighed, before producing the detention slip from my bag. "Because of this. I promised her I'd be home on time because she told me she was going to make me a really great birthday surprise, but..."

"Hey, we can figure out a way through this," Miss Lauriana said, stroking her chin. "What about this? You serve your detention here, and you ask Darko to drive you home?"

I shook my head. "Things between Darko and I aren't so good. I did... something near him the other day and he... well, he forgot my birthday. So, we're not really talking at the moment."

She sighed, before looking thoughtfully at the piano. "I'll drive you."

I beamed. "You would? Isn't that considered like, weird?"

Miss Lauriana scoffed. "Psh, the school doesn't care about me. I was best friends with your dad - I think he'd haunt me if I didn't at least offer."

I smiled. Miss Lauriana is more than just a teacher to me. She's like the auntie I never had.

She stood up, brushing off her ankle-long dress. "Now, I'm sorry, but I have a class to teach. Don't get any blood on my piano, or you'll be banned."

I smirked. "As if you'd ban your star pupil from their favourite instrument."

The bell rang, signalling the end of the school day. I quickly sent Ana a text before I went to the storeroom to grab a thick rubbish bag. 'I missed the bus, I'm sorry! I'll be roughly half an hour late.'

It's best not to tell her I got detention - there would be too many questions.

My phone sounded as I picked up some scrap paper. 'How dare you! You promised! That's it, I'm throwing your cake away! ;) '

I sniggered, gritting my teeth as Ana fell for the lie. 'Blame the stupid bus arriving and leaving early. I'll see you later. Love you'

"So," Miss Lauriana said, scribbling on a few papers behind her desk, "Did you get any presents for your birthday?"

I smiled. "Yeah, Bella got me one. Well, two actually - a present and a wax-sealed card."

I shuffled to my bag and produced the porcelain piano from its side pocket. Miss Lauriana rose from her desk and walked calmly to me, her eyes gleaming as she saw it.

"Wow, it's beautiful. I'm surprised - this seems more like something Darko would get you - I never even knew Bella appreciated your piano skills."

I smiled. "Yeah. Ugh, don't mention Darko."

I sunk into a desk, groaning. "I still can't believe he forgot my birthday-"

"I know, and I'm sorry I did."

Miss Lauriana and I both shot our gaze to the door. Darko stood there, tall, a gift bag in one hand and an envelope in the other. His cheeks were red, and he couldn't make eye contact with me.

Miss Lauriana looked at me, then back to Darko. "Should I give you two a moment?"

"Yes, please," Darko said, walking into the class. Miss Lauriana handed me the porcelain gift and walked briskly to the doorway.

"Be quick, I have assessments to mark." She said, slipping out of the door, closing it shut. I looked at Darko, eyes narrowing, arms folded.

"What are you doing here?"

Darko let out a long breath, before settling into a desk next to me. "I need to apologise. I feel like an idiot for forgetting my best friend's birthday. I hope your favourite snack and a heartfelt card would make up for it-"

"-And you think I'd forgive you instantly, through some food and a card? Darko, no, it's not just today that you've made me feel terrible - it's been going on for days! Why did you never respond to my messages? Did you ever get my voicemail after Lyra's party?"

He folded his arms, letting out a sigh. "I didn't want to talk to you! I hate Bella, you know that, and seeing you and her kissing each other made me so fucking angry!"

He shook his head. "I did get your voicemail, but my phone died midway through. It deleted itself when I charged my phone. What was the rest of it?"

I looked away, shaking my head. "I just wanted to tell you my side of things. The voice mail said for you to call me, or for you to message me, so we could sort everything out. I wanted to explain everything, like how it was my first party and I had no idea what I was doing."

I let out another sigh. "From your perspective, it looks like the kiss was a mutual thing. It wasn't. She filled my head with lies. She manipulated a situation to make it look like the person I'm crushing on was into someone else. I was drunk. I felt like shit, Darko. When she kissed me, I knew it was the wrong thing to do, but I didn't stop her. She made everything feel right for a split second."

Darko leaned back in his chair, a smug grin on his face. He snorted, before saying "And you wonder why I hate her."

"Why do you hate her?" I asked. He scoffed.

"Because of everything you just told me-"

"No," I said, furrowing my brows. "Pretend Lyra's party never happened. She's done nothing at all to you before then, so why the hate?"

He shrugged, letting out a long sigh before making eye contact with me. I couldn't shake the feeling that he knew why, but he didn't want to tell me.

"I just hate her," he said, after a few tense moments. "She wasn't a good boyfriend to Trent or a good friend to his underlings. I just get the vibe that she's toxic and up to no good at all - and the shit she pulled at the party is evidence enough."

We sat there for a few tense moments. "Why have you been hanging out with Owen?" I asked, my voice prickly.

Darko sighed again. "He came to my races on Sunday. He's a cool dude, you two would get along great."

I looked at him, creasing my brows. "And, what? You have talked to him for less than two days and you've already ditched me for him? Now I finally see how much our friendship means to you."

Darko groaned. "Taylor, don't be such a prick. The only reason I hung out with him is that I lost a bet - he wanted me to chill with him for the day at school. I was so caught up with him that it made me forget things, like your birthday, for example."

I let out a laugh. "Ooh, wow, next time, shoot me a text so I don't end up feeling like an expendable, used, idiot!"

We sat there for a few moments. My breath was rapid from all the yelling I was doing. Darko's face was beetroot red, and his breath was sped up too. We were both so angry at each other.

"I'm sorry for being a shitty friend," Darko said suddenly. "I'm sorry for everything, for ditching you today, for forgetting about your birthday, for ignoring your voicemail and messages, every-thing."

I made eye contact with him. His eyes were pleading. I could just make out a thin line of tears building up from the bottom of his eyes.

I felt guilty now. I felt selfish. Sure, I had every right to be, but I couldn't help it. I freaking love him.

I let out a sigh. "I'm sorry too. I'm sorry that I blew up on you just now, I'm sorry if I embarrassed you in physics class, and I'm sorry that you saw Bella and I kissing."

Darko looked up at me, the tears from his eyes almost gone completely. "I'll forgive you if you forgive me?"

We sat there for a few moments, his eyes lingering on mine. A smile crept onto my face, as well as a chuckle. His lips curled into his trademark smirk before he laughed too.

"I can't stay mad at you after you just apologised like that. Sure, I forgive you."

"Then, I forgive you too, my good sir."

I cringed. It was bittersweet hearing that horrid nickname. Darko chuckled again before I stared daggers at him.

"You're really testing my patience with that nickname."

We sat there, smiling at each other. Miss Lauriana opened the door, before squinting at us.

"Are you two done yet? I've had to pretend to be on the phone with someone in front of two cleaners now, It's getting kind of ridiculous."

I nodded. She groaned dramatically before pushing the doors open, striding up to her desk. She began marking tests.

"Anyway," Darko said, leaning behind him, "I believe you have presents to open."

He produced the gift bag and the envelope to me.

"The envelope is from Stefan and the parents. Some good cash in there, as well as some heartfelt stuff."

He delicately placed the bag on the desk. "This one is from me."

Miss Lauriana looked at us, a grin forming on her face. "Aww, you bought him a present! I doubt it's going to top Bella's gift though."

Darko lifted a brow. "Bella's gift?"

I smiled sheepishly. "Yeah, at lunch, she walked up to me and apologised about how she was acting at Lyra's. She handed me this tiny gift box and this wax sealed envelope."

I showed Darko the present. His eyes widened.

"It's beautiful, isn't it?" I said, smiling at the porcelain piano figurine. His eyes narrowed, and his eyebrows knitted together.

"What, uh, was in that wax letter she gave you?" He said, his voice shaky. Lifting a brow, I fished out the letter and read it to him. His eyes widened as I read her name last.

"She confessed her love to me. I don't know whether it's poetic or not, but yeah."

Darko froze. A sweat bead tricked down his forehead. His eyes were blank. His knuckles clenched white as his face began to go red.

"Darko? What's wrong?" I asked. He shook his head before he stood up and scrambled out of the room. His heavy footsteps could be heard as he ran down the hallway.

"What the hell?"

CHAPTER 18

D arko's pov

Monday evening, February 11th, 2014.

I cannot believe Bella stole my fucking gifts.

Entwined in Taylor's delicate fingers were my porcelain piano and my wax-sealed envelope. My heart fell out of my chest when he read me the letter. That piano figurine was one of a kind - I even engraved my initials to the base of it, so Taylor would always find it special. This gift was meant to be the thing that helped me come out to Taylor, and remove the crushing weight of my undying feelings for him.

And Bella's taken it all and used it for her own gain.

I'm fucking angry! This gift was personal. Bella doesn't even like the piano.

All I could hear was a loud, piercing white noise as I ran to my car, leaving a very confused Taylor behind me. Adrenaline coursed through my entire being as I had fished out my keys and switched on my car's ignition. How did she know I even had a gift in my glove box? Why did she have a knife?

Why does she love screwing with me?!

I had sped off, leaving long skid marks on the asphalt. Pitch black smoke billowed out of my exhaust pipe as I raced out of the school car park, narrowly missing the edge of the school's fence. Other cars beeped as I shot through red lights and took illegal turns.

I don't give a fuck about them. I'm going to Bella's house and demanding answers. I'm sick of her screwing with my life - this shit needs to stop.

"Your destination is on the left," my phone's GPS said. Hastily pulling over, I got out of the car before slamming the door and stormed towards her house, seething.

I've only ever been here once before, and it was to pick up Taylor. He and Bella had spent the afternoon at her house, studying for Biology. God knows if they studied - Bella probably tried to kiss him.

I rapped my knuckles on the grand oak door and folded my arms. Quick footsteps erupted from the house, before the lock on the door clicked. It swung open. I closed my eyes, knitted my brows and growled.

"Alright Bella, what the actual fuck? Why the hell did you decide to break into my car, take my glove box, steal my fucking present and my love letter to Taylor? How fucking dare you-"

I froze. Bella was not at the door.

Instead, there was a little girl, probably only seven years old, clutching the door handle with one hand. Tears welled in her eyes as she dropped a teddy bear she was holding.

"BIG SIS! THERE'S A SCARY MAN AT THE DOOR SWEARING AT ME!" the little girl said, slamming the oak slab. I could hear her sobbing through the door.

Oh, fuck.

I whipped out my phone and checked the address. Everything was correct - I got the right house. Maybe this was her little sister?

Suddenly, the door swung open, nearly making me drop my phone. The little girl was still there, although this time, she was hiding behind a very familiar woman.

"Hannah, go back to our movie. I need to talk to him," Bella said, her eyes not leaving mine. The little girl, who I assumed was Hannah, picked up her stuffed teddy and ran back into the house. Bella swung the flyscreen-door open, before shutting the wooden door behind her. A sardonic smile crept on her lips.

Why was she so evil?

"Okay, one, don't you dare talk to my sister like that again, and two: what the hell are you doing here?" She said, her eyebrows knitting.

"Oh, save your facade for some other gullible fucker. You know exactly why I came to your shitty house. You have five minutes to explain why you stole my gift before I march to the police station to file a burglary report."

"Ah, that isn't a good idea," she said, casually sitting on the couch that was on her porch. "If you do that, then I would have no choice but to out you to the entire school, and to your bible-loving family."

My hands clenched into fists.

"My family wouldn't listen to you! You're bluffing - there is no way you'd be able to spread this around the school-"

"Oh, save your breath. I have you in the palm of my hand, and there's nothing you can do about it. I'm not telling your family directly - I'm telling Lyra. Knowing her huge gossip mouth, she'd tell Stefan, and that boy will believe anything Lyra says. I have connections with the school's newspaper, and I have photos of your love letter that I think would look amazing on Facebook and every other social media in existence. Don't test me." She spat.

I stood there, glowering. Bella just smiled, before lying down on the couch. Of course she's blackmailing me - It's her trademark.

"Why?" I asked, my tone unsteady. "Why the fuck do you hate me so much?"

Bella smirked. "That's a simple answer. It's because I love Taylor, and you need to get out of the picture."

I scoffed. "Out of the picture? Why?! Taylor is straight, I'll never have a chance with him. How is my involvement hindering your chances with him?"

Bella stared at me, before bursting out into laughter. "Oh god Darko, you know absolutely nothing."

I lifted a brow. What is she talking about?

"What do you mean? What don't I know?"

Bella tapped her nose, before smirking. "That's for me to know, and for you to never find out."

I folded my arms. Of course she's cryptic.

"Care to at least explain the shitshow regarding you breaking into my car then?"

Bella rolled her eyes. God, if she weren't blackmailing me right now, I would have decked her.

"I will, but let me ask you this - when was the last time you spoke to Nicole?" Bella asked, her gaze blank.

"What has she got to do with any of this-"

"Just answer the damn question!"

I sighed. "Fine! I don't know, a week or two ago? She sent me a pic on Snapchat. I don't care about her in that way."

"Good. Then, you shouldn't find this explanation far-fetched then."

Bella put her phone away, before facing me, her face blank.

"It wasn't me that broke into your car. Nicole did it."

My brow had never creased that fast before. Bella, noticing that, smirked devilishly before continuing.

"After school two weeks ago, the same day Lyra invited you, Tay Tay and I to her party, I went to the school's bathroom, desperately needing to pee. As soon as I walked in, I heard sobbing come from one of the stalls. I knocked, and after some coaxing, Nicole stepped out, her cheeks streaked with her running mascara. She explained to me how much of a dick you had apparently been to her - ignoring her in real life and just being very apathetic towards her - and we bonded over our shared dislike of you. To cut a long story short - I told her to spy on you, she saw you hide the present in the car, I told her to get it, and she did."

"What the fuck," I said, running my hands through my hair. "I could file for attempted assault, or robbery, or vandalism-"

"Oh no, no, no," Bella said, waving a finger. "You can't prove it was Nicole and me without that fight ending with you coming out to your family. Either way, I win."

"She pulled a fucking knife on me, Bella! I could have died that night!"

"Oh no, what an absolute shame, oh my gosh I'm so upset about that!" Bella said, her tone tearing away at my tolerance. She grabbed her collar, her face searching inside her shirt before she looked up to me and said: "Oh gosh, there's nobody in this shirt that cares!"

That's it.

I ran up to her and grabbed her by the shirt, lifting her up and pinning her to a wall. Shocked, she gasped, but then furrowed her brows.

"Strike one, dick face. Drop me before I scream." She growled. I half-dropped, half-threw her on the ground, making her land with a thud on her wooden porch floor. She had scrambled to her feet before she dusted herself off. She snatched her phone out of her pocket and jabbed the screen with her thorny fingers.

"You shouldn't have done that," she said, shaking her head. "You should not have done that."

"What are you doing?" I asked. She scoffed, before shoving her phone into her pocket.

"You'll see soon enough. Consider this a warning. If you ever touch me again, or if you threaten Nicole, or if you tell Taylor any of this - you're going to find yourself thrown completely out of the closet."

She pivoted before entering her house, slamming the door behind me.

Oh God, what did she do?

I pounded the door with my fist. "What the hell? Get back out here; we aren't finished yet!"

Silence.

After a few moments of waiting, I gave up and trudged to my car, sinking into the seat.

Anxiety began to spike through my chest like a harpoon. I ran my fingers through my sweaty hair, before cranking the air conditioner. What did Bella do?!

I threw my phone onto my passenger seat, before turning on the engine. I reversed out of Bella's driveway and raced home, driving a little safer than I did before.

As I pulled into my driveway, my phone buzzed. It was Taylor.

'Dude, what the hell happened? Is everything okay?'

I sighed. I wish I could tell him that Bella was a toxic bitch. I wish I could tell Taylor that she stole those gifts from me and that she's trying to isolate me from him.

I wish I could tell Taylor how I feel. At least before Bella, I had a choice. Now, I don't.

'I'm sorry,' I texted, 'I don't know what happened. I just remembered something and panicked. I'll be okay.'

'Oh, okay.' He texted back. 'Let me know if there's anything I can do to help.'

'You can maybe start by getting rid of Bella and like me instead,' I thought.

Why the hell am I such a huge problem in Bella's love life with Taylor? Bella has him wrapped around her fingers. There's no other explanation for Bella's behaviour unless she sees me as a real threat to her love life with him.

Does Bella think I have a chance to be with Taylor?

That can't be! Taylor is straight. He kissed Bella at Lyra's party, and he loves girls.

Wait.

Bella said that I didn't know everything about him. Maybe the reason why Bella hates me so much is that I actually do have a chance with Taylor.

Taylor must be bisexual. If I were to think that two weeks ago, I would have slapped myself for being so unreasonable, but now, it's the only thing that makes sense.

CHAPTER 19

Taylor's pov

Monday Evening, February 11th, 2014.

"You know miss," I said, resting my head on my hand as I looked out her car window, "Today's been really shit. Just want to say thanks for not being horrible to me."

Miss Lauriana chuckled as she continued to drive. "Oh shush Taylor, you know I'm always going to be good to you. Side note; don't call me 'miss' outside of school - that's just... weird. Call me by my first name."

I smiled. "Sure thing, Dianne."

It was about six in the evening, and Miss Lauriana drove me home. We sang along to songs on the radio and had a heated discussion on who was the best classical pianist. We had just left a set of traffic lights when she spoke again.

"Did you ever end up finding out why Darko left my music room so suddenly?" Miss Lauriana asked, turning a corner. I whipped out my phone and read aloud my conversation with Darko.

"That seems fishy..." she said. "I hope things are okay with him. He hasn't been very stable these past few weeks."

I nodded in agreement. "So many things don't make any sense with him anymore. It's like he's hiding something from me. I just can't help shake the feeling that he's struggling with something and that he needs help."

She shrugged. "Maybe he is. Have you ever asked him if he's okay?"

"Well... no. Not in person."

She laughed. "Well, you better do it first thing tomorrow."

We sat in comfortable silence. Miss Lauriana's focus may have been on the road, but mine was on Darko.

"We're here," she said, snapping me out of my reverie. She pulled into the driveway as I reached in front of my seat, plucking my schoolbag from the car's floor.

"You know, you can stay over for dinner if you like. It would be cool for you and Mum to catch up - you haven't talked in a long time."

"Thanks," she said, looking toward the house, "but, I can't. I need to get home to cook for my kids."

"Ah right, I forgot about AJ and Micah. Tell them I said hey!" I said, earning a smile from her. AJ and Micah are twins, and the sassiest boys I've ever met.

"See you tomorrow, Dianne."

Miss Lauriana smiled. "Have a lovely birthday, Taylor."

I opened the car door and trudged towards the front of my house, waving her off as she reversed out of my driveway. The tiny turquoise car sped off, little liquorice-coloured puffs of smoke jetting out of her exhaust pipe as she turned out of our street.

While calling out to Ana, I knocked on the door. I had my own key, but I figured that Ana would want me to wait outside for her surprise to really have a good effect on me.

I held my breath. Although I had been bottling it in for the last half of the day, I was absolutely terrified of spending my first birthday without my dad. I don't know how any of us are going to handle doing something 'big' without him.

Only time will tell.

Almost instantly, I heard footsteps thunder down my wooden hallway, stopping abruptly at the oak slab in front of me.

"DO NOT, I REPEAT, DO NOT COME IN YET!" Ana had shouted before shuffling off. Chuckling, I sat on the porch and flicked through my bag, grabbing Darko's unopened present out.

I forgot about that. I've been so focused on why he left to remember that he actually got me something.

I opened the gift bag and fished out a wrapped, rectangular box. Shaking it lightly, I listened inside, anticipating what the gift was.

It sounded grainy and weirdly dense.

I started to preen the paper away when I noticed a card at the bottom of the gift bag. I put the present aside and grabbed the tiny card, flipping it open.

'You told me you were craving this before. Happy birthday, Taylor <3 Warning: DO NOT SHAKE PRESENT!"

My heart skipped a beat when I read the tiny heart he drew. It then tripled in speed when I read the warning.

Shit.

I hastily opened the gift and saw my present. A gross, soggy heap of broken sushi rolls.

Great.

"All right, you can come in, I just need to-" Ana said suddenly, poking her head out of the doorway. She stopped talking as she noticed my hand.

"What the hell Taylor? Are you okay?" She said, moving to sit next to me. She grabbed my wrist and inspected the gauze around my wound. I shrugged.

"Just a knife slip in woodwork," I said, "I'll be fine."

Ana nodded thoughtfully, before looking at the tray of 'sushi' on my lap. She started chuckling.

"Bro, I don't think that's how you eat sushi." She giggled. I rolled my eyes.

"It was a gift from Darko. I shook it before I read the card that said 'DO NOT SHAKE PRESENT'." I said, rocking my head back. "I was really looking forward to having some food..."

Ana beamed. "Well, that's a relief."

I lifted a brow. "Huh, what?"

My eyes glanced over Ana. Her hands appeared to be covered in a white substance, and she was wearing an apron smeared with what I hoped was chocolate. What was she up to?

Ana shook her head before tapping her nose. "In due time, you will know."

She pulled a handkerchief out of her pocket, showing it to me. "For my surprise to be perfect, I need you to wear this. I'll walk you in the house, so don't worry about crashing into furniture. I just need you to put this on."

I snorted. "Fine. Just, be careful."

I took off my glasses and hooked them on my collar, allowing Ana to wrap the silky-blue fabric around my eyes. She lifted the sushi mess from my lap and, judging from the crunchy noise the gift bag made, put it away. I stood up and let Ana lead me into the house. My lips bristled against the loose tips of the handkerchief that dangled in front of my mouth.

"Okay, you're doing great," Ana said, stopping. "Just a little furt her..."

"Where are you taking me?" I asked. I couldn't see her face, but I assumed she had smiled. Or, she had rolled her eyes.

"It's called a surprise for a reason," she said. Yeah, she definitely rolled her eyes.

"All right, just sit down here and I'll be back in a second."

I sat down at the chair Ana guided me to. I instantly recognised that it was the dining table chair - the squeak of my chair's backboard was distinguishable enough.

After a few minutes, I heard footsteps approach me. A chair squealed and shuffled over next to me, and the clink of cutlery could be heard as it was placed on the table. The sound of bowls clinking could be heard. Someone cleared their throat.

"Mum, would you do the honours of taking the blindfold off?" Ana said. After a few moments, I felt hands gently pry away at the knot Ana tied.

As the handkerchief came off, I had to stop my jaw from hitting the ground. In front of me was the most beautiful, two-tier cake I had ever seen in my entire eighteen years on this planet.

It was covered in creamy-white fondant, with tiny rainbow detailing around the edges. Dark caramel sauce and liquid chocolate dribbled from the top layer to the bottom, the liquids eagerly meeting with the buttery cookie crumble at the base. Iced crimson roses rested on top of the crumble, making my mouth salivate at the thought of tasting them. The scent of slightly burned caramel wafted in the air, like sea spray at the beach.

They began singing the birthday song, my heart filling with warmth as the tune filled the air. The eighteen candles burned a beautiful incandescent orange as I watched a wax bead roll down one of the shafts. I found myself grinning, eyes shut, lettting myself get lost in this moment.

"Make a wish!" Ana said, pointing to the candle. I chuckled to myself, leaning forward, eyes still shut.

'I wish...' I thought. 'I wish I could kiss Darko. Just once. Or a million times.'

I blew out the candle. Ana and Mum had smiled before Mum started cutting the cake. Ana told me about how she made everything.

"See the rainbows?" She said, pointing to one of the dozen fondant rainbows that covered the cake. "You can take a guess as to why those were included."

I sighed, smirking. "Gee, I wonder why."

We shared a laugh, before we looked at mum, smiling. Ana's face fell when she saw how many slices she had cut.

"Mum... you don't need to cut four..."

Mum looked at Ana, before looking at the slices she had cut. She forced a laugh out, before putting down the knife.

"I'm sorry, I didn't even realise. Just a habit that I haven't shaken off yet." She said. Her words sounded forced. Ana and I shared a look before I spoke.

"No, this is good. Here," I said, plucking the candle out of the cake's top. "I have an idea."

I got up and fetched a bowl. Placing the extra slice of cake in it, I put the bowl in front of the only empty seat at our table. The candle slid easily into the sponge insides as I lit the wick. The tiny orange glow brightened the dim dining room.

I gripped the chair, sighing, before looking at everyone. "This is the first birthday that we are having without Dad here. I... I don't know, I think this would be a nice, small sign of respect for him."

I sat back down. We all looked at the slice of cake with a candle wedged in it.

"You're right," Mum said, her voice a bit shaky. "This... this is nice."

We all stared at the candle. I could head mum's breath speed up as a few wax droplets rolled down onto the sponge dessert. I felt my cheeks burn up.

Ana sighed. "Come on guys, let's not turn Taylor's birthday into a sad episode... Dad wouldn't have wanted this. Let's just enjoy each other's company and the cake. Please?"

Mother and I nodded. Ana perked up, passing the cut slices around until we all had one each.

We talked about our day as we ate - it was a decent enough distraction. I explained to mum what happened with the knife, but nothing more than that. For some reason, I don't like it when mum knows about the drama between me and my friends. Part of me knows that I feel this way because I confided these things with dad, the other part just doesn't want me to tell anybody else.

Ana told us how her appointment with her psychologist went. She was told about the Five Stages of Grief, and that she was nearly through the fourth stage. Ana whispered to me that Mum was still stuck in stage one, while I'm at the acceptance stage. Stage 5.

"That cake was delicious," Mum said, smiling at Ana. "Where did you learn how to cook that?"

"Food Science class," Ana said, smirking at me. "I highly recommend it."

Ana and I shared a laugh while mum smiled at us. When we stopped, I found myself staring at the candle again. Half of the wax has melted onto the slice.

Mum noticed Ana and I looking at the candle. Her breathing was unpredictably fast at this point, and her face had gone red -

particularly her cheeks. She swallowed hard before she looked up at us.

I placed my hand on mum's hand. Ana glanced at us before I spoke.

"Mum? Everything is fine. Please don't cry."

"I-I'm sorry, I can't do this," she said. Before Ana or I could say another word, Mum stood up and shuffled out of the kitchen, her bedroom door slamming shut.

Ana and I looked at each other. She shook her head before following mum, presumably going to go check on her. I looked at the candle again.

Without a word, I leaned over and blew out Dad's candle.

"So, what else did you get for your birthday?" Ana asked. I shoved the cake into our fridge and took out the sushi pile. Grabbing a spoon, I shuffled to my room, a curious Ana trailing behind me.

"I got this sushi pile from Darko, a cute porcelain piano and card from Bella and some cash from Darko's parents," I called out. I sat on my bed and showed Ana the presents. Her eyes beamed at the piano as I scooped some of the sushi bits into my mouth.

Hey, it might not look like sushi, but it still tasted like it. That's all that matters.

"The piano is beautiful," Ana said, her eyes inspecting the figurine. "Darko went all out on this."

"Darko?" I said with a mouthful of sushi. "Darko didn't get me that. Bella did."

Ana lifted a brow. "Sorry, I assumed Darko did. His initials are scratched on the bottom."

I shrugged. "Easy mistake. Those initials are from the maker of the statue, I'm pretty sure. Must be a huge coincidence."

We shared a comfortable silence as I continued to eat my sushi mess. Ana counted the cash I got from Darko's parents.

"So, what are you doing for Valentine's day?" Ana asked, stacking the money. I knitted my brows, earning a confused look from her.

"Valentine's day? When's that?"

"Uh, in three days?" Ana said, scoffing. "Don't tell me you forgot."

I shrugged. Ana's eyes widened.

"Dude! How can you forget? Do you remember that you're performing on that night? In front of the whole school?!"

Oh shit. Right. My performance. I've been so preoccupied with things for the past month, I completely forgot.

"SHIT!" I said, running a hand through my hair. "I'm fucked! I haven't practised any of my songs in ages, and my hand is injured!"

Ana sighed. "Shit dude. I'm sure you'll be fine. Piano comes naturally to you."

I shook my head. Noticing my nerves, Ana spoke up, attempting to change the subject. "Look, forget about the performance stuff for now. What I meant before was, are you going to ask anybody out?"

I lifted a brow, then furrowed them when I noticed she was wiggling her's at me.

"Are you going to ask a particular boy to be your Valentine?" She said, her tone indulgent. I rolled my eyes.

"As much as I want to, you know I can't. He's straight. Besides, I think someone else is going to ask me out anyway."

"Ooh, who? Do I know them?" Ana asked, her voice bubbling with curiosity. I sighed before I fished out Bella's love letter.

"Read this."

Ana's eyes flicked through the parchment, her eyes widening as she looked up at me. She shook her head.

"Please tell me you're not actually contemplating a relationship with that witch."

I grimaced. "A relationship? No, of course not. A Valentine's dance though..."

"Why?" Ana asked, throwing the letter on my pillow. I groaned.

"Because maybe spending time with her will help me get over my feelings for Darko. Yeah, she's been a bit of a bitch for the past few weeks, but she apologised for everything today. I just feel she deserves a second chance."

Ana's eyes widened. "You do realise this is the same girl that made you drink eight cups of beer, the same girl that kissed you when you were drunk, and the same girl that grabbed your dick at Lyra's party? She's nothing but trouble bro!"

I sat there, letting the words sink in. "You're right... what am I doing?"

Ana groaned. "You're about to make one of the biggest mistakes of your high school life. Do not, I repeat, do NOT ask Bella to be your Valentine. I get bad vibes from her. Really bad vibes."

I rolled my neck toward her, sighing before leaning back onto my mattress. "Who should I ask out then? Darko?"

Ana didn't respond. She just looked at me suggestively, flicking both eyebrows up at the same time.

"Uh, yeah!"

CHAPTER 20

D arko's pov

Monday Afternoon, February 11th, 2014.

My tires screeched to a halt as I crossed the finish line. Owen turned to me, his brunette hair popping out of his helmet as he took it off, before switching off his engine.

"Dude, why'd you throw that race off?" He said, his face warped with confusion. "You were so far ahead, but you slowed down and let me win! Is everything all right?"

"I'm fine," I said, flatly.

I wasn't fine. I had driven away from Bella's house to my own, before firing up my motorcycle to meet Owen at The Tracks. I still don't know what Bella's done, and it's making me paranoid as all hell. Fuck Bella.

Owen had flicked his kickstand with his foot, before he walked to me, peeling off his biker gloves. "You can talk to me, dude. What's wrong?"

"It's really nothing. Don't worry about me." Can he stop please?

Owen lifted a brow. "Darko, please. Whatever's happening, you need to do something about it, or you could be a danger on the racetrack. If there's anything I can do to help-"

"I said I'm fine!"

Owen's eyes widened. I sighed sharply, before running my fingers through my dampened hair.

"Just pissed at someone, alright? Is that enough for you?"

He lifted a brow. "Dude, calm down. I'm just a concerned friend, worried about you."

I grunted, throwing my hands on my face. Groaning, I dragged them down my cheeks before I made eye contact with Owen, who was staring at me, his gaze lingering.

"I've never seen you like this - It's scary. Can I ask... what happened? You seemed fine at school today. Does it have to do with Taylor's outburst in physics?"

I shook my head. "Just... it's complicated, dude. I'm pissed at Bella."

Owen threw his head back, groaning. "Ugh, I don't like her. "

I lifted a brow. "You don't?"

Owen scoffed. "Of course I don't! She's so two-faced, and I've heard about all of the shit she's done to so many people."

I snorted. "I'm glad I'm not the only one that sees it. Bella's so fucking awful."

Owen smiled. "So, she's pissing you off. Did she do anything to you?"

I looked away, letting out a long sigh. "Shit's complicated dude. It'll take too long to explain, and most of it is just mind-blowing stuff."

Owen turned to me, his eyes widening slightly. "I've got time. Come on, tell me!"

"Nah dude..."

Owen frowned. "Dude, we may have only been talking for two days, but I do consider you a friend. Friends are there for each other, and I wanna-"

I sighed. "Look, I'll tell you so that you stop being sappy. But, you need to promise me you won't tell anybody, and that if you do, I won't talk to you ever again, and I will seriously hurt you."

His eyes widened. "Uh... I promise. Please don't tell me you murdered someone and Bella's gonna rat you out, or something like that."

I laughed. "Oh, god, no. I wish she were dead though."

Shutting my eyes, I rolled my head back, taking a deep breath. I looked at him, his expression waiting. Good god, why is this so hard?

"It's okay," He said, his smile reassuring me, "whatever the situation is, I'm sure it's not that bad."

I sighed. "It's just hard, okay? I haven't told anybody this, and for me to tell someone I've only talked to within such a small period... it's beyond difficult."

"It's okay. Take your time. I've got nothing except it."

Taking a long breath, I gripped the handlebars on my bike in a vain attempt to feel secure again.

Well, here goes nothing.

"I'mgayandIhaveahugecrushonTaylor." I gabbled. Owen raised an eyebrow.

"What did you say?"

"I'm gay," I said, saying my words slowly, "and I have a huge crush on Taylor."

As the words left my mouth, I realised that Owen was the very first person I had told about my real sexuality. Did I just make the biggest mistake telling someone so new to me something this personal?

He sat there, his face wrapped with a grin. He shook his head before staring off into the race track, tittering.

"The school's renown lady-killer is gay? Haha! Good one, mate. So, what was the real issue?"

I lifted a brow as he glanced back at me. Realisation dawning on him, he clasped his mouth, his eyes wider than the Grand Canyon after a category ten earthquake.

"Oh my God... you're serious..." he said, his words muffled against his palm. I sighed.

"Yeah... I am."

Owen continued to sit there, words unable to escape his open lips. I sighed.

"Bella found out that I like him, and she thinks Taylor feels the same way. She's threatening to out me in front of everyone - my family, my friends, the general public - unless I keep my mouth shut and I stay away from Taylor."

He shook his head.

"So, what are you going to do?" he said, his hands finally leaving his face. I tried to shrug non-nonchalantly, but I felt myself get anxious again.

"I don't know. I accidentally lashed out at her about an hour ago, and she's gone and done something bad. I still need to figure out what she did. I'm so worried about it Owen; what if she outed me to my brother? Or to the rest of the bikers? I don't think I'd be able to handle how you reacted several more times."

Owen looked at me, before looking at his own hands. He shook his head, before taking a breath and relaxing.

"Well, that explains why you've been out of it while racing..." He said, patting my back. "Take my reaction with a grain of salt. I just can't believe it - you had so many female options, and you've slept with girls before, and-"

"And," I said, cutting him off, "I felt nothing. I hooked up with them as a cover-up. I didn't enjoy one second of any of it."

I got up. "Look, just forget I said anything. It was a waste of time opening up."

I went to leave, but Owen grabbed me by the shoulder. "Dude, no need to be like that. I never said I hated you or that I don't appreciate your honesty. It's just mind-blowing, like you said. I'm sorry if how I reacted offended you."

I nudged his hand off and turned to face him. He had a welcoming smirk on his lips, before he tore his attention from me, and back onto the helmet that was on his lap.

"Tell me everything that's happened, Darko."

After about half an hour, I explained it all; the shit that happened at Lyra's party, the broken-into car, Nicole's involvement, and my stolen gift. Owen's face grew angrier as each moment passed.

"I hate her even more now," Owen said, glowering. "I didn't think it was possible, yet here I am, wanting to punch her in the face."

I laughed. "Tell me about it."

"So, let me get this straight," he said, "you can't be near Taylor, and you can't speak to him when she's around. She's got enough dirt on you to ruin your reputation and your relationships with your family, right?"

I nodded. He frowned, before sighing.

"He's clueless!" I huffed. "I even got my initials carved into the bottom of it - how stupid can he be?"

Owen shrugged. "You could always send him a photo of the receipt. Better yet, you could just message him, saying that it was your present and that Bella stole it."

I grimaced. "Why the hell would I do that?"

"Well, you said it yourself. If your theory of Taylor being into you is true, then what's the harm in saying it to him? Hell, even if he rejects you, at least you'll have closure."

I shook my head. "Even if Taylor felt the same, I wouldn't be able to act on it. Bella would get in the way, and I'd be thrown out of the closet faster than you can say 'Bella is a bitch.' Look, I'm just going to accept that Bella has won for the time being. There's nothing I can do that would help."

Owen stroked his chin thoughtfully.

"Yes, maybe there's nothing you can do! But what if..."

He trailed off. Narrowing my brows, I looked at him, his face wrapped in thought.

"I've got an idea."

He got up and walked to his bike. Confused, I followed him, grabbing my jacket as I got off of mine.

He was scribbling something on a sheet of paper he fetched out of his bag. Peering over his shoulder, I could barely see what he was writing.

"What are you doing?" I asked, unable to see. He folded the paper and got on his bike, putting on his helmet.

"You'll see. Just, trust me."

He sped off, a dust cloud kicking up from his back wheel. Coughing and waving the dirty air in front of me, I saw his hunched figure jet out of The Tracks. What on Earth is he up to?

I walked back and sat on my bike, pulling out my phone. The sounds of distant tires skidding the dirt from other races filled the air.

That's when it hit me. I just came out to someone about my sexuality for the first time - on my own terms.

It was weird - my friendship with Owen. We've only really talked to each other for two days at most, yet I feel more comfortable talking to him than I do my own family sometimes.

Hell, I don't even know his last name, yet I trust him more than my own father.

That flicker I felt when Owen and I first started talking died quickly. I love Taylor too much even to consider other guys.

Owen was right. Bottling stuff up was awful - I'm glad he got me to open up. It felt nice to confide in someone that wasn't Taylor, or Lyra.

My eyes drifted back to my phone. Reaching behind to my butt pocket, I fished out my wallet, prying it open. I produced the porcelain piano receipt.

Maybe Owen was right.

Regardless if Taylor liked me back or not, I needed his answer. I needed that closure, before I go and do something stupid again.

I was about to snap a photo when Connor appeared out of nowhere, laughing heartily with those three brutes from Sunday.

"See you around, lads," he said, chuckling. The three giants waved him off before walking away. Connor noticed me and smiled, before sauntering to me.

"Hey, DK boy. How were ya races today?" He asked, his grin wide. I shrugged.

"They were okay. What's with you? You're never this happy."

Connor laughed before cupping my shoulder. "I just bought the rights to own this place! You, my fellow racing enthusiast, are talking to the new owner of The Tracks."

I beamed. "Holy shit dude, that's awesome! Congratulations!"

He smirked before standing proudly. "Prepare to see some major upgrades around the place here, as well as more surprises, like celebrity appearances, more official races, and stuff like-"

My phone began buzzing, cutting Connor off mid-sentence. I glanced down at my screen - It was Stefan.

"Hey look, I gotta take this. Sorry dude."

Connor smiled. "No worries lad. I have to go and finish some paperwork. Great chatting to you!"

I waved to him as he walked off. Answering the call, I brought the phone to my ear.

"Hey Stefan, I'm at The Tracks, I'll be home soon."

There was silence on the other end. Feeling myself become antsy, I spoke.

"Stefan bud? You there?"

"Please tell me what Bella told Lyra is wrong."

I froze. Oh my fucking God. Did Bella actually fucking tell Lyra?

"Uh..." I spluttered. I heard Stefan scoff.

"Get home, now. We need to fucking talk about this, and I don't want to do it on the phone."

He hung up.

I felt my heart flare up as I ran my fingers through my hair. Dread trickled down my spine like a careful spider sliding down its silk. I gritted my teeth as I shoved my phone in my pocket, hastily revving my engine alive. My stomach tossed and turned, like the swirling, bubbly water inside a shaken drinking bottle.

This... this can't be fucking happening!

CHAPTER 21

D arko's pov

Monday Evening, February 11th, 2014.

I gnawed on the inside of my cheek as I shot through the neighbourhood, the wind tickling my torso as it whipped around me. My knuckles paled against the handlebars as my grip tightened, the white reminiscent of the wild daisies that littered the grassy patches I passed. I'm going thirty kilometres above the speed limit, but I don't care. My mind kept wandering to the phone call I had with Stefan.

"Get home, now. We need to fucking talk about this, and I don't want to do it on the phone."

My life is over. I want to kill Bella.

I can hear the disappointment in Stefan's voice. The betrayal. I'm the one thing he despises the most in this world - a male, homosexual human being.

My stomach knotted as I rounded a corner, my tires barely avoiding the curb.

Stefan wouldn't hesitate to tell Mum and Dad everything. I can see it now - I'm going to arrive home and they'll all be sitting on the porch, their faces etched with disbelief and anger. They're going to berate and curse at me until they think I'm straight again. They will never love me like how they used to.

Hell, I wouldn't be surprised if they kick me out.

I rounded a final corner and reached the beginning of my street. Dread filled every muscle in my body, paralysing me on my bike. It would be another minute or so before I reached my house, but it felt like time was speeding up the more I waited here.

My head is pounding. I sighed, hastily taking off my helmet.

This is it. The final stretch before everything changes.

I tousled my hair, letting all of the sweat drip free from my scalp, before fixing the helmet back on. As slowly as I could possibly go, I drove back to my house. There's no point trying to avoid it.

Stefan stood there, arms folded, on the porch couch outside our house as I pulled into the driveway. I took off my helmet, turning to face him.

He shook his head, before walking inside. His arms never uncrossed. I felt like vomiting.

They're probably all in the loungeroom, ready to give me their best intervention, or their 'being gay is bad! Come to church, before it's too late!' speech.

I shoved my key deep into my pocket, clutching my helmet in my hands. I opened the flyscreen door, welcomed by the familiar scent of roasted beef.

I knitted my brows, confusion permeating my nerves.

Stefan was nowhere to be found; from the front door, you could see the stairwell to the second floor, the kitchen, the dining room and the loungeroom. He wasn't anywhere. Mum was humming a tune to herself as she pulled the aforementioned beef from the oven, while Dad watched TV, completely unfazed.

What the hell is going on?

"Hey dear," Mum said, smiling as she looked up at me, "how was your motorcycling stuff?"

I smiled, a complete facade of how I was really feeling. "It was uh... all right. Where did Stefan walk off to just then?"

Dad gruffed, swishing his beer to the stairwell. "Think he went upstairs."

"Thank you," I said. I began walking when Mum called out.

"Dinner will be ready soon! Let your brother know."

Confusion consumed me as I crept up the staircase. Why aren't they screaming at me? I expected Dad to be at my throat already, with Mum giving me disappointed sighs and moaning about how corrupt I was.

What's going on?!

I looked around at the top of the stairwell. Stefan's door was shut, and no light was peeking through the slit at the bottom. He wasn't there.

I turned towards my room, and the door had been left ajar. Orange light bathed out of the room. I could hear Stefan muttering something to himself.

I swallowed hard. Here goes nothing.

I pushed open the door to see Stefan sitting on my bed, his jaw resting on the palms of his hands. He looked up at me and sighed, before gesturing me to shut the door. I did, before standing awkwardly in front of it.

"So? Care to explain why Lyra got a bitter message from Bella depicting how... gay you seem to be for Taylor?" he spat, hesitating at the word gay. I froze.

"I..." I said, stammering. Maybe denying it will help. "I don't like him in that way-"

He scoffed. "Bullshit. Don't lie to me - Lyra sent me the photo of your love letter to him. I recognised your handwriting and everything."

I felt my cheeks burn up. Stefan shook his head, forcing a sigh out.

"You're fucking disgusting."

I shot up at him. "No, I'm not."

He shook his head. "No, you are! How dare you go around, acting all gay and shit? Why did you choose to be like this? You've literally slept with an uncountable number of girls, and now you decide to like dicks?!"

I felt hot tears surface. "I didn't choose this! I can't help it, Stefan! The stuff with the girls was all fake - I really, really like him, and-"

He shuddered. "Shut up. Keep your gayness to yourself, freak."

I shook my head, the tears falling down my face. As much as I wanted to just shut up and cop the verbal assault, my voice wouldn't let me. "How can you call me that? Stefan, I'm your brother - you've known me for so long, I'm still the same guy! The only difference is that I love the same gender!"

Stefan shook his head. I let a whimper escape my lips as I wiped stray tears from my cheeks. I pulled my study chair out of my desk and threw myself into it, sitting in front of Stefan. He couldn't even look at me.

"Listen," he said, facing to the left of him, "I'm not saying shit to Mum and Dad, purely because I don't want them to feel shame. Imagine if word got out - the people at church would condemn us!"

I sobbed. He glanced at me, scoffing. "I can't believe that you're actually a fag."

We sat in silence for a few moments. Sadness and regret washed over me like an untamed ocean sweeping up a lonely kayak. Fear of rejection was replaced with despair that hugged my heart so tightly I thought it would burst and spill out of my chest.

It was that look that Stefan gave me. The furrowed, frustrated eyebrows that twitched with his every thought. His pursed lips that portrayed his disgust. His narrow eyes, piercing my chest with their judgemental glares.

Stefan hates me.

Mum's sharp voice shot through the house, making me jump. "EVERYONE! DINNER'S READY!"

He exhaled sharply out of his nose before standing up, briskly walking to the door, stopping as he opened it. He went to say something to me, but just as fast as he opened his mouth, it shut. He slammed the door.

I threw myself on my bed, letting my cries become muffled in my mounds of pillows. His words hit me like a runaway jet engine as I let them spiral in my mind. "You're actually a fag". "Freak". "You're fucking disgusting."

I sobbed harder. I know who I am, these things shouldn't be getting under my skin, but maybe...

Maybe he's right.

Mum's voice pierced the walls again. "DARKO! HURRY UP, WE CAN'T SAY GRACE WITHOUT YOU!"

"I'll be there in a minute," I shouted, my shaky voice betraying me. I sat up and wiped my tears away, before taking in a few breaths.

'Just eat and come back,' I thought to myself, 'just eat, and come back to your room.'

I waited till my sobbing stopped, before walking out.

"There you are," Dad said, half smiling. "Hurry up and sit down, we need to say Grace."

I sat down and took Mum's and Dad's hands. "Sorry... just had to do something really quick."

Mum glanced at me, her eyes inspecting my face. "Is... everything okay? You seem upset."

I glanced at Stefan, who was looking daggers back. Feeling a lurch in my chest, I snapped away, before faking a smile.

"Yeah, I'm all good."

Mum lifted a brow, before rubbing her thumb along my cheek. "Dear, your eyes are all red and your face is flushed. Are you sure?"

I nodded, suppressing the urge to snap. "I'm fine. Trust me."

She nodded.

Dad sighed. "Whatever. Close your eyes, everyone."

I did as told.

"Bless us, oh Lord, and these gifts which we are about to receive from your bounty. Through Christ our Lord we pray, Amen."

I repeated 'Amen' as did my brother and mother. I released my hands from my parents and opened my eyes, watching Dad carve away at the roasted beef.

"You did well, honey," he said, earning a smile from her.

"Thank you. Darko, fill up on veggies. I made extra mashed potatoes - one of your favourites."

"Thanks, Mum," I said, looking at the bowl she gestured to. It was in front of Stefan. Seeing him glower at me in his seat, I directed my fork to the vegetables instead. I pretended to eat when Dad spoke.

"So," Dad said, scooping up the slices of beef he cut up. "I hear you have a girlfriend now Stefan?"

I looked up at Stefan. His eyes darted from Dad to me. He smirked slightly.

"Yeah, I have the most beautiful girlfriend," he said, looking at me. "Her name is Lyra."

Dad hummed. "What a beautiful name. May I see a photo of her?"

Stefan giddily whipped out his phone, showing Dad a selfie of him and Lyra. I took this opportunity to grab the bowl of mashed potatoes. I lost my appetite, but if I didn't get some potatoes on my plate, Mum would grow even more suspicious.

"We met at a party a few weeks back. She's so sweet, I can't wait for you two to meet her-"

Dad cleared his throat. Glancing at him, I only just noticed that his eyebrows were tightly knitted.

"She's... black?" Dad said, earning a lifted eyebrow from Stefan. "Yeah? So what?"

Dad laughed. "So what? Are you joking? Women of their kind aren't dateable."

Stefan shook his head in disbelief. He looked at me, but I just sat there, eyebrows raised, a smug smile on my face.

"Dad - she's different. Just wait till you meet her - she's amazing, and sweet, and-"

"You think I want to meet her? Stefan, I forbid you from dating her."

"But-"

Dad slammed his fist down, making everything on the table clatter slightly. "No buts! Break up with her as soon as you can. We need to find you a pretty, white, lady before it's too late. We can't let you live and experience their customs - It would drive you away from God!"

"I can't help who I like!" He shouted. He stared up at me, his face washing over with realisation. Fucking hypocrite. Have a taste of your own fucking medicine.

He stood up and rushed upstairs, his door slamming against the doorframe. Dad shook his head, while Mum began to eat again, although a strong awkwardness hung in the air.

"It's okay," Mum said, smiling at me. "It could be worse - at least Stefan isn't gay."

I felt my grip on my knife and fork tighten at that statement. Mum and Dad continued to eat like nothing had just happened. I shook my head, before getting up.

"May I please be excused? I've lost my appetite."

Dad nodded, "Don't worry, I understand. Seeing Stefan like that has thrown me off too."

He turned to Mum. "I'm sorry, sweetie. Maybe we can have a midnight snack together."

She smiled. I thanked her for the meal, before rushing upstairs. I leaned my ear against Stefan's door and heard his sobbing through the cheap wood.

Now he knows how I fucking feel.

CHAPTER 22

Taylor's pov

Midday Tuesday, February 12th, 2014.

I let out a frustrated groan as I stared at the mounds of sheet music in front of me. After sifting through it for the past two hours with Ana, all I want to do is set the stupid stacks on fire.

I angrily picked up a sheet, my narrow eyes scanning the wrinkled parchment through my glasses. Shaking my head, I screwed it into a ball and ditched it at a wall. Throwing off my glasses, I buried my face in my hands as Ana patted my back.

"Why is this so hard?" I whined. I couldn't see Ana's face, but knowing her she probably rolled her eyes at me or shot me an incredulous glare.

"Look," Ana said, her smile reassuring. "We will find the right songs, don't get so worked up about it."

I shrugged, shaking my head slightly. "We have two days to find the right ones, otherwise I'm going to look like an idiot in front of the entire school. I have the right to get worked up about it."

Sighing, I let my head drop into my palm. "Maybe we shouldn't have taken the day off of school today - none of the things I know are good enough. I could have gotten advice from Miss Lauriana instead of doing this."

I shook my head and angrily shoved one of the sheet piles over, shouting. One of the paper's edge scraped against the wound on my hand, making me wince. I clutched my wrist as Ana frowned. It was Ana's idea to not put a bandage on it - she thought it would be good to 'let it air out'. I wish I didn't listen to her.

"God, you're such a drama queen! Breathe, Taylor - you're over-thinking." She commanded. I rested my face on the palms of my hands and groaned.

"I'm doomed."

I curled into a ball. I heard Ana groan, before hearing bits of paper shift around.

"Hey," she said, tapping my shoulder. "Why don't you play this?"

I looked at the sheet music. 'Kiss Me' - one of my original works.

"This song?" I said, my face scrunching up slightly. "Nah, it's too depressing."

Ignoring me, she sat there, her eyes scanning the lyrics. "Woah... this is really personal. Is this about...?"

I nodded. "Yeah... it's about Darko."

Her eyes widened. "Oh my gosh! Please play it, I want to hear it!"

I sighed, rubbing the back of my neck with my healthy hand. "I dunno... maybe. It's quite a long song..."

Ana grumbled. "Just play until the end of the first chorus. I fully expect you to sing, too."

"I'm sorry," I began to say. "I don't want to dredge up those feelings again. Wrote this when I was in a dark place."

With a huff, Ana snatched the sheet music out of my hands. We sat there awkwardly for a few minutes. Ana was about to say something, but she was cut off by her stomach grumbling. I giggled.

"I'll go make us lunch, then we shall resume the search for songs. I won't force you to play anything again- oh shit! Taylor - you're bleeding!" she shouted, pointing to my hand. I looked down, and sure enough, tiny crimson dots were racing down my palm. The cut must have reopened when Ana ripped the sheet music out of me grasp. I gritted my teeth, my face contorting with pain as Ana darted out of the room, fetching and tossing me a hand towel and some bandages.

"There," she said. "Would you like me to..?"

I shook my head as I dabbed at the cut. "Nah, I can do it. Go make lunch - I've got this."

She nodded, before exiting the room. Out of the corner of my eye, I saw my phone light up. Carefully putting on the bandage, I shuffled out of my seat to where my phone was.

'Hey, Tay-Tay! Why aren't you at school? :(' Bella sent to me. I picked up my phone and began to reply.

'Wagged so I could get ready for the Valentines Dance. Soz.'

Knowing her, she would have laughed at me for wagging. She replied with 'Wow. Mr Nerd is wagging school? How naughty.'

I half cringed, half giggled. Thanks, Bella, for that unnecessary observation.

As I wiped some stray droplets, my phone lit up again. 'So... have you thought about the letter I wrote to you?'

I sighed. 'Look - can I call you? I feel it would be better if you heard me say it instead of over text. Plus, it's annoying to type right now - my wound reopened.'

She replied 'yeah sure'. I quickly dialled her number before squishing the phone between my ear and my shoulder.

"Heeeeey!" she said, her tone flirtatious. I suppressed a groan as I adjusted the bandage.

"Look, Bella..." I said, hesitating. Hopefully, this doesn't bite me in the ass later on. It needs to be said before anything else happens. I've lead her on for long enough.

"I don't feel the same way towards you. I am hugely flattered, but I would rather we stayed as friends. I'm sorry Bella... I just like Darko too much."

There was a pause. The faint chatter of her classmates could be heard.

"Fair enough," she said, her voice uneven. "Who are you thinking of taking to the dance?"

I shook my head. Realising that Bella couldn't see me, I said, "I don't know."

I want to ask Darko so badly. With everything that's happened within the past two weeks, everything is pointing towards him liking me - but, I'm still so worried. What if everything just seemed that way because I wanted it to? I've known him my whole life, if he did feel something then he wouldn't have hidden it for this long.

Then again, I've hidden my sexuality for this long. Hm.

"Why don't we go to the dance together?" Bella said suddenly, snapping me out of my reverie. I sighed. She must have heard me because she began to speak again.

"Wait no, don't sigh - it's just a dance. I promise you that if we go together, I won't make any moves on you, nor would I do anything of the sort. No strings attached. Please?"

"I'm sorry Bella," I said. "I made a deal with myself that if I'm not going with Darko, I'm going alone. I've got nothing against going with you, but I'd much rather it be with him or just myself. Please understand."

There was another pause. I heard the faintest of groans from the end of the phone before a sharp exhale. I think she's pissed.

"Okay then. I've got class now. See you tomorrow."

She hung up.

I slid the phone down my cheek, before letting it fall onto my lap. She may be pissed, but it's my decision. She's just going to have to accept that.

'I wonder what Darko's up to,' I thought to myself. Grabbing my phone again, I unlocked it and opened my message box with Darko.

'Hey Darko, I miss you. The sushi was delicious btw - I accidentally shook the container, but I ate it anyway.' I hit send.

Ana called out to me from the kitchen. "Hey Tay - I'm gonna make some sandwiches - do you want salami or curried egg?"

I looked in the general direction of Ana's voice before shouting back the former option. She yelled 'thanks' as I turned back to the phone. Darko replied.

'You saw me yesterday, how can you miss me already? Also, I'm glad you liked it! :D why aren't you at school btw, my good sir? (Ps. my phone may die on me, I forgot to charge it.)'

I smiled. 'Wagging. Need to figure out what songs to play for the dance. Highkey freaking out about it.'

'Oh wow - you and Owen wagged today. Left me all alone. :('

I lifted a brow. 'What about Lyra?'

'She sat with Stefan. Usually, I would have gone and joined her but... shit's gotten weird with him. Stuff's happened - I got into a fight last night w/ him. Dw about it.'

I was about to reply, curious about the fight, but Darko double texted. 'Wish you were here. You never ditch school - I miss and hate you right now.'

My lips warped into a huge grin. He's so sweet.

I smirked, exhaling sharply out of my nose. 'Oh shush - you know you love me. There's no way on Earth can you hate me!'

'True - you do have a special place in my cold, frozen heart <3'

I sniggered. I felt my chest flutter when I saw the heart emoji.

Darko messaged again. 'Well, anyway, I have good news for you. The morning announcements said that the Valentines dance been postponed until Friday - something about the gym being gassed. Apparently, there are termites eating the walls.'

I grimaced, before sending back: 'Ew. Thanks for the heads up.'

'Shit gotta go, the principal just walked in class. Bye, my good sir. Love yooouuuuuuuu'

I smiled. 'Love you too. Talk later?'

'Can't. Have motorcycle racing tonight. We will soon, though.'

I sent a thumb's up. I leaned back on my bed, clutching my phone onto my chest, smiling contently. I heard a loud cough come from the doorway.

"Lemme guess," Ana said before delicately placing herself next to me, careful not to knock the plates of sandwiches over. "You texted Darko, he said something cute and now you're fangirling?"

I giggled, before letting out a long, happy sigh. "Yeah."

She rolled her eyes, her lips forming into a smirk. "God, you're so whipped. Eat your sandwich, you lovesick child."

Ana handed me my lunch before biting into her curried egg sandwich. "How's your hand?"

"Stings a bit, but I'll manage. Thanks for making me the sand-wich - it's delicious." I mumbled through a mouthful of food. She smiled.

"So, back to song hunting..."

"Uh uh," I said, turning my head towards her, showing her the messages. "Darko said that it's been postponed. We don't need to look as hard now - we have an extra day!"

Ana lifted a brow. "Uhm, no. We are still finding the songs today, whether you want to or not. I know you - you'd procrastinate, then next thing you know it's the day before and you're gonna freak out-."

I sighed, cutting her off. "All right, I get it. Fine."

We began to dig through the paper sheets again, but my mind kept wandering back to the conversation with Darko. God, I love him so much.

CHAPTER 23

D arko's pov

Midday Tuesday, February 12th, 2014.

Have you ever walked past a kid who's just sitting there, smiling like a tool at their phone and wondered why they were?

Well, right now, that's me - sitting right here, by myself, in the cafeteria with the biggest grin on my face. You can blame Taylor for my stupid grin.

I keep re-reading the conversation, but one bit in particular made me fangirl more than a thirteen-year-old teenager at a Justin Bieber Concert.

'Love you too dude.'

Taylor has no idea how happy that single message has made me. Today's been absolutely shit; Bella would not stop giving me bitchy side-eye all of Maths, Lyra's ditched me for Stefan - who I don't want to be around - and Owen's disappeared from the face of the Earth. I felt like crying before but after talking to Taylor for those short few moments, I felt so warm and loved.

I was so lost in my musings that I didn't even notice Bella plonk herself next to me. I was still smiling at my phone when I heard a cough come from her.

Her gaze was murderous.

"Uhm, what the fuck?" She said, whipping her phone out. "What did you do?!"

I furrowed my brows, the happiness from Taylor vanishing. "What the hell are you on about?"

She sighed heavily. "Don't act dumb! You got Taylor to reject me, didn't you? DIDN'T YOU?!"

"Reject you? I didn't! I didn't even know he did until just now!"

She rolled her eyes, before scoffing. Her lips curled into a sardonic grin. "You're full of shit, Darko."

I'm gonna hit her. "I swear on my grandpop's grave that I did not get him to reject you!"

She cocked her eyebrows in a mocking way. "Whatever. Watch your fucking back. If I find out that you had something to do with this, then you can kiss your closet goodbye!"

"Whatever," I said, returning back to my phone. "You aren't going to find anything, because I haven't told him jack shit."

"Then why is he so hung up on asking y-" She said, cutting herself off before she could finish her sentence. I lifted a brow, but before I could ask her to finish it, she picked up her things and stormed off.

Who?

"BELLA," I shouted, "Who does he want to ask out?"

She craned the upper-half of her body around, flipping the bird at me. She shot me a withering glare, before disappearing into the crowd.

Tuesday Evening

"Darko? Why aren't you racing?" Owen said, shouting up at me from the starting point. I shook my head before sighing, leaning against the backboard of the makeshift stadium stairs that lined the race track.

I wanted to race - I just couldn't. Every time I hopped onto my bike and went to the starting line, all I could hear was Stefan's dramatic commentator voice from the referee stand. He was acting so great these past two weeks, and now, it's all just been thrown to the wind.

Owen glanced at the other racers, nodding and mumbling stuff out of my earshot. He quickly parked his bike on the edge of the track before hurrying up to where I was sitting.

"What's wrong, mate?" Owen said, carefully sitting next to me. I shrugged.

"Did Bella do something else? Because if she did, I swear she's gonna get a face full of Knuc and Ckles."

I lifted a brow, a slight smirk teasing at one corner of my lips. "Knuc and Ckles? Who are they?"

He lifted up both fists in the air, wiggling his brows at me. I let out a laugh as he pretended to box an imaginary punching bag. God, I thought I was bad at nicknames. He's worse than both Lyra and I, combined.

"Mr Lefty is Knuc. He's the best at uppercuts. Sir Righty here is Ckles - a dirty fighter, but always a winner."

My smile faded. "Hey, Taylor calls his piano hands Mr Lefty and Sir Righty."

Owen's smile warped into a frown. He lowered his fists and placed a reassuring hand on my shoulder. "Is Taylor the reason why you're sad?"

I scoffed. "Nah. Taylor's actually one of the reasons why today was bearable."

He lifted a brow. "Oh. So, what's the reason then?"

I sighed. Quickly glancing around to make sure nobody was listening, I lowered my voice. "Bella outed me to my brother and Lyra yesterday night. Now they're both ignoring me."

Unsure of what to do or how to react, he just sat there, wide-eyed.

"What the fuck," he said eventually. "What a fucking bitch. Is that what she did the other day? Jesus, what happened?"

His face was plagued with worry. I sighed. "Five minutes or so after you left yesterday evening, I got a call from him, telling me to come home so we could talk. He said that Bella sent Lyra texts and photos of the letter, and Lyra blabbed to Stefan."

I felt tears well in my eyes. "He... he called me such shitty things, man. A failure, a freak, and disgusting to name a few. I really don't want to go home tonight."

Owen wrapped me in a hug. I felt a few tears seep onto his jacket sleeve. He tenderly stroked my back when my sobbing grew louder.

"Hey," he said, pulling away. "Let's get out of here. I know the perfect place to go - It always makes me feel better when I get upset."

I couldn't speak. I could only manage a nod.

"All right," he said, getting up. "Let's go, bro. You wait here, I'll go park your bike in the shed so it doesn't get stolen."

I tossed him my keys and he darted off. Looking around, I was getting a lot of strange looks from the other bikers. Some seemed to want to ask me what was wrong, while others gave me condescending glares. One even straight up pointed and laughed at me.

I was about to shout 'Fuck you!' to them when Owen reappeared, extending his arm out for me to grab. "Come on, it's been locked up. My bike's just down there."

"Where are we going?" I felt my lips say. He turned on his bike's ignition before tossing me a helmet.

"You'll see."

Soon, the salty smell of the ocean was all that filled my nostrils.

I peered around, keeping a tight grip on Owen's waist as I saw the rolling ocean in front of us. Tiny waves rippled and undulated on the sea surface. The sound of the sea crashing against the shore instantly relaxed me.

Owen parked the bike. Stepping off and taking off our helmets, I took a deep breath, letting the crisp brine air fill my lungs. Seagulls could be heard nearby, battling out who would get that greasy chip a girl threw at them. The sunset beckoned me to meet it halfway, but Owen grabbed me before I could nosedive into the water.

"We came here mostly for that, Darko." He said, pointing to a large ice-cream stand. "Unless you're skinny dipping, we can save swimming for another time."

I glanced over to the ice-cream stand Owen pointed out. It was built to mimic the shape of a giant waffle cone - the top exploding with plastic lookalike chocolate mint, vanilla, strawberry and caramel ice cream scoops. Two giant wafers protruded from the plastic blobs, making my mouth water.

"Hey, Darko," Owen said, catching my attention. "I need to make this phone call. Can you buy the stuff? I'll have whatever you're having."

He slipped me a ten dollar note before pulling out his phone. Smiling at me, he walked away, pressing his white fingers onto the number pad on his screen.

I walked over to the stand and was immediately assaulted by seagulls - one shat on my shoulder, another parked itself on my head, and a third tried to pry the money out of my hands. Waving my arms around like a madman, I shooed them. Damn, these birds are brave as hell.

The cashier at the ice cream stand was howling with laughter. He handed me a tissue.

"You have some bird poop on your-"

"Yeah, I know,' I spat, hastily rubbing off the bird shit. "Have you finished laughing at me?"

He shook his head before bursting into tears again. Groaning, I looked at the menu. Hopefully, he hasn't pissed his pants by the time I order. So fucking rude.

"Could I get a banana and caramel scoop on two waffle cones?" I asked. Barely stifling his giggles, he grabbed the money out of my hands and began scooping. I let out another groan as I turned around, looking at what Owen was doing.

Something wasn't right.

He was standing there, shouting at his phone. His face expression told me he was angry, but his eyes were red like he's just cried. Was he sad and angry? He shouted a few more times before hanging up and kicking his bike, earning him a few concerned glares from passersby's. I spun around and grabbed the towering ice creams from the cashier, before hurrying back to Owen.

"Hotman, is everything okay?" I asked, handing him the change and the ice cream. He cringed slightly at the nickname, but then shrugged.

"Let's go find somewhere to sit. I need to tell you something."

I lifted a brow, before scanning the area. "There's that sand dune under the palm trees over there. Nobody's near it, and it's secluded. Is that okay?"

He nodded. I gingerly ate my ice cream as we walked to the spot in silence. He pulled out his phone, reading a text, before hastily shoving it back into his pocket.

"You know, you never told me why you're almost always on that thing," I said, trying to lighten the mood. It did the opposite.

He started crying. He dropped his ice cream, the sand quickly enveloping it. I went in to hug him, but he quickly shoved away.

"Look, just... forget about me for now, okay? I took you out here so you'd feel better."

His phone buzzed again. We both snapped our attention to Owen's pocket, which he had clutched with his hand.

"No dude, forget about me. I've never seen you cry or ever be upset before - please, tell me what's wrong. I wanna help."

He scoffed. "Well, do you have the cure for dementia?"

I lifted a brow. He smiled, letting out a nervous laugh.

"It's my grandma. She has it. I'm always on my phone because I'm the only one that she remembers clearly - she's always asking me where the coffee is, where the tea is, what the name of my parents is. I just got word from her caretakers that she forgot who I was, and where she was. She won't stop messaging me, threatening to call the police and-"

Ding. Another message on his phone. He turned it off and threw it across the sand in front of us.

"She's forgetting me, Darko. The staff at the nursing home have told me that they're going to try and get her to a hospital. She hasn't got much time left. Soon, she won't remember how to swallow... or walk... or t-talk..."

I sat there, my jaw swung open. Owen began to weep again, which I responded by wrapping him up in my arms. He sobbed, harder and harder, thicker, wetter until the sleeve of my shirt was completely soaked.

"I don't want to lose my grandma. She's all I've got."

"What about your parents?" I asked. Owen sat still for a few moments, only moving to wipe the tears from his eyes. He looked out towards the sea.

"Let's just say that they prefer money over actually taking care of their only child."

A thick silence hung over us. The only noises that could be heard were Owen's slowing sobbing and the soft lapping of the sea water hitting the shore. I stared at Owen, who was still gazing out to the ocean. For someone that's always so happy, so strong, I never expected him to have shitty parents and an ill grandmother. I honestly thought he was the luckiest of us all.

I glanced out to the ocean. The sun had just vanished below the horizon, leaving a beautiful violet-orange sky behind. The clouds above us twisted and curled like cotton candy dragons waging a thousand year long battle. I heard a soft giggle come from Owen.

"Dude, I think your ice cream is melting."

Suddenly feeling the cool drips from the dessert, I glanced at my hand. Half of the ice cream has fallen off into the sand; the other half has melted onto me. Groaning, I threw it on the floor and flicked the drops away from me, all while Owen laughed.

Owen fished out a water bottle from his bag. "Wash your hands with this, dude."

Taking it, I opened the lid and dribbled the liquid onto my fingers.

"Thanks." He said quickly. I looked at him, and he had the smallest of smiles on his face. "I don't usually open up to people, but I feel like I can trust you with this. Thank you for listening to me, man."

I smiled. "Of course Owen. It's the least I could do for you - you've done so much for me."

He grinned.

"And Darko," he said while putting his drink bottle away, "if things get too hard at home, my door is always open. I'm the only one that's ever home, so there's plenty of room for you if you want to stay for a couple days."

A wave of comfort washed over me. I grinned so widely, I was worried that my lips would crack.

"Thank you, Owen. I really appreciate you offering that."

Owen smirked. He stood up, extending his arm to me. I clasped it and he hoisted me up. Owen quickly darted ahead and picked up his phone, before we began walking back to his bike.

"Just don't want my best friend anywhere near Stefan."

I smiled. I'm so lucky to have Owen as a friend.

"So," I said, putting on my helmet. "I'm going to guess that's why you weren't at school today?"

Owen side-glanced me, before scoffing. "Nope. I was busy getting that idea ready, the one I mentioned to you yesterday before walking off."

I furrowed my brows slightly, but then relaxed them when I remembered him doing that. "Oh yeah. What was the idea?"

Owen smirked devilishly. Growing somewhat nervous, I furrowed my eyebrows.

"You remember how you said YOU couldn't tell Taylor that you were the one that originally bought him the gift and the love letter?"

My chest sank. "Oh no... you didn't-"

"You bet your ass I told Taylor. I left a note on his doormat. I told him to text me when he's seen it."

"And that took you the whole day because..?"

Owen scoffed. "I didn't know how to write in calligraphy."

CHAPTER 24

Taylor's pov

Midday Wednesday, February 13th, 2014.

"Hey, Taylor. Can I talk to you for a second?" a voice asked me. I glanced up from my piano and saw Owen standing there. He awkwardly held his guitar at his side, while he clutched a small yellow piece of paper in the other.

"Uhm," I felt my lips say, lifting a brow. "Sure?"

"Cool. Come out to the hall with me."

I left my piano, confused, and followed him out into the school's hallway. What's he doing? He never talks to me in music.

He turned to face me. "Look, you were meant to find this note earlier this morning, but you never did. I think I hid it too well."

He handed me the folded sheet of paper. I lifted a brow at him. "What's this?"

"It's something good. Hopefully. I need to show you that b ecause... he can't. Ignore the last half of it, that stuff was only relevant because I thought you'd find it, and the stains. I'm terrible at calligraphy."

I opened the piece of paper.

My eyes widened. They flicked at Owen before they cast back down onto the sheet of paper.

The porcelain piano and the love letter? That... that was all Darko?

Owen coughed. "I couldn't say that out loud, for obvious reasons. Bella may have some of her underlings lurking around the place. You can never be too careful."

I barely nodded at Owen. I was too busy remembering what was written in the note. Bella wasn't confessing her love to me, it was Darko. It all makes sense.

All these weeks, its all been my personal speculation that Darko's crushing over me. But this? this was proof. Physical proof of his feelings.

"He... he definitely feels something for me?" I managed to say through my grin. Owen nodded.

"He sure damn does. And you..?"

I looked up at Owen. "What do you think?"

He considered me for a moment. I felt his eyes scan my blushing face, my happy tears streaking down my cheeks, and the wide grin that's probably permanently there now. He nodded.

"This is surreal. Am I dreaming?" I asked. Much to my relief, he shook his head.

"No, you're not. This is all real."

"Woah."

Owen looked back into the classroom. "I think Miss Lauriana is looking for us. I'll head inside; I'll be by your piano. I think you need a moment out here to calm down. There's a lot we need to talk about. Just, do not message Darko."

Owen flashed me a quick smile, before heading back into the room. I glanced down at the note, re-reading it.

'Darko meant it all.'

I pulled out my phone and went through my camera roll. I remember taking a photo of the letter - god knows why. I'm glad I did.

It makes so much more sense now that I'm reading it from Darko's perspective. Holy crap.

"Dear Mr birthday boy, I'm not going to bore you with the gritty, cheesy nonsense that I've blessed you with every year prior to this one. Actually, this card has a much deeper meaning to it.

Why didn't I notice that sooner? Bella has NEVER made me a cheesy birthday card. All she does is get me a bottle of cologne and aftershave.

I... I've been meaning to tell you something important. It's been eating away at me for a long time now. I... I have no other way of saying it without beating around the bush. Brace yourself, you're probably never going to expect what I'm going to say next. Taylor... I love you.

Even this makes more sense! I'd have expected this from Bella after the party incident happened. It's much more surprising from Darko.

Why am I so stupid!?

I know, we're best friends, we should tell each other everything, blah blah blah - I didn't feel comfortable sharing this with you, mainly because I never knew how you'd react to it. I should have come clean about who I was and about who I am. I figured you'd hate me, or you'd just stop talking to me, or something like that. I just needed to tell you, my feelings were beginning to get in the way of my academic life, as well as my social life. God, I feel like such a coward for telling you through a letter. Hopefully, after I have given this to you, you'll still talk to me. Love, your best friend, Bella.

Now I know why I saw a K there before - it's fucking Darko's name, erased.

I creased my brows. What other shit has Bella done?

"Okay, so put simply, you need to stay as far away from Bella as possible."

I played a few notes as Owen talked to me. "Yeah, no shit. I can't believe she's done that to him!"

I joined Owen back at the piano. He explained to me everything that's been going on - the outing to Stefan, the blackmail, the break-in. Everything makes sense.

Bella's been plotting behind me this entire time. I should have known to keep an eye on her after the party, and to not be so lenient when she apologised on my birthday. She's cunning, ruthless, and manipulative.

No wonder Darko hated her this whole time. Bella needs to leave him the fuck alone.

"She's obsessed with you. She wants to keep you all to herself. If only there was a way to take her down a few pegs, and to get with Darko. She seems to be one step ahead of all of us-"

Miss Lauriana began to shout, cutting Owen off mid-sentence. "For those that are playing on Friday - you better have your songs perfect by tomorrow - otherwise, you aren't performing!"

I furrowed my brows. That gives me an idea.

I got out of my seat and walked towards the bookshelf, prying out my booklet. Flicking through it, I noticed Owen poke his head over my shoulder.

"Dude, what are you doing?"

I caught myself poking my tongue out slightly as I flipped over the plastic covered sheets. "Trying to find a song I wrote- ah, there we go!"

I have all my other performances ready - all except one. I was going to spend this afternoon figuring it out with Miss Lauriana, but with everything that's happened within the past hour, this song needs to be for Darko.

What better way to tell someone you love them on Valentine's day?

Plus, this is the perfect opportunity to have a dig at Bella. It's probably not a good idea to poke the bear... but this is too good of an opportunity. Bella won't suspect a thing.

I fished out the paper and showed Owen. "I have an idea. Tomorrow, I'll perform this. Bella would never suspect me to sing this, and it'll show Darko exactly how I feel."

Owen skimmed over the sheet. "This requires two performers though - a pianist and a guitarist."

I lifted a brow, smirking. "That's where you come in. You think you can learn this by tomorrow night? Afterschool, I'll be here, practising. Maybe you can join me? I just need to re-work some lyrics, but the chords will be the same."

Owen smiled. "Of course I can learn this. This is going to be one hell of a performance, I can already tell."

I smiled. No wonder Darko trusts Owen so much - he's lovely.

"From now until tomorrow evening, pretend nothing's happened. Tell Darko that you've gotten no news of me seeing the note, and I'll pretend to like Bella for the time being. It's the only way this is going to work perfectly."

We walked back to our station. Owen practised a few chords, while I tried to think of new lyrics. After a few attempts, Miss Lauriana came walking over, a small smile on her lips.

"What are you two practising?"

I showed her the sheet music. Her eyes lit up, then narrowed.

"Why is Darko's name written on the top?"

We glanced at each other, unsure of what to say. She lifted a brow, before leaning in closer to us.

"So, you two are performing your love song for Darko, aren't you? Which one of you is asking him out, hm?" She said softly, making sure nobody else but us heard her. Her tone was rhetorical. Owen looked at me straight away. I sighed.

"You took your damn time, Taylor."

I lifted a brow. "What? You knew?"

She scoffed. "You're kidding? That kid's the only one that shows up to hear you play every Thursday afternoon. I've seen the sparks fly when you two are in this class together - especially when you taught him Fur Elise. It was pretty obvious."

I didn't know what to say. Owen looked at me and Lauriana, before getting up.

"I'll go uh... get a drink. Be right back." He said, quickly walking off. Miss Lauriana sat in his seat, her expression curious.

"What are you thinking, Taylor? Come on, say something. I'm getting worried." She said, her tone concerned. I side glanced her, unable to keep eye contact.

"I don't know what I'm thinking, to be honest. I think so highly of you, and I consider you a part of my family - I didn't want to disappoint you or change the way you thought of me-"

She shook her head. I stopped talking at her gesture. She glanced around the room, before leaning in, so only I could hear her.

"Taylor honey, don't you dare believe for one second that I think any less of you. You are an amazing person, and your sexual preference isn't ever going to change how I perceive you. I know I'm not your mother or anybody that's directly related to you, but I'm the best goddamn godmother in the world - I just want you happy."

Without thinking, I leaned in for a hug. She wrapped her arms around me, tenderly patting the top of my head. After a few moments, she lightly pushed me away from her and grabbed both of my shoulders.

"This performance is going to be the best damn thing this school has ever seen. You and Owen are going to do absolutely amazing, I can already feel it. If you ever need to talk or help, you know I am here for you Taylor."

She stood up and smiled at me. "Now, I gotta go back to being a teacher. Keep your chin up, all right?"

She walked off. A short moment later, Owen returned.

"Everything okay?" He asked. I smiled.

"Better than okay."

Owen grinned. "All right, great. Now, back to the matter at hand - we have practically less than a day to learn this. Let's get a move on."

CHAPTER 25

O wen's pov

Wednesday Afternoon, February 13th, 2014.

'Owen, what's your last name again, sweetie?' Grandma texted me. Swallowing back the lump forming in my throat, I texted her back as I walked towards the music room.

'It's the same as yours, gran. It's Prietto.' I texted back. I felt my phone buzz before I could put it back into my pocket.

'That's such a lovely name. When are you coming to see me next?'

I frowned. 'I saw you yesterday. I'll probably come and visit in a few days.'

'You visited me yesterday?'

Stifling back a sigh, I texted her back. 'Yes. Look, I'm busy right now, I'll call you later tonight. Love you <3.'

'That's okay. I can't wait for your call. I miss you, dear. x'

I slipped my phone into my pocket.

I rounded a corner. I was about to open the door of the music room when I heard a scream erupt from the girl's toilets.

'The hell?' I thought to myself. Nobody should be here after school. That's either a teacher or a student that's snuck in. Why are they screaming?

I inched closer to the bathroom. I began to hear muffled cries and the annoyed groan of another female.

"He's not taking me to the dance. What a fucking prick. I told him I loved him - what else do I need? A dick?!"

Instantly, I recognised the voice. It was Bella. The second voice began to speak. It was Nicole. Whipping out my phone, I pressed record, just in case they said something interesting.

"Can you shut the fuck up, or at least, quieten down? Did you forget that he's, like, two classrooms away?"

Bella blew her nose. "Sure. Whatever. Fine."

"What do you even see in him anyway? Taylor isn't that attractive, and he has the social skills of a dying cat. What's he got going that I don't know about?"

Bella scoffed. "He's cute, and one of the sweetest boys in the world. But, most importantly, he's got talent. Have you ever heard him play the piano?"

There was a short silence. Either Nicole shook her head or stared at Bella blankly. Regardless of what she did, Bella continued to speak.

"He's gifted, both instrumentally and vocally. One day, he's going to be fucking famous. Rich beyond anything I'll ever become."

"So what? You want to get in with him so you can mooch off of his success?"

"Not entirely, but yeah. I'm not working a 9-5 hour job - screw that. Plus, I'll be famous by association with him. There's literally no downside."

I cringed. Thank fuck I intervened - I would hate to see Taylor being used by Bella like that. That's horrible.

"What do you see in Darko? There are a million things I could call him, but dateable isn't one of them." Bella said to Nicole. I assume she shrugged.

"I don't see anything, did you forget? He broke my heart by never talking to me; all I wanted him to do was notice me. This is all revenge."

I shook my head. Grudges are pointless and just make you seem like a terrible person.

Bella gasped. "I just came up with the best idea. Why don't you ask him out to the dance tomorrow?"

"Why the hell would I do that?"

Bella sighed. "Uh, for petty reasons? He's going to be super uncomfortable the whole time. Plus, it'll further instil the idea that Darko is straight in Taylor's eyes. It's a win-win situation for the both of us!"

I rolled my eyes. At least Bella doesn't know that Taylor knows how Darko really feels.

"You're a genius!" Nicole said, squealing.

I heard a tap turn on. Nicole began speaking again. "Remind me - why are we waiting here? I really want to go home and make sure my outfit for the dance is perfect."

Bella scoffed. "We're hiding here to wait for the right opportunity for me to go and try and persuade Taylor to take me to the dance. You're here to keep an eye out for me-"

Suddenly, my phone began to beep loudly. The ringtone seemed to pierce through the silent hallway - and the female girl's toilets. I heard one of them gasp.

"Fuck, fuck, fuck!" I mumbled, fumbling through my pockets. I heard the girls scramble.

"Shit, someone might have heard us!" Bella spat. Panicking, I stopped recording, silenced my phone, and quickly scrambled away, ducking into the closest classroom. Bella has seen me hang out with Darko before. If she catches me, she's going to link my eavesdropping to Darko somehow, and she's probably going to do something stupid. Hiding underneath the teacher's desk, I pulled out my phone and checked who called.

'One Misscall from Grandma.'

Ah great.

'Sorry I couldn't pick up,' I texted. 'What did you need?'

Loud clicking streaked past the classroom I was hiding in. "Damn it, what if that was Taylor that heard us?" I heard Bella say.

"It couldn't have been. We can hear him playing the piano still. Someone else must have heard us."

Bella groaned. "I swear to fucking God if it was Darko, I'm gonna-"

My phone vibrated loudly. Nearly shitting my pants, I turned it off before precariously covering myself in textbooks.

"Did you hear that?" Nicole said. Through the tiny gap I left for breathing, I saw Nicole poke her head into the classroom. I sat as still as a statue, muffling my breath with my shirt.

"Hear what? You're going crazy. Come on, let's just go back to the bathroom. I'm sure it was just a cleaner walking by, or something."

Sighing in relief, I turned my phone back on as the sound of their footsteps faded away. Peering down, I shook my head, burying it in my free hand.

"What was your last name again, Owen sweetie? xx'

Taylor's pov

I plonked my head onto the keys of my piano. Repeatedly. Sharp twangs of sounds exploded from the instrument. Why is it so hard to learn this damn song?!

I sighed, running my fingers through my hair in frustration. Mere moments later, Owen opened the door to the room, letting himself in.

"Sorry I was late, had to call someone. Warning, Bella may show up soon. Just caught her sneaking into the bathroom."

I grunted in response. He grabbed his guitar from a rack, and a chair, and sat next to me.

"Okay, let's take it from the top. You start, and I'll join in."

"Sure, whatever."

I flicked back to the first page of the sheet music and began to play. For about ten seconds, everything was going smoothly. I closed my eyes.

I imagined myself playing this on stage with Owen by my side. I scanned the crowd. Everyone was booing us. Darko locked eyes with me, a frown forming on his face. He shook his head before turning away.

I snapped back to reality. I was playing the wrong notes. Angrily, I shoved the music sheets off of my piano, scattering them on the floor beside me. I ran my palm down the side of my face before grunting.

"Woah dude, why so angry?"

I let out a long sigh, before shaking my head. "It's... it's nothing. Ugh."

"Are you sure? Are you maybe... worried about fucking up on stage?"

I shrugged. Owen shook his head.

"Mate, nothing in this world is perfect. If you're worried about getting it wrong on stage, forget about it. You're really good at playing the piano, and -"

"You know how much pressure that puts on me?"

Owen lifted a brow. "What?"

I folded my arms, glowering in my seat. "I always get shouted with praise by everybody when it comes to piano playing. 'Oh, wow, you're so great!' 'You're so talented!'! You know how much pressure that puts on me to not fuck up? One mistake and I'm reduced to nothing. Not to mention, that this performance is going to change everything between Darko and me. If I screw it up, it's not gonna be as special. It's gonna ruin everything!'

I placed my elbows on the keys, resting my face on the palms of my hands. "Ugh. You're right. I don't want to screw things up."

"You need to let go of your worries, or you are gonna mess up," Owen said. He played a chord on the guitar, making me sit up. "Stop with the self-pitying, Taylor. This isn't like you. "

'This isn't like you,' I thought to myself. He's only talked to me for less than a day, how could he know what I'm really like?

"And before you start with the 'How isn't this like me? You don't even know me,' garbage, you're right. I don't know you. But, I do know how you are on stage. You are amazing, Taylor. You could make up a #1 charting song on the spot if you tried. Your insecurities are the only thing that's stopping you."

"Well then," I began to ask, side glancing him. "How do I stop worrying?"

"Simple. Channel your emotions for Darko into the piece. Don't focus on the future, don't think about the crowd - just pretend you're alone in your bedroom or this class, just practising. If you do that, you'll do amazing."

"All right, fine. I'll try it."

Owen grabbed the sheet music from the floor and put it in front of me. "Just, breathe," he said.

My hands quivered over the instrument. I inhaled slowly, then exhaled sharply. "I can do this," I mumbled to myself.

I began playing again. Unlike before, my fingers seemed to dance on the keys, hitting each one with perfect precision. I closed my eyes, foregoing the sheets, playing by ear. I caught myself smiling when a comfortable warmth flooded my veins. I let out a long breath of air, one I didn't realise I was holding, as I heard Owen join in. His guitar chords synced perfectly with my playing, even though I wasn't following the sheet music anymore.

My feet alternated between the pedals at the bottom of the piano as the song picked up in pace. Owen's strumming added a new layer of bliss to my ears - soon, I forgot that I was at school. All that I cared about was the piano and Owen.

We played the final notes. Hearing a small applause start suddenly at the door, I opened my eyes.

"Colour me impressed, boys," Miss Lauriana said, smiling.

Owen turned to me, a wide grin on his face. "Told you you'd do fine."

I grinned. "That was the best thing I've ever played. We are going to smash this performance!"

Miss Lauriana shut the door before walking towards us. "I'm sure you two didn't notice, but while you were playing Bella and that Nicole girl were waiting by the door. They ran off when they saw me. You have any clue why they're here?"

Owen and I shrugged. "Dunno. Maybe she wanted to talk to me?"

She shrugged. "Oh well, they're both gone now. Keep practising."

"If they come back," Owen began, "please don't let them, no matter what they say. We don't like them."

"Sure thing." Miss Lauriana said, smiling warmly. She walked over to the other instruments, making sure they were tuned and working correctly for the performances tomorrow.

"All right," I announced, earning Owen's attention. "Let's play again - I'll try to work on the vocals this time."

CHAPTER 26

D arko's pov

Midday Thursday, February 14th, 2014.

I angrily shoved a tater tot in my mouth as I watched a random girl ask a guy out. She pulled him aside, out of the nauseating love nest that the cafeteria has become, and popped the question. Overjoyed, the boy swallowed up the girl in his arms and they walked off, hand-in-hand.

Lucky straight fuckers.

I glanced over at Bella's table. She had her arm draped over Taylor, who was smiling at something Nicole told him. I rolled my eyes before groaning dramatically as Owen joined me.

"Hey bud," Owen said, plopping down next to me, indulging in a heart-shaped cookie. "How are you holding up?"

I glanced at Bella and Taylor again. She fed him a part of a cookie. "I highkey want to die. Does that count as holding up?"

Owen patted my back as I dropped my head on the cafeteria table. "I'm sorry he didn't see the note, dude. Maybe I should have given it to him in person. I feel terrible."

I turned my head to face him, half frowning. "Don't say sorry. In a way, it's good that he's over there and not here. Don't think I'd be able to contain myself near him."

Owen giggled. It's true - if he were to talk to me, I'd probably try something stupid, like kissing him. I'm so sick of Bella. I just want Taylor.

"Uh, heads up dude..." Owen mumbled. I lifted my head slightly.

Nicole was walking over to us.

Stifling a groan, I sat up, locking eyes with her. She slid into the seat in front of us, a smile on her dolled-up face.

"Hey, Darko. Owen." She said, nodding to both of us. Owen smiled in response.

"What do you need?" I asked, my tone catching her off guard. She sighed quickly before running her fingers through her blonde hair.

"Do you... do you want to go to the dance with me tomorrow?" She asked calmly, a small smile forming on her pink-washed lips.

After breaking into my car and assisting Bella with her blackmail against me, she think's I'd say yes?! Is she denser than a stack of concrete slabs?

I was about to shout 'No!' at her, but Bella was staring straight at me. I made eye-contact with her, and she shot me a withering glare, piercing my bravado. She mouthed 'do it' before mimicking a phone with her hand. She returned her attention back to Taylor after nearly catching on to what she was doing. I groaned, running my fingers through my hair, before nodding.

"Yeah, sure. Whatever."

Nicole beamed. "Sweet! I'll be with Lyra tomorrow. Meet me there with Stefan?"

'Ah yes, my three favourite people,' I thought to myself. Realising that I needed to respond to her, I nodded. She flashed a quick smile before getting up and walking back to her table. I dropped my head on the desk, groaning loudly as Owen rubbed my back.

"Hey, at least she's gone. Can't get any worse than-" Owen said, stopping abruptly. He leaned in closer and whispered, "I take that back. Brace yourself, Stefan's coming."

My eyes widened. Stefan sat where Nicole did, unable to make eye contact with me. He faced Owen, half smiling.

"Hey, Owen. Could I talk to Darko, privately, please?" He asked. Owen looked at me, then Stefan, then lifted a brow.

"He's having a shit day. Are you going to make it worse?"

Stefan's eyebrows furrowed. "No. Hopefully not."

Owen reluctantly nodded, before getting up, pulling out his phone. "Fine. I needed to call someone anyway. Text me if you need me, Darko."

He walked off. Stefan looked up at me, his expression perplexed, and somewhat nervous. He glanced around the cafeteria, before standing up.

"Let's talk somewhere less noisy. Follow me."

By the time we reached the oval bleachers, my heart was in my throat. What the hell has Stefan got to say? Can he just spit it out already?

He sat down, looking out towards the oval. Feeling my hands begin to get clammy, I wiped them on my jeans as I sat next to him. I cleared my throat.

"What do you need to talk to me about?"

Stefan lowered his head, letting out a long sigh. He turned it, making eye contact with me for the first time in days. He shook his head.

"I'm sorry."

I lifted a brow, my expression unimpressed. "Sorry about what?"

He scoffed. "You know what about. Me being a dick regarding your... preference. I'm sorry."

I rolled my eyes. "What has made you come to this grand conclusion? I assumed that you made your mind up and that we weren't going to speak to each other, ever again."

"Part of it was me, and dad's, but most of it was Lyra."

I groaned. Of course.

"What did Lyra do?"

"She didn't know that I was ignoring you. Believe it or not, I didn't tell her how I felt about the situation. All she did was text me what Bella told her. She wanted to come and talk to you about it - she was really excited to talk about boys with you. But..." he paused, sighing. "Lyra noticed that you and I stopped talking. She assumed that I was just being a good bro, giving you some space before talking to you about it..."

"Lemme take a wild guess," I said, cutting him off, "she found out that you're a homophobic asshole and told you to fix things with me?"

He shook his head, earning him a confused eyebrow lift from me. "Not exactly."

"Elaborate?"

He sighed. "Half of what you said is true. Lyra did find out about what I said to you, thanks to your friend Owen. She ended up confronting me about it. Basically, she called me out on all of my shit and told me to be a better brother. She even threatened to dump me if I continued to be like this."

He shook his head, before resting his face in his palms. After a few moments, he let out a groan before sitting up and looking at me. "She got me thinking really hard about this, Darko. All my life, I've believed that being gay means you're a shitty excuse for a person. I'm so conflicted because I know you're not that. You're my brother, you're amazing, and my closest friend."

There was a small silence after he said that. I felt myself begin to tear up, but I fought them back as Stefan began to speak again.

"Look, that was... messy. All I wanted to say was sorry to you, Darko. I know now that I treated you like shit. If I could take back everything I called you that night, I would in a heartbeat. I'm trying my hardest to learn and be more understanding, for your sake. I just need more time."

Without even thinking, I fiercely wrapped Stefan in my arms. Shocked, he tensed up as I embraced him, but eventually returned it. I felt happy tears streak down my face.

That's all I wanted to hear from him.

He patted my back, before laughing awkwardly. "All right, pull yourself together, dude. The footballers are giving us weird looks."

I got up and stuck the finger up at the footballers, who just shrugged and continued to play. Stefan laughed at my gesture.

"Anyway..." Stefan said, leaning back to rest his arms on the seats behind him. "I need some advice."

I lifted a brow. "What do you need?"

He forced out a short laugh. "The dance is tomorrow. Dad's going to be at my throat if I don't break up with Lyra by the time it's finished. I'm so fucked."

"Just disobey him?"

He shook his head. "You saw how powerless I was at dinner the other night. I don't think I can resist his influences forever-"

Suddenly, the lunch bell rang, cutting off Stefan mid-sentence.

"Ugh," He said with an exasperated sigh. "Look, I'm going suit shopping this afternoon for the dance. You wanna join me? We need to talk more and I don't think home is the safest place. Plus, if what Owen said was true, then I guess this'll be the fix to your shitty day."

I smiled. "Sure thing."

Thursday Evening

"So, explain me this," Stefan said, pretending to search through a rack of suit jackets, "how does being gay work?"

I lifted a brow. "What do you mean?"

He let out a short laugh. "I don't know; are the stereotypes true?"

Furrowing my brows, my expression warped into further confusion. "Stereotypes? Which ones are you referring to?"

He picked up a jacket and held it against his body. "There's the first stereotype - are all gays great with fashion?"

I shook my head, smiling slightly. "Oh my god, no! Well, kind of. Not all gay guys are good at fashion, but some are. I'm no spokesperson for all of us, but in my opinion, gay guys are generally more willing to try new styles of clothing - all straight guys do is wear the same crap."

"The same crap? Like what?" Stefan asked, putting the jacket back down on the rack. I eyed down his outfit - a t-shirt with a skating graphic on it, cargo shorts, flip-flops and a cap.

"Look in a mirror."

Stefan scoffed. "What do you mean? I like the clothes I'm wearing."

I folded my arms, my lips turning into a smirk. "Fine, go outside the store and look around the shopping centre - I bet you you'll find at least ten other guys with the same style as you."

Stefan rolled his eyes, smirking too. "Whatever, jackass, I doubt that other people-"

He was suddenly cut off by a random guy colliding with him after turning the corner. Recovering, the boy apologised before running away. Stefan eyed his outfit and surely enough, it was the same thing he was wearing.

"My god, you're right."

I picked up a jet-grey suit set. "See? My point was made and you didn't even leave the store! Straight guys tend to just follow the trend of what other guys wear, or they just throw on whatever is nearby. In my opinion, the stereotype shouldn't be that gay guys are good with clothes, it should be that straight guys don't give a fuck."

He smiled. "Hey, kind of random, but this gives me an idea. You wanna play a game?"

I lifted a brow. "Uhm... sure? What's the game?"

"It's a really simple game. 20 questions. The catch is that I'm the only one that's going to be asking the questions."

I scoffed. "So, an interrogation?"

Stefan laughed, earning a glance from passing shoppers. "No! Well, yes, technically, but It's going to be fun. It'll help me understand you better."

I grabbed a black suit set from a rack and faced him. "Sure, whatever. What's your first question?"

Stefan smiled. "How many guys have you liked since you realised you were gay?"

Furrowing my brows, I thought about it. "Well, I've found several guys attractive, but I've only liked one guy."

Stefan hummed. "Interesting. Okay, question two..."

I rolled my eyes. This is going to be a long shopping trip.

One suit shop, 17 invasive questions and a drink later, we got back into Stefan's car and drove out of the parking lot.

"Okay, final three questions," Stefan said, stroking his chin thoughtfully.

"Haha yeah," I said, my tone amused. Although the previous questions were personal as fuck, this game is entertaining. "Ask wisely."

He turned a corner. I started sipping a drink I bought as he asked the question.

"So, does anal hurt?"

Taken aback by the question, I began choking on my drink. I heard Stefan laugh like a maniac as I dry heaved onto my lap, forcing him to pull over. He was still laughing by the time I recovered.

"Stefan, what the fuck? You can't just ask that so casually! Warn me next time, holy shit!"

Stefan continued to giggle. "Jesus Christ, that was hilarious. Please do not answer that question, I only asked it because I wanted to see your reaction."

'Like I was going to answer it anyway,' I thought to myself. He began driving.

"Two more questions, then I am NEVER playing this game with you ever again," I said, earning a smirk from him.

"Okay, I've got a question," Stefan declared. "When did you know for sure you liked Taylor?"

All of a sudden, I found my chest warm up at the thought of that day. Smiling warmly, I looked out the window, my face periodically bathing in a golden orange light as Stefan passed the streetlamps. "That day was amazing. I'll never forget it."

"Care to explain?"

I turned to face him, a grin refusing to leave my lips. "You remember my 13th birthday?"

Stefan narrowed his eyes, seemingly lost in thought. After a few moments, he shook his head. "Nope."

I lied back and closed my eyes. "Well, I think it was after the birthday party that the 'rents put together - Taylor wanted to sleep over. We were watching a movie in my bedroom when he shot up, remembering that he had a second gift to give me. He darted out of the room, fetched it from his bag downstairs, and ran up to me, shoving it in my lap."

"So you realised you liked him after he got you a gift? That's borderline gold digger behaviour, dude." Stefan said, teasing. I punched him lightly in the arm.

"Let me finish!"

"Okay okay, fine! Keep going."

"He handed it to me and I peeled the paper off. It was a box with an envelope in it, wax sealed, with handwriting on the front of it, saying 'Open me'. I opened it, and it turns out, it was a glitter bomb, and rainbow glitter exploded all over me and my bed. Taylor was bouncing up and down on the bed, clapping like a seal, absolutely howling with laughter at the sight of me fuming, covered in glitter. That's when I started noticing it. His smile was perfect. His laugh made me feel so warm and happy. That's when I started liking him."

We pulled into the driveway. Stefan turned off the engine, before turning to me. "Okay, final question."

I half smiled. "Shoot."

"Do you love Taylor?"

I slightly furrowed my brows. "Huh?"

Stefan rolled his eyes, before grinning. "Just answer the question. Do you love Taylor?"

I looked away, toward our porch. Catching myself smile, I knew the answer to his question.

"Yes. Absolutely. One hundred percent."

Stefan nodded, before smiling contently. "You love him..."

I lifted a brow. "Did I answer wrong?"

Stefan shook his head almost immediately. "No! This just gives me another reason to get over myself and forego my upbringing."

He softly grabbed my shoulders, locking eyes with me. "Darko, you know I'm a sucker for cute romances. I'm a strong, passionate believer in true love. You know that. Do you know how bad I'd feel if I got in the way of you and him? I'd feel fucking terrible!"

Stefan loosened his grip, sighing. "I've kind of said this earlier, but imma say it again. The point I'm trying to make is that if you believe you love him, then I have no right to get in the way or force my beliefs on you. You are your own man and you do not need your naggy older brother condemning you to hell for having a different perspective to me. I fully support you now, bro. Fuck our parents. Love has no gender. If you like dicks, then I'll just have to accept it. You are my little bro, and I'll always love you, unconditionally."

He wrapped me in a tight hug. Who knew that Stefan could make me cry twice on the same day?

"I fucking love you, Stefan. That's all I've ever wanted to hear from you." I mumbled into his shoulder. He gripped me tighter.

"I love you too."

He released me, nodding once, before flashing a reassuring smile. He popped the trunk open.

"Okay, let's go inside. Today's been exhausting."

CHAPTER 27

D arko's pov

Friday Evening, February 15th, 2014.

After looking at myself in the mirror for way longer than I should have, a soft knock on my bedroom door earned my attention. Fixing my tie for the millionth time, I shouted "come in!" before turning around.

Stefan walked in, silver and black suit on, grinning widely. He did a twirl before posing awkwardly in front of me.

"On a scale of one to ten, how great do I look?"

I smirked. "If I say ten, will you say the same for me?"

"Of course. Are you ready?"

I turned to face the mirror again. While physically I'm ready, I'm definitely not mentally prepared for the evening. I don't know how I'm going to handle seeing Taylor perform tonight. On one hand, it's going to be magical seeing him do what he loves, but on the other, I'm going to be miserable the entire night knowing I'm not going to be able to stand near him without Bella or Nicole threatening me.

Can't she find some other dude? Or, since she and Nicole are so close, date her instead? They're already a match made in hell, so why not take it up another notch?

"Dude," Stefan said as he walked closer, checking his watch. "Snap out of it, we've gotta go soon. Meet me downstairs when you're ready."

"Wait," I said, making him pause at the door. "How are you feeling? Are you ready for tonight?"

Understanding my implication, he turned around and softly shut the door. "No. I'm not ready to break up with Lyra. I don't think I ever will be."

I frowned. "You gotta make a choice then, bro. Rebel, or comply."

He nodded, pausing for a moment. He left the room shortly after, shutting the door lightly. I took one last look at me in my suit, before walking out.

"Both of your suits look lovely on you two," Mum said as we stood in front of the front door. She brushed off a few specs of stray lint that gathered on Stefan's shoulder. Dad smiled proudly at my suit, while barely cracking a smile at Stefan's.

"Not the... traditional suit like we planned, Stefan," Dad said disapprovingly. "You should have worn the same thing as Darko - he looks very dapper."

"Maybe I wanted to try something different," Stefan declared. "Not everything has to be traditional."

Dad's eyes widened. "I hope you're only talking about your attire here, young man."

Stefan sighed. Knowing that he'd be forced to stay home if he bickered any more, he relented. "I am. I'm sorry if I implied anything else."

Dad smiled. "Then you know what to do before the night ends. Make the right choice."

After an awkward pause, Stefan and I said our goodbyes and climbed into his car. He turned on the ignition and reversed out of the driveway when I began speaking again.

"So, what are you going to do?"

He scoffed, before turning to me. "Have you ever heard the phrase, 'love has no barriers'?"

I nodded. He turned to face the road, a grin on his face.

"I love Lyra. There's no way I'm letting Dad get between us. I'm rebelling. Besides, what's he going to do if he catches me? I'm an adult - I can make my own choices."

Smiling warmly, I clapped his shoulder. "Well, you made the right choice, bro."

He shook his head, still smiling widely. "I swear you're a bad influence on me. I'm glad."

We shared a laugh before popping on the radio. Apart from our very manly duets to Selena Gomez songs and whatever else came on, the car ride was silent. He turned it off when we arrived at Lyra's house.

"Let's go get our girls."

I sneered. "I don't want mine, can you take her from me?"

Stefan laughed. "I'm good, bro."

He knocked on the door. A few moments later, Lyra stepped out, a beautiful black sequin dress clinging to her petite frame. It glistened as her porch light shone on it. She beamed before wrapping her arms around Stefan, of whom picked her up and spun her around.

"Oh my god Stefan! You look so hot!" She said between squeals. He laughed before setting her down, kissing her tenderly.

"Only for you, babe," he said, flashing a smile. Their embrace was interrupted when Nicole stepped out of the house, shyly smiling at us.

If she didn't break into my car and get on my bad side permanently, I wouldn't have minded taking her to the dance. Unfortunately, she did, so the only thing I was thinking as she made eye contact with me was to pick her up and throw her in Lyra's dumpster.

"Hey everyone!" she said before doing a small twirl, "and hey, Darko."

She walked over to me and scanned me, her eyes trailing over my suit. Breaking a sweat, I couldn't help but feel uncomfortable as Nicole scarily inspected every corner of me.

"Uh," Lyra began to speak after noticing me begin to panic, "where's that bag I lent you?"

Nicole tore her attention away from me, before her eyes widened in realisation. "Oh! I left it inside. Be right back."

She zoomed back into Lyra's house. Seizing the opportunity, Lyra looked between Stefan and I.

"I'm assuming you two have talked?" She said, her tone serious. We nodded. Her expression changed instantaneously - her whole being becoming animated. She ran straight to me and wrapped me in a tight hug.

"We need to talk, Darko," she said. She pulled back and locked eyes with me.

"Not now, obviously. Owen's informed me of Nicole's involvement, and there's no doubt that she'd out you out of spite if we talked about Taylor in front of her. God, I miss you so much, it's like we haven't talked since my party a few weeks ago."

I smiled. "Yeah, thank you. A lot's happened since then. We'll catch up soon. I missed you too."

We hugged again. Stefan let out a dramatic cough.

"Um, she's my girlfriend, Darko."

We all shared a laugh. A few moments later, Nicole reappeared, her borrowed bag in tow.

"Okay, I'm ready. Let's go."

Before we could get into the car, however, Lyra's mother stepped out of the house, a camera in her hands. "Wait! I want photos of Stefan and Lyra!"

We laughed. Stefan and Lyra posed for photos, while Nicole and I stood awkwardly, waiting for them. After a few painful moments, she leaned in and began to whisper.

"Just a warning. If you do anything tonight regarding Taylor, Bella will not hesitate to call your parents and let them know. Watch yourself."

I turned to face her, my face warping with anger at her threat. All she did was smile innocently, before letting herself into Stefan's car. Glowering, I gritted my teeth as Lyra's mum finished taking photos.

"I'll get these printed tomorrow morning," she said, her smile wide. "You two are so adorable - I hope things go well tonight."

They turned to each other. "I hope so too," Stefan said, grinning from ear to ear.

They said their goodbyes before climbing into the car. I drove while Nicole sat in the front seat. Stefan and Lyra sat in the back, alternating between whispering sweet nothings between themselves, kissing and giggling. I smiled contently, listening to my brother and friend being so happy.

Nicole kept trying to talk to me. As much as I didn't want to get on her bad side, I couldn't help being rude. Apparently, giving her one worded answers and grunts in response to her words wasn't enough, because she wouldn't shut the fuck up.

Finally, we arrived at the school. We made our way to the gymnasium, where the dance was being held. Stefan and Lyra linked arms as they walked through the doors. I stiffly walked next to Nicole as we entered.

The place was set up beautifully.

We arrived ten minutes late, so the event had already begun. A few musicians from Taylor's class were performing some love songs on a makeshift stage. In front of the stage was a large dance-floor, complete with spotlights and a Disco-ball. Around the dance-floor and spread to the back of the gym were tables draped with white cloths, kept down by heart-shaped paper-weights and vases full of roses. A large buffet had been set up on the edge of the room, near the exit.

This is all amazing, given the small budget the school allowed for this event. The school council had outdone themselves.

Nicole branched off from our group, much to my relief. Her excuse was to go to the bathroom, but she's full of shit (no pun intended). She most likely broke off to go update Bella.

Stefan and Lyra walked to their table, the former plucking a rose from the vase, offering the flower. She took it from him, gingerly smelling it, before grinning and pulling him in for a kiss.

God, they're so cute together. I'm so happy that they're happy.

I was about to go join them when I saw Taylor. Standing near the stage, he stood confidently, his hair neatly combed back, contact lenses in (I assumed so, he wasn't wearing his glasses) and his face was freshly shaved. I can't describe how amazing he looked in his suit. It fitted his frame so perfectly, amplifying his thin but fit build.

My favourite good sir.

Scanning around quickly, I couldn't find Bella or Nicole any-where. Making the most of the opportunity, I began walking towards him.

Miss Lauriana beat me to him, though. Before I could come within speaking distance, she ushered him to the musician's table, where the other kids in his class sat if they were performing. Dejected, I began walking toward where Lyra and Stefan were, when a familiar voice called me.

"Hey, Darko! Wait up!"

I spun around, smiling at Owen. He was running toward me, earning him some puzzled looks from other classmates. I admired his white suit as he caught his breath.

"I need to give you this," Owen said, panting. He reached into his pocket before fishing out a condom.

Wait, what?

"Uhm," I began, furrowing my brows. "Hotman, why the hell would I need this?"

Finally catching his breath, he sat up, composed and relaxed. He smirked at me before slipping it into my jacket pocket.

"Just in case things go well tonight." He said, winking.

Before I could protest, he scuttled off, joining Taylor at the Musician's table. Still confused, I frowned when I saw Bella sit next to him - he smiled when he noticed her. Her red dress stood out among the sea of black and white suits.

She really is the devil.

I sat down next to Stefan. Adjusting the cutlery at my seat, I grabbed the set-list for tonight.

Of course Taylor is performing last. I was secretly planning on sticking around just to hear him then leave, but now that's out of the question. I have to endure a long, painful night of romance.

Yay me.

CHAPTER 28

T aylor's pov

Friday Evening, February 15th, 2014.

Tonight's been a blur.

Apart from enduring Bella's endless showering of compliments and Miss Lauriana's panicked barking about who's performing when, I don't remember a thing. Hell, I haven't even seen Darko yet - or, maybe I have and I don't remember. Ergh.

I'm standing backstage, peeking through the garnet curtains separating me from the rest of the school. The performance that's currently being presented was a beautiful jazz song led by a girl in my class. She played the final notes from her saxophone before stopping, earning a round of applause from the audience as she bowed. I closed the curtain and sighed deeply, knowing that I'll be up there soon, confessing everything about myself to everybody, especially Darko.

Fucking hell, this is daunting.

Outing myself to the school isn't what's terrifying me - I'm proud of who I am. If anybody has a problem with me, then they'd have to get through Owen first (he showed off his fists to me yesterday - I'm assuming that Darko nicknamed them, because the nicknames were both terrible and amusing). What's terrifying to me is that even though I have proof of Darko's feelings, I still feel a slight fear of rejection. I guess that's going to be there no matter what. I'm not letting that stop me, though. It's too late to stop.

I suddenly felt a hand on my shoulder, which simultaneously snapped me out of my thoughts and made me flinch. Turning around, I realized it was Owen, who was noticeably out of breath.

"I'm... here... sorry..." he said between huffs. I furrowed my brows and grinned in amusement.

"Why're you so exhausted?"

He sat on a chair, attempting to catch his breath. "Had to give Darko something, and had to make sure Bella kept her mouth shut. The damn girl knows how to disappear. Took me ages to find her. Had to run because our performance is so close."

"Dare I ask what you gave to Darko and how you got Bella to stay silent?" I asked, a little worried about the answers. Owen, finally composing himself, smiled at me.

"If things go well tonight, you'll see what I gave to Darko. And, as for Bella..." he said, pulling out his phone. He opened the voice recorder app and showed me a recording.

"Before I met up with you yesterday to practice our song, I heard a scream come from the girl's toilets. Turns out Bella and Nicole were in there, conspiring and plotting. At one point, Bella said why she loves you so much - she wants to mooch off of you when you become famous. I recorded it and told her I'd show it to you if she tried anything. There's no doubt shes going to try and ruin Darko after your performance. The recording shut her up immediately and will continue to shut her up, so long as my phone isn't broken."

I turned around, peeking through the curtain again. I could see Bella from here - she seemed nervous, judging from they way she fidgeted in her seat and was frantically looking around for something (probably me). I smiled smugly to myself, knowing that she finally got blackmailed. Karma is a bitch.

"Why doesn't she want me to know?" I asked rhetorically. Owen, ignoring my tone, answered me.

"Who knows dude. Maybe she knows how scummy she is and doesn't want you to see that side of her anymore. Or, maybe she's actually in love with you. Or, maybe, she doesn't want to jeopardize her chance of getting rich. It could go either way."

I closed the curtain and turned towards him. "Owen?"

"Yeah?"

I flashed him a warm smile. "Thanks... for everything."

He smiled. "Don't thank me yet. You and Darko aren't together - thank me then."

He checked his watch. "Look, before we perform, I've gotta call my grandma. I'll be back in a few, okay?"

I nodded. He flashed a smile before walking off, pressing his fingers onto the screen before bringing it to his ear. I turned back around and watched as some staff prepared my piano on stage. I grinned when I began remembering the time I taught Darko how to play Fur Elise.

Wow. Now that explains why he left so suddenly - I knew his excuse sounded like a load of bullshit. I probably nearly broke him with my teaching method. Thank god he left though; I have no idea how he didn't notice my boner when I sat down next to him. I also have no idea what made me think to lean over him and teach him in that way, but I'm so glad I did.

"Your suit looks amazing, my good sir." A voice said behind me.

'Darko?' a confused voice said in my head.

I whipped around to see Darko standing behind me, much to my surprise. My eyes widened, but softened when he flashed his perfect smile. I smiled brightly, exposing my teeth.

"Oh my god! Darko!" I shouted, my voice betraying my excitement to see him. Without even thinking, I wrapped him in a hug. He was surprised at my gesture but eventually returned it.

"I was just thinking of the time I taught you Fur Elise," I mumbled into his suit jacket. He laughed nervously, releasing me from his warm embrace. Damn, he smelled really nice - a strange mix of sandalwood and musk.

"That was a good day. You're a great teacher." He said. I giggled, punching him lightly.

"Look," he said, before looking around backstage, as if searching for someone. "I can't be back here for long, I think Miss Lauriana would throw a drum-kit at me if she finds me. I just wanted to say good luck before you started your performance. I know you'll do great."

I grinned, beginning to blush. "Heh. Thanks, Darko. You'll love the performance, I'm sure of it."

He smiled. We stood there, not saying anything to each other for a few moments. I just gazed into his eyes, as did he with mine.

"I uh," He said, running his fingers through his hair, "I wanted to just see and talk to you. I haven't been able to for a while and I miss you."

I smiled, my cheeks most likely a bright red - I certainly felt them warm up. "I've missed you too, dude."

We stood there, just gazing at each other. After a second, he stepped closer to me, our chests nearly touching. His eyes flicked down to my lips, making my heart nearly stop.

"Taylor, I..." he whispered, the corners of my lips curling into a smile. I felt a stirring in my groin as he stood there, studying my face. I nearly lost myself in his eyes.

Snapping both of us out of our spell, Miss Lauriana's voice erupted from the stage, making us both jump. He regained his posture, before taking a step away from me.

"I, uh.. I better go..." he said, his expression dejected. I reluctantly nodded, causing him to purse his lips, frowning. Before I could speak, Darko began walking away, his cheeks a very obvious bright red. Soon, he was lost in the crowd of teenagers outside of the stage area.

Hopefully, he isn't too embarrassed. Whatever's running in his mind right now is going to change within the next ten minutes, permanently.

Miss Lauriana's voice grew louder. Accepting that Darko's left, I turned around, facing her.

"And now, for our final performance," She said excitedly into the microphone on stage, "it's your favourite pianist, Taylor James Ferguson!"

I walked onto the stage, a round of applause following me as I smiled toward the crowd. I grabbed the microphone from Miss Lauriana before fixing it onto the stand that was attached to the piano. I sat down, cracked my knuckles, and faced the crowd with my most confident-looking smirk.

"Okay, I'm going to be playing two songs tonight. The first one is a cover, while the second one is going to be a song I wrote myself." I said, speaking into the microphone. The crowd cheered.

I smiled as I waited for their excitement to die down. I was meant to play four songs, but as the night progressed, Miss Lauriana advised that I only played two. She didn't limit just me;

everyone that performed had to drop some songs. Maybe she had to cut back due to time constraints, but who knows?

"Anyway, this first one is for the couples and potential couples-to-be. I hope you've all heard of Ed Sheeran's 'Tenerife Sea'," I said, the crowd cutting me off with a round of excited cheers at the mention of the red-headed artist. "If you have a special someone with you here tonight, or you've been dying to ask that one person out, now is the perfect time to ask them for a dance. Happy belated Valentines day, everybody!"

I began to sing. Couples bustled out of their seats as I began playing my piano cover of the famous song. They all began slow-dancing to my voice and music. I glanced at the crowd when I could, noticing that after the second chorus the audience had moved to the outskirts of the dance-floor, allowing a giant circle just for Stefan and Lyra. They danced perfectly to the song, swaying in time, twirling and eventually ending their 'routine' with a passionate kiss. The crowd cheered for them. I grinned widely.

I ended the song, earning a near earsplitting applause from the audience as I bowed, filling me with confidence and putting a permanent smile on my face. I make eye contact with Darko, who shot me a quick smirk, raising his hands toward me as he applauded harder.

"Okay, okay, everyone, take a seat," I said. "The next song will be played in a minute. As I've said, this one isn't one any of you will know - I wrote it myself. Get ready, because I'm also going to dedicate this song to a special somebody. My real valentine."

I scanned the crowd as excited murmurs and high pitched awwww's echoed off of the gym walls. I met eyes with Bella, who shot me a panicked expression. Her face was paler than normal, and she was noticeably distressed. I giggled to myself before breaking eye contact, focusing my attention on Darko. He looked at me, confused. I smirked at him.

His face paled. Before I could give away any more information, I forced myself to look away. My phone vibrated in my pocket, startling me.

'I'm done with the call. Waiting on standby behind the curtain. Ready when you are.' Owen texted. I smiled. I took in a deep breath.

This is it.

"Of course, I need help from a good friend of mine to help perform this song. Everyone give it up for my mystery right-hand person, Owen Prietto!"

He burst out from behind the curtain, his classical guitar in tow. He smiled warmly, striding towards the seat that was prepared for him. The crowd clapped furiously at his entrance. Owen and I locked eyes before nodding. I looked out towards the crowd, the biggest grin on my face. I locked eyed with Darko as I began to speak.

"I dedicate this song to Darko Ulyanov."

The audience gasped. Confused murmurs grew louder and louder. I heard Trent and Duncan holler slurs at me. There's no going back now.

CHAPTER 29

Darko's pov

Friday Evening, February 15th, 2014.

"I dedicate this song to Darko Ulyanov"

At the sound of my name, my hand clenched tighter around my drinking glass. Scanning the room, I saw half of the crowd turn to me, while the other half stared at Owen and Taylor on stage.

Dedicated to me?

I looked at Owen on stage, who was grinning widely at me. He turned to Taylor, who was taking in the reaction of the audience. As they all quietened down, Taylor turned to me with the faintest glint in his eyes.

"It's called 'I got you'. Darko... I love you." Taylor said, never leaving my gaze. I felt my cheeks burn up at his words.

He loves me. He fucking loves me.

Taylor tapped his mic and began playing on the piano. His fingers delicately tapped the keys, sending beautiful clicks of sound throughout the gymnasium. After a few moments, he began singing.

I am tired of living a lie,

I am sick of keeping a straight face.

I look at the fake me and I cry,

Then I met you in a real place.

If I knew what I know now,

I wouldn't think twice to kiss you.

These piano keys told me somehow,

Home is when I'm with you.

Damn you emotions for betraying me.

I felt my eyes water at the sound of his voice. The tears fell when I listened to the lyrics. Taylor feels the same. This time, I didn't hear a rumour or have to decipher some body language to figure it out. Taylor admitted it to me and meant it.

As the lyrics rolled off of Taylor's tongue, Owen joined in, his soft acoustics complementing Taylor's piano. I felt light-headed as Taylor began to sing again.

Who knew I'd end up loving you,

like the way that you loved me?

All this time I've been so blue,

but now I got you, baby.

And you got me.

I was getting a myriad of looks around me. Some people were grimacing - those people being Trent and Duncan - while others were swooning over the entire situation. A group of girls kept alternating their attention between Taylor and I, clapping, grinning, and squealing at my reactions and Taylor's vocals.

Then I made eye contact with Bella.

She tried to crush you,

she tried to break us apart.

She tried destroying

what I felt for you from the start.

It took me forever to know

the part of you I failed to see.

The closet was so dark and cold,

the open door lead you to me.

I folded my arms, smirking at her. I pulled out my phone and waved it at her, taunting her. Come on, Bella. Do something!

What's stopping you?

I shot her a text. 'Why aren't you exposing me?'

Her face flipped like a switch. Her panicked expression disappeared and in its place was a devilish smirk. She began texting.

'I will, when Nicole gets Owen's phone.'

Oh lord. Why does she need his phone?

Who knew I'd end up loving you

like the way that you love me?

All this time, I've been so blue,

but now I got you baby,

and you got me.

'Its got blackmail on there about me. If I destroy the phone, I'll be free to out you to your parents.'

I looked up and her, catching a wink she sent my way before focusing back on stage.

All I want to feel is happiness. Everything I ever wanted from Taylor is happening - he's coming out, confessing how he feels and shutting Bella down - but I can't. Bella has a plan, and when Bella makes a plan against me, it happens no matter fucking what.

I saw Nicole slip backstage out of the corner of my eye. Owen's phone is on the floor of the stage, about a foot from the stool he's sitting on. As long as he picks it up when he's done performing, Bella won't get her satisfaction.

And I'll be safe.

I need to stop thinking about them and focus on Taylor. If everything goes wrong after this song ends, I'd never forgive myself if I didn't let myself enjoy this song.

He stopped playing the piano - instead, he unhooked his microphone and stepped towards the very front of the stage, looking straight at me, a soft smile spreading on his lips. A spotlight lowered on him, and Owen began delicately plucking his guitar strings, a beautiful melody emanating from it.

Taylor's crying. Happy tears, of course. I hope.

Hush now, you're safe with me.

I've been waiting to kiss you

waiting to hold you

but now we're free

He carried that last word for a few moments, his falsetto making my heart pound against my rib-cage. He rushed back to the piano and began playing the chorus again, his energy amplified by Owen's enthusiasm.

Who knew i'd end up loving you

like the way that you love me?

All this time I've been so blue,

He looked at me, wiping a tear from his cheek. The music stopped for a split second, before Taylor played a short melody as an outro.

But now I got you, Darko.

And you got me.

He played the final chord on the piano. He looked out towards the crowd, who was dead silent. A few moments passed, the air tense. Sweat beads trickled down my head as faces flipped from Taylor to me. He just smiled at me, puffing out of breath. I smiled back.

Suddenly, one person started clapping. Slow clapping.

A spotlight revealed that person to be Ana, a mess of tears. She hollered at Taylor and I, smiling as much as a crying person could.

Another set of hands began clapping. This time, it was Miss Lauriana.

Stefan and Lyra stood up, the former applauding me and the latter clapping for Taylor. Soon, more and more people stood up, and soon, almost all of the audience began cheering.

Taylor gestured for me to join him on stage. I went to, but then I noticed Nicole sneaking behind Owen.

Shit!

Nicole lunged forward, snatching up Owen's phone in her dainty fingers. Owen, bewildered, paled in realisation when she saw him with his phone.

"Don't, please, don't! I won't be able to talk to my grandma without it!"

Nicole smirked. With a deadpan expression, she dropped Owen's phone onto the stage, before stomping on it several times. Her heel dug into the machine, shattering the LCD, smashing the glass and bashing the insides. The audience gasped.

My heart dropped. I stared straight at Bella, who already had her phone up to her ear. She sardonically grinned at me before she started talking into it.

I shook my head. Taylor's observed the entire thing. I felt my face heat up, my shoulders grew heavy, my stomach felt like it was being mixed with a whisk.

"Bella. Don't you dare."

Everyone snapped their attention to Taylor on stage, Bella included. She lowered her phone when she saw the rage on Taylor's face.

"I already know. Owen knew that you were going to try and pull a stunt, even with the blackmail he had against you. I know everything - all the bullshit you've put Darko through. All to just to get on my good side. Bella, you're a monster. Put that phone away, or I'm never going anywhere near you again."

Bella hesitated for a moment. She went to put it away, but she steeled herself, staring Taylor straight in the eyes. "No. Taylor, you don't understand, I can't lose you-"

"Too fucking late for that. This isn't about you liking me, Bella. You could have done this all civilly. You didn't need to go through all this! Put the phone away. Last chance."

She shook her head. Glancing around to see bewildered students switching attention from me to her, she began crying. "Taylor..."

She clutched her phone and stared straight at me. For the first time in the five years I've known her, I saw fear in her eyes. Pure, irrational, genuine fear. Her usually cool, cold and collected self was gone.

She stood up. Her phone fell into her purse. She hung her head low, defeated, before sprinting out of the gymnasium. More confused shouting erupted from the other students.

I looked back towards the stage. Sometime during the chaos, Miss Lauriana appeared on stage. She gestured for Taylor and Owen to go backstage. She began saying something, but I was too preoccupied with what Taylor was mouthing to me. He was at the exit door, beckoning to me.

"Come here."

I stood up, ignoring what Miss Lauriana was saying on-stage, and walked towards the door.

I walked out of the school exit, peering out into the darkness. Taylor was facing out towards the school oval, his back to me. I caught myself grinning as I walked slowly toward him.

"Well," I began, making him crane his head slightly toward me, "That was a surprise."

Taylor chuckled before turning around to fully face me, his smile making my heart race. "A good surprise, I hope."

I walked closer to him, a tiny gap between forming between us. The air was electric, our eyes unwavering from each other. "It was an amazing surprise. The best surprise I've ever experienced."

"Are you ready for another surprise?" He asked, flicking his eyes towards my lips. I cocked an eyebrow.

"I have a feeling I know what this surprise is."

"Good."

Taylor cupped my cheek in his hand, before leaning forward, kissing me. His lips were so warm. They moved over mine with the softest touch, nothing I could have ever imagined - and I've done a lot of imagining.

I tasted tentatively with my tongue. Taylor opened his mouth slightly, letting out a low moan. Worried about what I'd do if I continued, I broke away from him, my eyes hodded. Ecstasy filled my entire being as I smirked at Taylor.

Breaking into a grin, Taylor looked up at me, his eyes nearly sparkling under the streetlight. "You have no idea how long I've been waiting to do that."

I smirked. "Likewise."

He looked back towards the gym. He squinted through the wide-open doors, the students still audibly confused. "I think I caused a hellstorm in there."

He glanced back at me, flashing that beautiful smile again. "Did you like the song?"

"Eh, it was all right. Not your best..." I said sarcastically. He giggled, feigning offence.

"Well, if you dislike it, I'll never write you a song ever again..."

"Like that's never stopped you before."

He let out a short laugh. The way his eyes crinkled and the way he snorted made me love him that tiny bit more.

He stopped, and once again, we found ourselves in that calm silence, eyes unwavering from each other. After a few more moments, Taylor seemed to snap out of our gaze faster than I did, because he stepped closer to me and flicked his eyes between mine and my lips again.

Before I could react, he softly weaved his hand into my hair and pulled me into another kiss, this one more passionate. Shutting my eyes, I cupped one hand over his jaw, eventually allowing it to make its way across the back of his neck. The other hand found its way to his ass. He let out a small moan in my mouth as I squeezed. His free hand travelled to my back, sliding up and down my spine.

'Fuck, it feels so good to grab it.' I thought to myself.

After what felt like ages, Taylor eventually pulled away, eyes still shut, grinning from ear to ear. He let out a short giggle before exhaling. I let go of a breath I didn't realise I was holding.

"What do we do now?" I asked. As if to answer my question, A loud cry erupted from around the corner. Taylor and I looked at each other quizzically before walking towards the source. We stopped behind a wall and peered around the corner.

My eyes widened. Out in the cold by a dumpster was a teary Bella, on her phone, completely broken down.

"I think she's on the phone with your parents." He said grimly. We looked at each other.

"I think it's time we all had a talk. Together." I said to Taylor. After a few moments, we both stepped away from the wall and walked towards Bella. Noticing us, she hastily wiped away at her face before standing up, brushing her dress down.

"Bella, we need to talk," Taylor began. After a few moments, she nodded. Stifling back a sob, she leaned against a wall, slipping her phone back into her purse.

"Before you ask, no, that wasn't your parents, Darko. I called a cab."

I sighed in relief. "Why didn't you call them?"

She scoffed. "Can you please just leave me alone?"

I shook my head. "No, not until we get some answers-"

Taylor lifted his hand up, gesturing for me to stop. I did. Taylor walked away from Bella and towards me, a worried expression on his face.

"Is it okay if I talk to her by myself?" He asked. Flicking my attention from Taylor to Bella, I furrowed my brow in confusion.

"Why?"

He let out a sigh. "This is going to sound fucked up, but I still see her as a friend."

Involuntarily, my face screwed up in disgust. "Seriously? After everything she's put us both through?"

He nodded. "Yes. Darko. Please, just trust me."

I hesitated. A part of me wants to pick Bella up and drop-kick her into the dumpster next to her. Another part of me wants to just walk away and to never speak to her again. But a part of me wants Taylor to make sure Bella doesn't do this again. Maybe a genuine talk with Taylor will finally put Bella at ease.

"I'll be around the corner. Come find me when you're done."

EPILOGUE

T aylor's pov

Friday Evening, February 15th 2014.

I sat down next to Bella. She had stopped crying a while ago, but judging by her crooked frown, her pale face, and the hitch in her breathing, she was still upset.

"You remember that time when we snuck out of our house to go to the circus carnival a year back?" I asked her. Hesitantly, she nodded.

"We had so much fun. I remember you nearly threw up on the merry go round after you had too much cotton candy. Do you remember going on the Ferris wheel with me, and we were gazing at the entire carnival from dozens of metres up?"

She flashed a smile, before returning to her frown. "That was a fun day."

"And," I continued, "when we got home, you threw every single excuse you could think of at your parents but only I knew the truth?"

"Yeah. I still can't believe that they fell for it all."

I smiled reassuringly. "Bella... I've heard so many stories from so many people as to why you've been doing this. Blackmailing

Darko, threatening Owen, lying to Lyra, and manipulating Stefan. You've always been truthful to me, no matter what it was about. Can I know why you've done all of this? The real reason?"

She rocked her head back, resting it on the wall behind her, closing her eyes. "Everything I've said to other people is a lie. I lied to Nicole when I said I wanted to date you because you'd become famous. It's all lies."

She turned to me. "It's been a reoccurring thing in my life, Tay. I've lied to my parents since as far as I can remember. I've never had any friends, and my last relationship, the one with Trent, is based on false statements as well. I don't know, I just get a thrill from doing it. It's a great feeling convincing others."

She looked up at the sky. "Then you came along. For some reason, I couldn't lie to you. You were and still are the sweetest, kindest boy I've ever met. All my life I've been manipulating others and telling others what to do to live. When I'm with you, I didn't have to do any of that. I felt so free."

"Somewhere along the way, I... I fell in love with you."

"I thought I had a chance. I genuinely thought I did. Then you came out to me and told me that you were head over heels over Darko. Of course, I became resentful of Darko because his presence was a threat. I became scared. I didn't want to lose you. So, I became ruthless. Stopping at nothing until Darko's reputation was destroyed and you were all mine again."

She wiped another tear from her face, smearing her makeup. I placed my hand on her hand, causing her to flinch for a moment. She relaxed when I lightly squeezed it. "That... that all changed tonight though. I heard your song, then you told me off on stage. I realised two things."

"What were those things?" I questioned. She smiled.

"The first thing was that I needed to stop being so angry about it. I let vengeance consume me. I was so afraid of losing the one person that let me be happy, that I ended up losing myself."

"The second thing was that I realised you and Darko really do love each other. I feel so terrible to have gotten between you two."

She faced me again, tears streaking down her cheeks once more. "Taylor, I know my actions were horrible. Blackmailing, manipulation, exploitation and threatening to out someone is some of the worst things you can do. I'm a bad person."

Her voice cracked. She hastily wiped her nose. "But I am pleading for one more chance. I know everything I've done is wrong. I don't want to risk losing you again, Taylor-"

Cutting us off, her phone rang. She picked it up, and groaned loudly, angrily hanging up. She let out a sigh before looking back at me.

"I... I gotta go."

I nodded. We both looked at each other. There was a glint in her eyes. You could see the sorrow she was feeling. The sadness. The regret. It was wrapped around her entire face.

I opened my arms, gesturing for a hug. Bella, confused at first, realised what I was doing and reciprocated, hugging me tightly.

"I'm sorry Taylor, for everything," she mumbled into my chest. I hugged her tighter as a response. After a few moments, we broke apart.

"I can't forgive you, Bella. Not right now. Things have changed and I don't think things can go back to the way they were immediately." I said. Bella looked down, nodding sadly.

"But, that doesn't mean we can't try and make things better."

Her head shot up immediately. Her eyes widened. "What?"

"Bella, I'm giving you one last chance. One final chance. I want to be your friend again. But not immediately. We need to fix everything you've done. Starting tomorrow."

For the first time tonight, she smiled. For the first time in a long time, her smile was genuine. Full of happiness. No snide remarks hiding behind those lips, nor any catty insults or fake expressions. Pure happiness.

"Okay. First thing tomorrow."

Her phone buzzed again. She looked at it, then looked back at me.

"I really need to go now," she said.

"Don't let me keep you."

She walked off. I smiled, knowing that Bella won't harm Darko again.

"What happened?"

I walked towards Darko, kicking a bit of dirt on the way. "I talked to Bella and got her side of everything. Long story short, she's going to leave you alone and she's never going to threaten my friendship with her again."

He shook his head. "So, she's not going to out me to my parents?"

I nodded. He grinned, before crying out in celebration. Surprisingly, he picked me up and spun me around, earning him a joyous laugh from me.

"I'm free! I'm free!!" He chanted gleefully before setting me down.

"She's also really apologetic about everything. She's going to try and be a better person – she's going to start fixing things with everybody she's hurt. I want to fix things between me and her too."

He nodded. "That's fair. I can't see you cutting anybody out of your life. You're too sweet for that."

I smirked. "That's what she said."

He wrapped me in a hug, his strong arms making my heart ache.

"So, what do we do now?" Darko asked, mumbling into the groove in his neck. I smirked.

"Come on," I began, grabbing his hand. "Let's go home. I wanna spend the rest of the night with you."

He laughed. "Just the rest of tonight? Ouch."

Snorting, I lead him to the car park, hands linked. I took him to Owen's car. Owen stood there, frowning over his broken phone until he noticed us walking toward him. He quickly crammed the machine into his jacket pocket, before flashing us a smile.

"There are my favourite lovebirds," he said, sticking his hand into his pocket. He fished out his keys before handing them to me, smiling.

"I'll come by tomorrow to get my car. Just tell me the address before you go - here's my home phone number," he said to both of us, giving me a tiny slip of paper. "Darko, could you give me and Taylor a moment alone?"

Darko nodded, climbing into the car. Owen turned toward me, before fishing out his phone. He looked at me, clearly upset.

"Look, I'm sorry Tay. Tonight was meant to be perfect for you and Darko, but fucking Bella had to do ONE thing to ruin it..." he said. He shook his head, laughing mockingly. "I'm sorry about Darko's parents. Can you remind him for me that if things get hard, my place is still open to him?"

I smiled. "Bella didn't call his parents."

Shocked, he furrowed his brow in confusion. "Come again? Bella was nice?"

"Yep," I stated. "She's about to get a hell of a lot nicer too. Expect a new phone sometime this week from her."

He grinned. "Sweet!!"

"I'm gonna go head back to the gym and help the staff clean up. I'll see you on Sunday?" He said, beaming. I nodded.

"Of course, Owen."

He leaned in closer, his voice a whisper. "Don't forget about the gift I gave Darko."

He smirked before walking off. I completely forgot about the gift. He waved to Darko before disappearing back into the school.

I got into the car, sitting in the passenger seat. Darko switched on the ignition, before turning to face me, eyes expectant.

"Let's go to my house," I suggested, "Ana's sleeping over at her friend's place, and mum's out with a therapy group. It'll be just us."

Perfect.

We finally reached my house. Climbing out of the car, we headed for the front door.

"We should talk about everything that's happened," I said, fumbling with my keys. "We haven't sat down for a long time and talked about it. Hell, we haven't talked about a lot recently."

He nodded in response. Finally unlocking the door, we walked inside. Darko lingered in the hallway as I locked the door behind me.

"What should we talk about first?" He asked. I turned to face him, throwing my keys on the table next to the door. He walked closer to me, his eyes flickering to my lips.

"Because I don't feel like talking right now. I want to do something else."

Feeling my face flush, I playfully pushed him away. "No, not yet."

He frowned, his expression mirroring a sad puppy. I laughed at him, before walking past him, sitting in the lounge room. "That ain't going to work against me."

"Please? Come on, Tay. That's not fair."

I shook my head. Although all I wanted to do was tear that suit off of him, I needed answers, and what's a better time than the present?

Darko sat down, grumbling. "Fine, I'll do it, but I'm only answering one question."

I rolled my eyes. "Fine. You ask first."

"How did you figure out I liked you?"

I smiled. "That's easy. Owen told me the truth about the birthday card. Your birthday card."

His expression turned quizzical. "The hell? He told me you didn't see it yet."

A moment passed, and Darko was dumbstruck. "Damn, he's good."

I laughed. "What you said was very sweet, by the way."

He smiled. "Anyway. It's your turn. Only one question."

I stroked my chin. "Owen told me he gave you a gift at the dance. What is it?"

A smirk slowly spread across Darko's face. He got off of the couch, and before I could register what he was doing, he was on top of me, sitting on my lap.

"Uh, Darko, what are you-"

He reached into his jacket pocket, before fishing out a condom. "This is what he gave me."

My eyes flicked between the condom, Darko's seductive smirk, and his body that sat perfectly on my lap. Biting my lip, I struggled to think of anything other than Darko using that with me.

Darko leaned forward, closing the distance, and gently kissed my lips. Not a heavy, passionate kiss like the one in the parking lot at school. His lips barely graze mine, only allowing contact for a few brief moments before he pulled away.

"Have you got any more questions?" he asked me, his tone teasing. I shook my head.

"Fuck the questions!"

I leaned forward and kissed him again. My lips grew hungrier as they fervently brushed against his, the kiss deepening as Darko explored my mouth with his tongue. I wrapped my hand around the back of his neck, pushing him closer to me. My fingers tangled in his brunette hair.

After a few moments, my hand moved away from his neck, trailing down his suit jacket to the buttons keeping it together. I undid it without breaking away from his lips, and he managed to take it off without pulling away either.

I started unbuttoning his undershirt as he started undoing my suit jacket. We broke apart for just a second to tear our shirts off. Darko's bare chest almost glistened as the moonlight shone on him through the tiny slits in my blinds. My jaw fell at the sight of him.

Muscly, but not brawny. Fit, but not skinny.

Snapping me out of my gaze, Darko unbuttoned my undershirt. He threw it across the room.

I pushed him off, causing him to sit on the couch spot next to me. Before he could recover, I was on his lap now. He wrapped his arms around my waist, bringing my body closer to him. I dipped my head into his neck, kissing his skin tenderly.

Pulling away to catch my breath, Darko slipped his hand around my back, kissing my neck with his warm lips. I let out a moan as he travelled down my bare skin, his face meeting my chest. He delicately kissed one of my nipples, earning him a moan.

"Darko... I need you so badly..." I said to him, my mouth centimetres from his ear. Hearing him laugh, he lightly pushed me off of him and laced his fingers into mine.

"Let's go to your room."

Darko's pov

Saturday Morning, February 16th, 2014.

I woke up to the light chatter of morning birds outside, and the soft snores from Taylor. Light bled through my curtains, filling the room with a hazy golden colour. Taylor's sprawled like a starfish next to me, belly down, the blanket barely covering him.

Last night's events came rushing back to me, and I'm filled with happiness. Pure happiness. Everything went so right.

Turning my body to him, I roll onto my side and wiggle closer to him. I watch as his shoulders rose and fell with every breath he took. I lifted my arm, stroking his back's bare skin.

"Wake up, my good sir," I mumbled to him, tracing lines with my thumb around Taylor's shoulder blade. After a moment, I felt him stir underneath me. With a small moan, he turned his head to face me, his eyes opening ever so slightly.

"Good morning," Taylor said, yawning. After a quick stretch of his arms, he lifted himself toward me and planted a tender kiss on my lips.

"How are you feeling? Last night was..."

He pressed a finger to my mouth, shushing me. "It was good. It's still good. I can't believe we went that far."

I smirked. "I can't believe everything that's happened. I mean, everything."

A soft chuckle filled the space between us. "Me too."

The air seemed to swell to a stop, nothing but the warm morning sun, birds, and neighbourhood traffic filling the room. Taylor's with me, in ways I couldn't have ever imagined, and I'm glad. Blissful. Peaceful.

Both of us can hear our phones going off, but those worries were far from us. Sure, Bella told Taylor that she won't tell my parents about us, but that's one person compared to the hundreds that were there at the concert. Either by rumour, social media, or something else, my parents are going to find out, one way or another, and... well, I dunno. Plus, Taylor did just out himself, so bullies are going to be on him like sharks.

Beyond these bedroom doors, hell's waiting for me. For us. But, I don't really care anymore. And, judging by Taylor's expression, he doesn't either.

I only care about the boy that's wrapped in my arms, softly smiling at me, the morning sun glinting in his eyes. My good sir. One look at his face and nothing else seemed to matter. Plus, we have Lyra, Owen, and Stefan in our corner. Bella will come around as she promised. As long as we have each other, we can survive anything.

"I love you," I said. Taylor shuts his eyes and buries his face on my chest, my skin warming up instantly. A soft hum reverberated against my heart.

"I love you too, Darko."

www.ingramcontent.com/pod-product-compliance
Lightning Source LLC
Chambersburg PA
CBHW070626170726
48291CB00003B/893